ALSO BY CHARLOTTE BENNARDO
& NATALIE ZAMAN

Sirenz Back in Fashion
Sirenz

Blonde OPS

A NOVEL

Charlotte Bennardo
& Natalie Zaman

THOMAS DUNNE BOOKS ST. MARTIN'S GRIFFIN 🦌 NEW YORK

This is a work of fiction. All of the characters, organizations, and events portrayed in this novel are either products of the authors' imaginations or are used fictitiously.

THOMAS DUNNE BOOKS.
An imprint of St. Martin's Press.

www.thomasdunnebooks.com
www.stmartins.com

Designed by Anna Gorovoy

The Library of Congress Cataloging-in-Publication Data is available upon request.

ISBN 978-1-250-03039-9 (hardcover)
ISBN 978-1-4668-4988-4 (e-book)

St. Martin's Griffin books may be purchased for educational, business, or promotional use. For information on bulk purchases, please contact Macmillan Corporate and Premium Sales Department at 1-800-221-7945, extension 5442, or write specialmarkets@macmillan.com.

First Edition: May 2014

10   9   8   7   6   5   4   3   2   1

Prologue

Zip tie handcuffs—not my best accessory.

For one, they didn't go with the hot pink dress and crystal-studded heels I was wearing for the interview. Worse, though, was that they'd been used to tether me to a decorative wrought-iron window screen between my coworkers, and at the moment, neither of them made for good company. Sophie looked like she was going to lose it—very bad in a crisis situation—and Kevin swore until he was out of breath.

Boarding school didn't seem so bad anymore.

We all heard the distant slam of the door that led into the alley. Our captors had left us.

"This is great. Just great," Kevin muttered, and banged his head in frustration.

"It could be worse," I said.

"A *lot* worse," added Sophie. "We could be dead."

She was right, and that meant we could still do something. Kevin wrestled in his ties, shaking the iron screen. I thought I heard the cracking of plaster.

"That's not helping," I snapped. "Do you want this thing to come crashing down on us? Every time you move, you make the zip ties tighter. These things are hard enough to get out of."

Sophie laughed quietly. "What are you, some kind of a ninja? What type of boarding school did you go to?"

"Probably juvie," Kevin said not so under his breath.

"Well, my education is going to be worth more here than your extensive knowledge of fine Italian leather."

"Can you really get us out?" Sophie asked, serious and desperate.

I felt a little smug. "I can." The question was, did I have enough time to free all of us before the First Lady disappeared completely—or worse?

There are worse things than being yanked from the middle of lunch, dumped onto a plane to fly cross-country in a stupid school uniform that made me look like an anime reject, and be told that I *really* effed up this time.

But I couldn't think of any at the moment.

I unfolded the crumpled paper Dean Harding gave to me before I was dismissed and read it again. Printed on school letterhead, it was officially scary.

Does not adhere to school dress code.

Violates "No Cell Phones in Class" rule.

Does not perform to expected academic and social standards.

"Hacked" into school computer network and changed third-quarter grades.

Yeah, that last one did it—the infraction that sealed my expulsion from Anaheim's prestigious St. Xavier's Academy.

In less than three years, I'd been in and out of four—or was it five?—prep/boarding/private schools. This would make St. X's number six.

Mom's going to be pissed.

Correction: *was* pissed. I hadn't heard a word from her since I'd gotten called down to the dean's office: no phone call, no e-mail, no personal messenger with papers putting me up for adoption. Just a car sent to shuttle me to the airport and this flight to New York where she was probably waiting to escort me to the next polo-shirt-wearing / rowing-type school where I would finish my junior year. I didn't think there were any left I hadn't been kicked out of—on either coast.

The sudden jarring of the wheels as the plane landed churned up the worry in my empty stomach. Closing my eyes, I tried to think calming thoughts, but all I saw was Mom, her perfect brows arched like sickles, ready to cut down any excuse I had to offer.

I turned on my phone and winced. There was an unread message from her. I decided not to look at it yet. It was only going to be more bad news.

Not wanting to fight the crowds or my mother, I waited until the aisle was empty to grab my carry-on and laptop case, then stumbled off the plane, barely acknowledging the forced brightness of the flight attendants' good-byes.

I lingered in the airport bathroom, staring at my pathetic reflection in the mirror over the row of sinks: mussed pink braids; wrinkled oxford shirt; the cringe-worthy school-issued brown, beige, and taupe pleated skirt and burgundy tie that wasn't flattering on anyone. My sudden departure left me no time to change into normal clothes. For a second I was tempted to nip into a stall and ditch the uniform and put on my beloved combats and favorite tee, but I had a feeling that I wouldn't be able to spare the time. Curiosity overcame me and I read Mom's text—it was curt, and not open to interpretation.

Get off the plane. Find the limo. We have places to go.

A knot formed in my stomach. *Where?* I wondered. *To what new sleepaway school hell?*

I spotted the driver quickly, a large man in a gray suit holding a sign with my first initial and last name neatly printed in jumbo black Sharpie.

I waved. "B. Jackson, right here."

He looked me up and down, his eyes lingering on my neon hair for half a second before sweeping up my bag with a big paw, but he left my laptop to me.

The stench of diesel fumes and rain hit me as the exit doors whooshed open. Of course it would be raining. We headed for the taxi stand, where a long line of dark cars and cabs idled. The driver stopped at a long black Mercedes with tinted windows and popped the trunk to load my luggage. This was it. I opened the rear passenger door and let myself in.

"Rebecca."

My full name. And another layer of scary: the Quiet Voice.

"Hi, Mom!" I chirped and gave her a huge "I miss you" smile. She wasn't fooled. Everything about her—makeup, silver-gray power suit, black pumps, slicked-back hair—and pursed mouth—told me this was going to be a tough negotiation.

"I'm very disappointed in you. I thought we had an agreement, and you were doing so well—until this hacking episode." She frowned prettily, a talent I wished I could learn; when she did it, all anyone wanted to do was please her—even me.

The driver slid into his seat and tilted his head, his face reflected in the rearview mirror. "What airline, ma'am?"

"United," said Mom and turned to me. "You have really bad

timing, Rebecca. Your father is about to close on a property in the Hills and I have to travel. I tried to change my plans—" A ringing cell phone cut the admonishment short. She plucked it out of her bag, tapped a key. "Tam!"

Tamora Smith was Mom's personal assistant, responsible for making her travel arrangements, fetching her coffee, and remembering birthdays—mine included. Tam was amazing and paid close attention to details. She really impressed me with the original, factory-sealed Cap'n Crunch Bo'sun whistle—a trinket highly prized by the hacking set and hard to find—that landed in my mailbox at the dorm. On my actual birthday. The card was a nice touch too, even if she'd forged my parents' sigs; I'd done it enough, I *knew*.

I tugged at the neon yellow nylon cord around my neck and pulled out the whistle; I wore it everywhere. Mom caught me doing it and shook her head. What would she say if she knew Tam paid $250 for it? What would she do if she knew what it was for? Probably something worse than complain about my bad timing.

"You weren't able to change the flight?" Mom went on, clearly annoyed. "That'll mean getting into Belize at eight in the morning."

Belize?

I fought to suppress the instant giddy feeling that came over me. I'd be going along with Mom for once, to stay in one of her sweet beachfront hotel rooms with twenty-four-hour room service and *bronzed lifeguards*. . . .

I gazed out the window. Rain pelted the glass as the car snaked slowly around the airport. The sun-drenched shores of Belize would be a nice change from Cali—and way better than this chilly East Coast drizzle.

Mom hung up and tilted her head at the window. "I don't have a lot of time." She dropped her phone back into the pit of her purse. "I convinced Dean Harding, when I talked to him last week, to allow you to complete your junior year off-campus in an independent study."

Last week? Mom had been in cahoots with Dean Harding for

days and I'd had no idea? Wow. She was better than I thought. I tried to look contrite, really, I did, but inside I was screaming, *Belize, here I come!*

"He'll be sending the coursework requirements"—she peered at me over the top of thin, sleek glasses—"and all your assignments have to be printed out and mailed in—no technology. Not after what you did to his e-mail."

"Seriously? Oh my God, Mom, that is—"

"—very *generous* of Dean Harding," she interrupted, and narrowed her eyes at me. "Let's forget about the hacking for five seconds. You're a bright girl. Why are you giving your teachers a hard time? And getting a D in World Civilizations?"

I twisted in my seat. *That* wasn't on the list of violations—okay, it's why I had to adjust my grade, but I deserved at least a B+ for that last paper. It was a work of political genius.

"Mr. Benning doesn't teach. In fact, he doesn't have a clue about anything—especially current events. You're just supposed to agree with him. Whatever happened to independent thinking?" I slumped back into the leather seat. "What does he want, a robot?"

Mom sighed, not impressed. "You're not always going to like who you have to work with."

Here we go . . .

She eyed me sharply. "Or for."

I got it. It wasn't the time to argue. "Okay."

"That's better," she said, but tapped my knee with a French-tipped nail. "And don't you dare miss a single assignment. There won't be any second chances this time, understood?"

"I promise," I said, figuring I'd gotten off easy. She could have confiscated all my devices or sent me to a tech-free "retreat" for wayward teens. One of my off-grid pals, R2Deterent, was sent to one of those when his parents caught him tapping into his neighbor's wi-fi to cover his illicit activities. When he didn't show up in our weekly chat room, DR#4, haxorgrrrl, and I—Cap'nCrunch—knew something was up. When we finally heard from him again—three months later—he told us what happened. He'd been caught, all of his technology was confiscated, and then he was carted off to somewhere in Lancaster, PA. He'd been lucky to find a power socket out there, let alone a cell phone signal.

The car rolled to a stop in front of the Alitalia departure area. Didn't Mom say United? From her purse, she dragged out two tickets and handed one, along with my passport, to me. "You land in Rome at—"

WTF?

My heart sank. If Mom was going to Belize, who was going to Rome with me?

"Rome? I'm not going with you?"

She looked at me like I was insane. "No. What would you do in Belize?"

I shrugged. "Homework?"

She laughed. "I'm going to be in meetings for the next three weeks. Daddy may join me at some point, but with his schedule . . ." She put a hand to her temple, then stared at me with a very serious expression. "I don't have time to keep an eye on you."

"Come on, Mom! I don't need watching."

Up went that cutting eyebrow. "Really?"

"You know what I mean."

"The decision's been made. You aren't in any position to bargain, Rebecca. My friend Parker from college owes me a favor and agreed to watch you until Daddy and I are back in the States."

I ran down a mental list of Mom's friends. "Parker?"

"Parker Phillips. She's the editor in chief of *Edge* magazine. I really think you'll like her. She's a good role model. Successful, respected—"

Basically, everything I'm not. I shrank down in my seat, smarting inwardly at the unintentional barb, and looked away from her.

"I think you're making out quite well, *all things considered.*" She fished her wallet out of her bag and pulled out a few bills and a credit card. "Do *not* go crazy with this," she warned.

The driver opened the door, letting in the roar of the airport.

"You'll be fine," she said. Not a reassurance but an order. "Be good, and I'll call you once I've landed." She kissed me, giving me a little nudge out the door. "Love you!" Then her phone rang and she was back in full executive mode again. I should've known better than to get my hopes up. Numb, I slid out and retrieved my carry-on waiting for me on the curb. The driver shut the door behind me, got back in his seat, and sped away to the next terminal.

Ciao, Mama.

It had been a full twenty-four hours since I'd taken a shower.

And forget about sleep.

I didn't even bother looking at myself in the bathroom mirror when I landed in the Fiumicino Airport in Rome; I was just relieved to be in a stall that was larger than a broom closet. I considered hiding out in the sleek marble and chrome sanctuary forever. What would happen if I just . . . disappeared? No. Trouble on one continent was enough. I didn't need my face to go on a viral milk carton.

I checked my cell—no service. Damn. Bad, bad, *bad* decision not to make some adjustments to my cell phone plan before I got on the plane. Now I had no school, no phone, and no human connection. Making my way through customs and out to arrivals, I hoped that Parker knew I was coming, or had her own version of Tam to come and get me. I was in no mood to hunt down my probation officer, and in a foreign country no less.

But there was no need to worry. An older man in a well-fitted suit and fedora held up a sign with my name in a scrawl. I waved and he walked over, smiled, and took my carry-on, holding his free hand out for my laptop case.

"*Signorina*, please, may I?" he said, and reached for it.

I shook my head—"No, that's okay"—and pressed it closer to my chest. I didn't like anyone touching my equipment. He shrugged and turned away.

Squished into the back of a Fiat, I gripped the seat edge with sweaty hands as he wove in and out of traffic on the highway, dodging a truck that looked too rickety to be legal, then daring to race a blue Ferrari. He had amazing reflexes for an old guy. I was relieved when we finally got on a road where he had to drive slower, a street called Via Portuense that ran along the Tiber River.

Despite the haze of exhaustion, I gazed out the window. We passed countless statues, fountains, churches, and temples that looked older than time. I was really in *Rome*. I'd been to Europe before with my parents but usually got stuck at the hotel while they were in meetings. I'd seen a little of Prague, got glimpses of Barcelona, Munich, and Cannes. I'd only flown by myself to and from boarding school over vacations.

I'm in Europe.

Alone!

How could they do this to me? I got into trouble at school. Aren't they afraid of what I'll do when I'm an ocean and two continents away?

Bright flowers popped out of window boxes, and terra-cotta roof tiles added warm color to the clear blue sky as we snaked and bumped over cobbled streets that were hair-raisingly narrow. Vespa scooters putt-putted next to us, the drivers gesturing or yelling if the Fiat got too close.

We pulled over in front of a row of pale stuccoed buildings that looked left over from the Renaissance. When I stepped out of the car, the driver handed me my bag with a small bow. I fumbled for my wallet and handed him a twenty; I only had American dollars.

He shook his head, smiling. "*No, signorina, buono.*" And he slipped back into the car and shot away before my brain remembered that *grazie* was the word for thank you.

He'd dropped me in front of a large house. A shiny plastic sign with "*Edge* Magazine" emblazoned across it in bold black letters had been stuck to the door. Someone answered as soon as I knocked, a pin-thin girl in black skinny pants, a long-sleeved tee shirt in vivid geometrics that clung to her tiny frame, and outrageously high stilettos with wicked pointy heels. Her pale blonde hair was pulled away from a face with skin so perfect I doubt it had ever experienced a pimple.

Taking a sip from a bottle of mineral water, she said, "Rebecca?"

My name rolled off her tongue with a Euro-flourish of vowel. I liked the way it sounded.

"Just Bec is cool." I managed a smile, hoping my lack of Italian wouldn't be a problem. Her answer was a quirked finger and a wide berth as she stepped aside to let me enter.

Oh man, did I smell *that* bad?

Throwing my backpack over my shoulder, I entered a spacious brownstone-type house that was reorganized to be office-friendly. People milled around on the bottom floor. One worked a behemoth espresso machine in the kitchen toward the back. Others were curled up on the sofas and chairs in the front room, busy with laptops and sketch pads.

Skinny inclined her head toward an open set of stairs without looking at me. "*Al piano de sopra,*" she said.

Piano? I didn't see one, but I guessed she wanted me to go up.

When I got to the top, I found the hallway filled with a line of freakishly tall and expressionless models in various states of undress, waiting to go through an open door to the left. All the others were shut. Each model had a much shorter and harried-looking companion holding stacks of clothes over his or her arms and canvas bags with belts and hair clips and scarves and other accessories frothing out of the top like foam on a fizzy drink.

"Excuse me?" I said, trying to get someone's—anyone's—attention. "Does anyone speak English?"

I got a few odd looks. Then one of the model-handlers said in a thick Italian accent, "Are you here with the missing accessories from wardrobe?"

"No. I need to find Parker Phil—"

"So does everyone," she said, and turned her attention back to her model.

I maneuvered around them to squeeze into the room.

What lurked on the other side of the door was a sartorial war zone. Clothes were strewn about as if Neiman Marcus had exploded. An elaborate but small setup of white screens and lights dominated the room and centered on the window, which provided a spectacular view of the city beyond the river. Fans were humming and blowing from all directions and the model at the center of it all, a skyscraper of a girl with flawless caramel skin, stood absolutely still, the artificial wind billowing out the voluminous silk sheath that draped her body. From my angle, I could see it was fitted in the back with a row of black binder clips.

"No no no! Too much wind!" shouted a small steel-haired woman in a too-bright daffodil yellow dress.

Everyone froze. She pushed through the crowd, strode right up to the model, and peered at her through eyes ringed with glittering orange liner. In the few seconds of silence, I did a quick mental count. Madame Eyeliner—she couldn't be Parker, could she? A pleasantly plump photographer stood next to a younger bald man holding accent lights for him. Another guy, short but built, in jeans and a super-fitted polo shirt, hung back at a polite distance holding a can of hair spray, and next to him, another similarly shaped and clad guy clutched a fat Kabuki brush: Tweedle-buff and Tweedle-dee, ready to beautify the world. A panic-stricken assistant, a dress in each hand and a belt slung around her neck, looked like she wanted to run and hide. And then there was the model. It took this many people to take a picture?

"Serena," a voice drawled from the back, and Madam Eyeliner turned around. Okay, not Parker. Something inside me was happy about that. The photographer and his lighting assistant moved out of the way. The voice belonged to a man, deeply tanned, with perfectly styled white hair. He covered his eyes and mumbled something. Lounging back on what looked like the only comfortable chair in the room, he sighed dramatically and proceeded to talk to Serena in rapid Italian, pointing at the model and a pile of clothes on the floor. Serena said nothing, only nodded at his every word. When he was finished she said, "Of course, Gianni," and clapped her hands at the assistant, who first jumped like a scared rabbit, then started unclipping the model's outfit. Through it all none of them even looked at me.

Time to find Parker. I moved forward and bumped into one of the makeup tables, watching in horror as it teetered in slow motion. The guy with the Kabuki brush made a dive, saving it just before everything slid off.

"You can thank me later," he said, holding up his hands in triumph. Now everyone was staring at me. I backed away, hoping I wasn't going to have to spend a lot of time here. It would be a disaster looking for an opportunity.

Gianni pointed a stubby finger at me.

"Who. Are. You?"

"Uh, Bec Jackson."

"Do you belong here?"

"Yes! I'm looking for Parker—"

His imperial nose sniffed. "If you're not part of this shoot, wait over there." He motioned to the door with a sweep of his arm. "Out of my way."

I edged carefully toward the hall, wondering if I'd successfully blended into the wallpaper, when I nearly stepped on a tall guy in a tailored jacket and trousers, his shirt unbuttoned enough to prove that he was ripped, his eyes on a tablet. When he tore his attention from his device it was to give me an up and down. He was blindingly stunning, but the curl of his lip told me he didn't think the same of me.

"The schoolgirl look only works in Japan," he said—in American English.

"I'm—" I started.

He rolled his eyes heavenward. "Bec Jackson. Also known as my latest headache."

Hey! I was a compatriot!

But he stalked off, stopping a short distance away, then turned and huffed. "Stop gawking. I don't like to be kept waiting. Come on!"

If I apologized nicely, would Dean Harding take me back?

Not a chance.

I hurried after him to a back room where he pointed to a dusty corner.

"Put your stuff there. Trust me, no one will touch it," he said.

I wondered how he was so sure, but instead I asked, "And you are . . . ?" I wanted to know who I was dealing with.

"Kevin Clayton, managing editor. Now, as the newest *intern*," he said as if saying the word left a bad taste in his mouth, "your job is to tend to the models. They want water? You get it. They need a neck massage, you do it with a smile. You deny them carbs, no matter how much they beg—it makes them look bloated in pictures. But do it nicely, and make sure they eat something. They need to be kept happy and focused—if they aren't, no one around here will be happy or focused. Got it?"

I held up a hand.

Whoa.

Wait a minute.

"Intern? I think there's been a mistake. I'm *staying* with Parker—uh, I mean, Ms. Phillips. She's expecting me."

"Parker delegated you to me," he snapped, killing any hope of a reprieve. "You'll see her later."

I blew up my frazzled pink bangs so he'd see how annoyed I was.

"I just got off a plane. Where's the bathroom? And I need something to eat."

"Bathroom." He threw a hand over his shoulder, indicating a room behind him. Then looking at me as if lunch was something I should reconsider, "The caterer was here earlier. There might be some fruit left in the kitchen downstairs, which you can look into *after* I'm done with you."

As soon as I got out of the bathroom he crooked a finger at me. "Let's go."

I followed him, hoping I didn't pass out from hunger or dehydration.

"I'll introduce you to everyone," he said, as if he didn't relish the task. "Unfortunately Parker couldn't bring everyone over from New York. Titles don't matter here, so everyone pitches in where it's needed." He paused at the open door of the room where my not-so-fun encounter with Gianni the White had taken place.

"First rule, never interrupt a shoot, for anything, not even lunch. The models are expensive, and they get paid by the hour, so every second counts. I heard you already met Gianni," he said, tilting his head at the designer, who was back on his throne. "Don't even speak to him unless he asks you a question or tells you to do something. The photographer is Angelo, his assistant is Aldo. Ugi does makeup, Joe does hair. Serena is the executive editor, has first say on styling the photo shoots. I handle the details of everything else.

"That's Taliah." He pointed to skyscraper-girl from the photo shoot I almost ruined, now twirling around in a slinky fuchsia dress. I could see her skeleton poking through. Kevin's fingers grabbed my shoulder and he swung me around to face several doors across the hall. "That office is Parker's."

The one with the nameplate that says "Parker Phillips"? Thanks for the info.

"The one to the left belongs to Serena and me. There's the bathroom, and then the wardrobe and changing rooms. That last small door is a storage room." He walked over to the balcony and leaned over, pointing. "Francesca is our receptionist. Toward the back is the kitchen, to the left is the common area where we edit copy and photos, write and fact-check articles, do research and administrative work. It's not a big place and there aren't too many people. Even you won't get lost."

"You mean like you did when we first got here and Serena sent you to look for the extra binder clips?" said a female voice, softly sweet.

I turned around to find myself face-to-face with a pretty girl—red hair, creamy porcelain skin, and green eyes. She smiled. "We never have enough binder clips. Seems the models get thinner every season." She held out her hand. "I'm Sophie."

Kevin looked like he was fighting being annoyed and amused. "Show her how to work the espresso machine. She'll be using it. A lot." With a final dark look at me, he turned and left.

He so needed to chill.

"Don't mind Kevin. He's a little high-strung, but he's not so bad once you get used to him," Sophie said when we were safely out of earshot.

I didn't plan on being here long enough to get used to him or anyone else. I followed her down into the kitchen. Thankfully there was a lot more than fruit. A large tray of sliced meats and cheeses rested on the counter, along with a basket of biscotti next to the monster espresso machine. I filled a plate while she worked.

"Cappuccino?" Sophie asked, filling one of the filters with ground espresso. The rich smell of ultra-strong coffee snapped me awake. I could use a gallon of the stuff, I could feel jet lag settling in.

Nodding, I said, "I'm Bec, by the way."

"Nice to meet you. I hear you're staying with Parker." She snapped the filter into place and switched on the machine. "And that you'll be interning here."

"That's a surprise to me," I said.

She raised pale brows at me as she tipped two small porcelain cups under the spout to catch the steaming espresso. "You didn't know you were interning?"

"Not exactly."

She pressed her lips together into a sympathetic smile. "Well, it's not so bad. I'm an intern too. I help Parker with the copyediting. She runs a tight ship, but she's fair. I think you'll like it here."

Francesca poked her perfect face into the tiny kitchen.

"Make me a cappuccino. I was out all night and I'm so tired," she said, then looked over her shoulder. "I'd do it myself but . . . I have to stay at the desk." And then she was gone.

"Like the models, Francesca can't figure out how to use this thing, but she can work every free app and game on her cell phone." Sophie made a face in the direction of the front desk. "Poor thing has to stay up front—unless Angelo is screaming for a model who's late. Then she offers to 'fill in.'" Sophie struck a model pose and blew a kiss. "She's a little unfulfilled as a receptionist."

I giggled and Sophie joined me.

"I can tell we're going to be friends," she said.

Sophie spooned a thick dollop of frothy milk onto the top of each cup before handing me one and sipping from the other. For the first time since Dean Harding called me into his office, I started to relax. It felt good not to be alone.

"Where are you from?" I asked, taking a sip.

"Boston. I'm in Italy for a semester and staying with a host family not too far from here. What about you? What's your deal?"

The truth? I got kicked out of school and Mom banished me here because she knows Parker.

"My mom and Parker went to college together. She had a long business trip and couldn't take me along. Dad's traveling too." There. The truth, but only the part she needed to know.

She eyed my whistle, dangling outside my shirt. "That's an interesting accessory. What is it?"

"A Cap'n Crunch whistle."

"You mean you got it out of a cereal box?"

"Not exactly. It's kind of like . . . an antique."

She squinted at it like she was trying to understand. "Does it work?"

"Sure," I said, and picking it up, blew a blast on it. A few people turned around. "Sorry!" I said. "But that's not what it's for." *How to explain* . . . "Okay, so the frequency of this whistle was the exact same frequency the phone company used to route calls before everything went digital. If you blew the whistle into the phone when you dialed the operator, you *became* the operator."

Sophie's eyes widened. And I steeled myself for the inevitable eye roll and possible "You're a freak" look that would follow, but she smiled and glanced at the nearest phone.

"Let's try it!"

I laughed. "We can't. Not anymore. Phone systems have changed a lot since this whistle was made."

"What could you do, if it did work?"

I shrugged. "Make free long-distance calls, get information . . ."

She gave me a knowing look. "So you're a hacker."

I grinned. "I prefer *information vigilante.*"

"I see. Well, your secret is safe with me, but for the record, I think it's cool. You'll have to show me something sometime."

I gave a noncommittal nod. I didn't hack on command, or to show off. Draining my cup I said, "You totally missed your calling."

She struck a dramatic pose, her long hair drooping seductively over one eye. "Model?"

"I was thinking barista. Or maybe comedian."

She snorted. "I have enough material from working in this place to do a stand-up routine. Interning here is the price of getting my foot in the door to be a fashion writer." She rolled her eyes at one of the models passing by. "There are days when I have to remind myself that I really want to do this work instead of being a dog walker."

I spent the next four and a half hours fetching bottles of water, cell phones, and other items within two inches of each model's fingertips. They came and went: in the door, into Ugi's makeup chair, then to Joe for hair, and then in front of Angelo and Aldo and out the door again.

Around 4:30, Sophie looked at the clock and prodded me, her eyes lighting up. "Maybe we'll get lucky and there'll be a delivery today."

I was about to ask her what she meant when a buzzing hum tore through the open front window, louder than the usual traffic. I knew that sound. It was an open carburetor modified to let more gas into the engine, increasing the speed over what a vehicle straight off the assembly line could reach. Dad insisted on setting the one on his classic Harley bike the same way. The neighbors hated it when he took it for a ride.

"We just got lucky!" She giggled and dragged me over to see.

I looked into the street to see a yellow Vespa pull into an empty spot and idle down. Then the driver took off his helmet and *holy cannoli*, did I start to feel lucky.

Windblown blond hair, faded jeans, and a tight blue tee shirt outlined a totally *delizioso* body. He looked up, and catching Sophie's eye, waved. Then his gaze shifted to me.

I. *Melt*.

Sophie leaned on the sill next to me. "He's sooo hot! And sweet too. Come on." She dragged me downstairs. Didn't have to tell me twice.

The messenger-god walked into the downstairs area the same time we did, a fat envelope under his arm.

"*Ciao*, Dante," said Sophie, a bright lilt in her voice.

Dante. Like the poet. I was definitely feeling the inferno.

He smiled and winked at her.

Um . . . my turn?

Dante turned a glorious, blue-eyed stare at me. "*Sto cercando . . .*" He looked at the package, "Rebecca Jackson?"

I didn't know what the first part meant, but at least I recognized my name, and it sounded oh so luscious rolling off his tongue.

"That's me."

He smiled shyly and handed the envelope over. Promptly, I dropped it.

Laughing, he scooped it up from the floor and presented it to me as if it were a bouquet of red roses. I dragged my eyes away from him and checked the address. It was from Dean Harding. Oh joy—my homework. He must have put it all together last week when he and my mother had their secret meeting.

Dante carelessly tossed his hair, but it slid right back, making a curtain over one sexy eye. I was thinking that things weren't going to be so terrible, independent study notwithstanding. With a crooked grin that left me speechless, he turned and left.

Breathe, Bec.

"Such a waste," said Taliah, moving next to me, a disbelieving look on her face.

I turned to her. "What?"

"Do you know how many times Angelo tried to get him to model? I've seen agents chase him down to put a business card in his hand." She quickly peered over to where Francesca sat at the front desk flipping through a binder fat with model photos. "She'd kill for an opportunity like that, but she'll never get one—not with that beak."

I tried not to stare at Francesca's slightly hooked nose. It didn't seem *that* bad. Other models had imperfections—a space between their front teeth, eyes two different colors, or a beauty mark—and that didn't stop them from making it to the runway or a front cover.

Taliah shook her head and threw up her hands. "He could be making twenty times what he's getting being a delivery boy. He won't even date a model! So stupid."

With an exaggerated swing of her hips, she strutted away. I glanced at Sophie, who shrugged helplessly. I decided that messenger-god Dante was someone I wanted to get to know better.

"Bec!"

I looked up to see Kevin leering down from the balcony like a vulture.

"Parker wants you in her office. Now!"

"She's here?" I gasped. "Why didn't anyone tell me?"

He looked bored. "She had important things to do. Hurry up."

I tried to remember the many faces I'd seen during the day. One of them had to be Parker's, but which? "Where?" I asked.

"You forgot already?" His voice was snide. "Maybe the door with the sign that says 'Parker Phillips'?"

As I trudged upstairs, I thought it might be a good idea to learn some low-down, insult-your-mama Italian that I could use on Kevin.

Better yet, Dante could teach me.

"Come in!" called a muffled voice.

I opened the door, steeling myself to meet Parker Phillips.

A petite dark-skinned beauty rose from behind a cluttered desk to greet me. Her hair was sleek and cropped close to her head in tight-set curls. She reminded me of a glossy blackbird, bright-eyed and quick.

"Hi, Bec. I'm Parker. It's nice to have you here." She stuck out a firm hand for me to shake. I took it, mine soft in her tight grip. "I'm sorry, I should have met you at the airport myself and introduced you to everyone, but things have been crazy." She swung an arm around her office, which was crammed with a large desk; boxes overflowing with papers, photos, and fabric samples; and shelves stacked with back issues of *Edge* and other magazines. "Rome isn't New York, no real office space to be had, so we had to rent this town house."

"It's homey," I said, and I meant it. Definitely not a "corporate" type of place. I liked that.

She grinned. "Isn't it? Maybe I can convince our publisher to change things up back home. First, though, I'd like to start with extending our stay here."

I tilted my head at her. "Has anyone ever told you—"

"That I look like the First Lady?" She laughed and sat back down. "Yes, I get that a lot. Go get your things while I shut down my computer. Then we can talk on the way to the hotel."

Finally! Mom never said anything about me working for fashionista fanatics. I hoped Parker would set this all straight. Maybe I'd still come back to visit Sophie, though—say, around 4:30 . . . when Dante stopped by.

I retrieved my backpack and laptop case from the corner where Kevin had told me to stash them. He was right about no one touching them. After spending an afternoon at the *Edge* office, I understood why no one there would have any interest in me or my gear. No labels. No leather. No logos. In other words: L. A. M. E.

Parker exited her office, wrapped in a brilliant orange shawl and carrying a coordinating Birkin. I followed behind. Mostly everyone was gone—except Kevin and Sophie. They sat on opposite ends of the vast common area, bent over their laptops with papers and photos spread all around.

"You're still here?" Parker said.

Sophie looked up. "Just going over these last edits."

Parker smiled. "Kevin!"

He raised his head.

"In the morning, we need to go over the ad proofs," she said to him, and slid an eye in Sophie's direction. "Now, lock up and go out on a date or something."

He looked stunned. And embarrassed. "But what about—"

"Kevin," She threw up a hand and now looked directly over at Sophie as if the message was meant for her too. "It'll get done tomorrow. You're in Rome. Go fall in love, throw coins in a fountain, or visit a museum."

"But—"

"Go. Home."

Kevin smiled tightly, and although he looked taken aback, nodded and said, "We're leaving. See you tomorrow."

I followed her outside. The sky had just started to darken, and the sun glinted gold over terra-cotta rooftops.

"My staff might be small, but they're dedicated. And Kevin"—Parker sighed—"he's so . . ."

"Intense?" I offered dryly.

She smiled at me. "That's the word."

Well-dressed men and women strolled by us as we walked to the hotel, nodding and smiling as they passed. The late spring air was warm and scented first with strong espresso and the sweetness of toasted hazelnuts as we passed a crowded café, then with the sharp snap of garlic that wafted out of an open restaurant door. My stomach rumbled. Parker kept up a steady stream of chatter as we walked.

"We're staying at the Hotel Beatrici while we're working on the September issue," she said, keeping a brisk pace in what had to be three-inch heels over the cobblestones. At this point my brain was too weary and underfed to do more than keep one foot moving in front of the other, but I somehow managed to appear interested and paying attention. "We do the location photography on-site except for some indoor shots. At the office we handle all administrative and editorial tasks." She paused, giving me a sympathetic look. "I'm sorry, you're tired and you must be starving. I called ahead for room service, so we shouldn't have to wait too long."

The Hotel Beatrici looked like a miniature palazzo with ornate, whitewashed colonnades, floor-to-ceiling windows, and elaborate lights that hung over the doorways like giant stars. The yellow stucco walls glowed invitingly in the golden aura of the lamps, and an impeccably uniformed doorman swung open double carved oaken panels, letting us into a posh lobby with black-and-white checkered marble floors and high ceilings. I wondered if Mom had it so grand in Belize, but all of it, the elegant entryway, the crystal chandeliers, and Parker's Italian banter with the concierge, blurred together into a muffled mash of sight and sound. I didn't care about the architecture, the history, or the opulence. I just wanted to eat, shower, and sleep. Or sleep, eat, and shower. Whatever order, it didn't matter.

I barely registered getting into the elevator and following Parker into our suite like a tired puppy on a leash. When I stopped moving, though, I gaped at the room and let my bag and laptop slide gently to the floor.

"It's . . ."

"Pretty magnificent," said Parker, setting her things down.

Okay, I'd go with that, but *ostentatious* was the word that came to my mind.

We were in a small sitting room. Inlaid tables and delicate chairs with tufted velvet cushions in jewel tones were artfully arranged in the center and along the walls. Heavy jacquard drapes that matched the foiled wallpaper framed tall windows that looked out over the city, capturing the soaring columns of a centuries-old church across the street as if it were the central subject of a painting—but one that changed depending on the light. Each window offered a view of a different scene. I could've stood there for hours staring at each one, watching the light slip lower as it ran like fingertips over the tops of the buildings.

Parker laughed. "It's a little overwhelming, isn't it? Why don't you take a quick shower while we're waiting for the food. That"— she pointed at the door to my left—"is your bedroom. Towels and everything you need should be in your bathroom. I had Sophie run out and get pajamas, a robe, and a change of clothes for you. Your luggage should arrive tomorrow. Your mom made arrangements for it to be shipped from your school."

"Thanks," I said, wondering what else Mom had told Parker— about school and about me.

Inside, I found everything just as she'd said. I was glad Sophie had been chosen to go shopping for me; she had decent taste. She'd bought a knit dress and a pair of wedge sandals, both black—guess you couldn't go wrong with that—and in the right sizes. There was also a hot pink silk scarf. On closer inspection I could see that the floral pattern was a photographic print; black-and-white images of circuit boards, wires, and other hardware—totally me. But how could Sophie know?

Mom must have talked to Tam, who talked to Parker, who talked to Sophie.

A little lump welled in my throat.

Mom.

I was overtired and choked it down, turning the shower on full blast.

The hot water was bliss on my grimy body and gritty hair, the shampoo delicately scented with lavender, the towels fluffy. Slipping into silky-cotton pj's the same color as my hair, I sauntered out into the sitting room, where a silver serving cart had arrived. It was laid out with dishes of sliced chicken, bread, salad, fruit, and a bottle of wine.

"Here." Parker handed me a plate piled with a bit of everything and a glass of wine. "Shhh! No need to mention this to your mom. It's an Italian custom, and our little secret."

Trying not to wolf down the food was hard, but I forced myself to take human-sized bites. I sipped the wine slowly. It was dry and tasted like wood. I smiled weakly, not getting what people saw in the stuff. But it was followed by a mellow warmth that wasn't so bad. I wasn't a fan, but I swallowed. Several times. To be polite.

Parker's intense gaze made me leery and I looked away.

Was she gearing up to lecture me about the thousand things I must have screwed up today at the office? With the dirty looks Kevin gave me all day, I was sure he handed her a list of my bads before we left. If things didn't go well she could ship me back home. . . .

And face Mom and Dad? Not my best option.

"Wine is supposed to relax you, not make you worried."

My head snapped up; I must've looked as surprised as I felt.

"I'm around young people all the time. I don't have any children of my own, but sometimes I can read them better than their own parents." She took a sip of wine. Me too—for my nerves, of course.

Parker slipped off her heels and curled her legs up on the chair, swirling the ruby red liquid in her glass. "Your mom is one of my best friends, although we don't get to see each other much anymore. We're both too busy."

I wondered why Mom didn't talk more about her friends. Maybe then being here wouldn't seem so weird, like I was dumped with a stranger. Although being dropped off at a boarding school wasn't much different.

"Your mom's always talking about how sharp you are. It doesn't take long to see that."

I could feel a "but" coming next.

"This is the deal, Bec. You're not here for me to babysit. Besides doing your schoolwork, you'll intern for me."

"I will?" I asked.

I didn't mind having a job, but please! Not one with demanding models, overbearing designers—and Kevin. Anything but that—but I didn't have much of a choice. And what would I be doing all day, and for how long? Did Mom fill Parker in on my special skill set?

Parker looked surprised. "Didn't your mother tell you?"

I stared at my half-finished plate, no longer hungry. "We didn't have a lot of time to talk."

"No matter. There's so much to experience here. The designer boutiques, open-air markets. Every street has something historic if you're into that. There's always the usual tourist stops or a million other fabulous little places you won't find in the guidebooks. This could be the most wonderful summer of your life."

"Summer?" It was only late April! I thought Mom and Dad were going to be home in a few weeks.

Parker set down her goblet carefully. "She told me if things worked out, a little time away from home would be good for you—*if* there are no problems. I don't have my full staff with me—not even my personal assistant—and these Italian segments are only one part of the September issue. Thank God for the locals and temps Serena managed to find to help us out."

"Like who?" I asked.

"Aldo, Ugi, and Joe, not to mention the models. This whole trip would be a disaster if it wasn't for Serena. There's so much to do that everyone's pulling double and triple duty. You're going to do a bit of everything. You may assist the photographers one moment, type copy the next, and then arrange meetings for me. After Rome, we'll be back in New York. Are you up for it?"

Her dark eyes were direct and probing. I swallowed reflexively; I knew what that look meant. She kept a high-profile magazine running smoothly, navigated through a foreign city like a native, *and* agreed to take me in with my less-than-stellar reputation. She wasn't afraid of anything.

I considered the alternatives. Run away? No. Cry to go to Belize with Mom? Not possible. Make an illegal dip into the credit card for a return ticket to Cali? Don't even think about it! I was stuck here, though it seemed like an okay deal and Parker seemed pretty chill— *seemed* being the operative word all around.

"I'm in," I said, not without reservations, though I hid them well.

She smiled, then yawned and stretched, almost catlike. "You don't remember, but I stayed with your family once for a week. I believe you were just 'excused' from that private school in Massachusetts."

The memory of the embarrassment from two years ago came rushing back—I'd been caught making unauthorized changes to my schedule.

Parker laughed. "Keyboarding class is overrated." Then she grew serious. "None of that hacking stuff in my office, understand?"

"Okay," I said—like I had a choice.

She nodded with approval. "So this will be home base for you. The entire hotel is rented out to the magazine. And we'll be seeing some world-famous people pass through, starting with Theresa Jennings. She'll be joining us here in three days."

"The *First Lady*?" I said, incredulous.

Parker laughed again, then fixed me with a serious stare. "She's coming to Italy for the Fashion Fights Famine gala, but she'll be taking some time to do some photo shoots and an interview with us. Theresa Jennings handpicked *Edge* for this exclusive. She likes that we have a diversified staff—and I'm sure the fact that *Edge* is one of the few high-profile fashion magazines steered by a fellow African American woman isn't lost on her."

"That's so cool."

She nodded. "It is. And I probably don't have to tell you that Mrs. Jennings—or any celebrity guest's privacy—must be respected. You're not to discuss magazine business with anyone outside the office."

"I promise." I kept lots of secrets—various PINs, access codes, how I broke into my parents' telecom carrier to get more minutes on my data plan for free. I had enough secrets already to deserve a high security clearance—or be on a government watch list.

"Good." She picked up her cell and dialed. "Eat," she said while she waited for someone to answer. "Ortiz, will you and Nelson step in? Thanks."

A few moments later there was a knock on the door and a woman and man stepped into the room. She had golden skin and dark, thick hair. He was stern-faced with brown hair buzzed very close to his head. They both wore basic black suits.

"This is Special Agent Maria Ortiz and Special Agent Bradford Nelson. They are the Secret Service advance security team for the First Lady. You will cooperate with them, understand? This is very important, Bec. We can't have any problems with Mrs. Jennings coming here."

I nodded vigorously. People like me, with slight "smudges" on their records, didn't argue with the Secret Service. "Yes."

Parker stood. "Thanks, Ortiz, Nelson. See you tomorrow." They left and she turned to me. "Now, you need to catch up and reset your internal clock. Finish that glass of wine. There's no drinking age in Italy, but I trust you won't abuse it." She tipped her glass at me, and I felt myself relax. I could do this.

"Get a good night's sleep. I'll see you in the office by ten."

"Good night, Ms. Phillips."

"Parker, please." She gave me a warm smile.

Back in my luxurious room, I slipped into bed and was immediately swallowed up by the down mattress.

It was.

So.

Soft.

I never did finish my wine.

Hello Darling,
I landed safely and hear that you did too.
We'll catch up soon.
xxx Mom

I read Mom's e-mail out in the sitting room while the hotel maid was busy in my suite. I wondered if she sent the message when she knew I'd be asleep and unable to respond right away on purpose. Well, I guessed we were all where we had to be.

I found a note from Parker and a phone in a designer case on one of the tables. She must've put them there before she left. The note instructed me to have breakfast and then meet her at the office. The number for room service was scribbled on the bottom, along with walking directions back to *Edge*. After our dinner talk the night before, I was looking forward to getting to know her a bit better. Maybe with a couple more glasses of wine, she might spill some really good Mom stories.

Refreshed, I got a better look at my room. The ceilings were painted with a mural full of fat cherubs and bare-breasted women in opulent gowns and ribbons. The walls, covered in foiled and textured paper, were framed by scrolled and gilt woodwork. The furniture with its inlaid paneling and fluffy bedding and cushions looked like it belonged to a contessa. It was like living in a jewelry box.

Before I called room service, I customized my new phone and synched it with my laptop, then looked up an online English-Italian dictionary. If I was going to be here for a while, I'd better start learning the language. After a few listens to the autotranslate, I called in what had to be the worst-accented breakfast order they'd ever heard. Then I took another shower to wash away the fuzziness of sleep. It was going to take me a little while to get over the jet lag and time difference.

I had just finished rebraiding my hair, noticing the blonde roots starting to peek through under the pink, when there was a knock on the door. I opened it up to find an attractive older woman in a stiffly starched black uniform.

"*Buongiorno,*" she said. "Good morning."

Before I could reply, she slid a serving cart into the room and proceeded to pour espresso and uncover dishes for my inspection. There was a small plate of artfully arranged prosciutto, the meat sliced so thin that I could see the pattern of the china underneath; a cup of melon; and a plate with one golden, crescent-shaped roll that looked worth every bad-boy calorie.

"*Scusi.*" I went over to my backpack, found my purse, and pulled out the twenty the Fiat driver refused.

She waved her hands, refusing my offering, then smiled at me.

"Thank you," I said, adding hurriedly, "*Grazie,*" and smiled back. She nodded approvingly and left.

The buttery pastry melted in my mouth, and the espresso was so strong each cup required three teaspoons of sugar. The stuff could fuel jets, it was so intense.

Showered, fed, and outfitted in my sleek new clothes, I felt human again—and determined not to be at anyone's "Bec and call." As nice as Parker and Sophie seemed, I didn't want to tend to models—or deal with Kevin Clayton, Office Dictator. And was I getting paid for this internship? No one had mentioned a word about a paycheck. Resigned to a long day, I packed up my laptop and left the glittering hotel, strolling along and taking in the scenery I'd missed the night before. Budding flowers and tiny curled vines crept over the stucco walls of ancient houses, and I took care walking over the uneven pavement, inches taller in my cool wedge sandals. Could I get used to this?

At first I wasn't sure because there were so many cars, Vespas, and motorcycles that it was hard to tell one sound from another, but after a few seconds, I was certain: I'd heard this particular droning buzz before. And I tried not to smile.

A yellow Vespa putted until it was next to me, keeping pace. I turned my head to the driver.

"*Bec, come sta?*" Dante pulled up to the curb and, taking off his helmet, shook out his shiny blond hair.

"Hello, Dante," I said, unable to keep the delight out of my voice. "What's up?"

"Busy day," he said, looking over his shoulder at a pile of envelopes and boxes bound to the back of the Vespa with a bungee cord.

I'd rather be rolling around Rome, my arms wrapped around you and delivering packages, than going to certain servitude at Edge. Parker would be too busy to spare any time for me so I'd be delegated to Kevin as soon as I walked in the door.

"You working at the magazine?" he asked. "I thought you might . . . be a student."

"Yeah, I'm kind of doing both. What about you?"

"I go back to school soon. Need to save some money first. You want a ride over?"

I looked longingly at the Vespa. I wouldn't mind taking it for a spin around town—but I didn't just go riding around with guys I barely knew, gorgeous or not. Besides—what would Sophie say if

I showed up clinging to Dante on the back of his ride? She might not appreciate it if she was into him. Common sense prevailed.

"I want to walk around a bit and see everything," I said, not wanting to hurt his feelings.

He tilted his head at me and flashed the smile that made my stomach do flip-flops.

"Okay. Next time," he said, and putting his helmet back on, turned the Vespa into the road and disappeared in the traffic.

I hurried through the crowded street. It was a sunny day, but the occasional chilly breeze made me long for my hoodie, which was en route with my other things from school arriving who knew when. At lunchtime maybe I could go shopping with Sophie.

Francesca was on the phone when I walked in, speaking so fast I couldn't catch any words but "Parker." Looking up and seeing me, she impatiently waved at me to go upstairs.

The place was even more hectic than yesterday. Downstairs had been calm, but now people rushed around, yelling, bumping into each other. When I reached the top of the steps I spied Taliah in the big room fussing with the wardrobe racks, and another model looking semicomatose as Ugi slapped a palette of color onto her face.

"No more late nights!" he scolded her. "You want these dark circles to be permanent?"

"But Gianni gave me a personal invitation to that party." She sniffed. "No one says no to Gianni!"

"You start to look like an old lady and you'll be lucky if Gianni will let you carry his shopping bags. No more crazy parties! You wait until after the shoot!"

A series of bright flashes startled me; Aldo was adjusting a light for Angelo, who was clicking away on his camera.

"*Sinistra! Sinistra!*" he shouted at the model in front of him. She pouted, and swayed to the left.

Seeing me, Sophie hurried over and pulled me to the balcony. Below I could hear the espresso monster gurgling away. The rich aroma of roasted coffee beans wafted up to where we stood. I was already full of coffee but suddenly craved more. I hoped they had lots of sugar.

"Parker's not here. Everyone's going crazy," Sophie said, sounding anxious.

I frowned. "She left me a note and told me to meet her here, but maybe something came up—a last-minute appointment or a meeting."

Letting go of me, Sophie shook her head. "She did have an appointment. *Here.* Parker never does a no-show. And she's *always on time.*"

I didn't understand what the big deal was. Everyone was late sometimes, reputation or not. Parker probably stopped somewhere to field a phone call. I was willing to bet she got just as many as Mom. Or maybe she stopped in one of the bajillion cafés I'd passed on the way to the office and decided to indulge in an early cappuccino. And wasn't life supposed to be more relaxed in Italy? One wouldn't be able to tell by looking at this office. Here it was never-ending mayhem on a colossal scale.

"So call her," I said.

Sophie regarded me gravely. "I did. So did Kevin and Francesca. She didn't answer—and Parker *always* answers."

Again with the "always."

"I'm sure she'll be here soon."

"You don't understand." Sophie lowered her voice when a lanky model slunk by to go downstairs, probably to the kitchen. She gave us the evil eye—poor thing had to get her own water! We stood there, not saying a word until she was out of earshot.

"There are a million things to do, and Serena's not here either. That means until one of them gets back, Kevin's in charge."

I could see how that would be annoying. No—more than annoying. But I was sure Parker would show up soon, and when she got wind that he went all tyrant in her absence, Kevin might find himself on the next plane to you're-fireds-ville. Before I could assure Sophie that everything would be okay, Kevin stepped onto the balcony and sharply demanded quiet from everyone.

His expression grim, his mouth tight, he said, "Parker's in the hospital."

The air rushed out of my lungs as the shock hit. Kevin waited while people gasped and fretted. Some of the models just stood there, looking clueless or unconcerned.

My heart sank as I thought of Parker; the connection we'd managed to make in our brief conversation. Although now I was . . . *free*. What or who could stop me from buying a plane ticket to anywhere? No one. I'd have to call my parents, but it could wait a few days. . . .

"Serena just called. Parker and Agent Ortiz were in a car accident early this morning and were taken to the emergency room," Kevin said. "Apparently it's serious."

My grand plan to escape curled up into a ball that wedged itself in my throat. There was no way I could leave now, not if Parker was—

"Is she okay?" I asked.

Everyone started talking at once and Kevin tried to shush them.

"I'll pass along any information as soon as I find out," he said quietly, "but the order from Serena is to stay on schedule. The First Lady will be here the day after tomorrow and Serena said to keep things running as usual, so until *she* gets in, *I'm* keeping things organized."

Grumbles of discontent erupted all around, but everyone dispersed. And if Serena said to keep things going, it might not be *that* bad, although car accidents could be harrowing experiences. No one knew that better than me. That time I took Dad's new Lamborghini to get a latte? I really should've figured out how to drive a stick shift and parallel park before I got behind the wheel. Traumatic—most def.

It was a relief that Kevin wouldn't ultimately be in charge, but

I hadn't really seen Serena in action. It would be best to keep busy with a low profile and not think about the possibilities of what could happen. I shuffled behind Sophie, unfortunately still catching Kevin's eye.

He motioned to us. "Sophie, Bec—you're with me."

Sophie and I followed Kevin into Parker's office.
He did have the decency not to sit in her chair, but he pulled something off her desk to show us. Something big.

"Is that a—" I started.

Sophie shook her head. "No. You didn't. Kevin, that's not a—"

"It's a chore chart," he said, holding it up with obvious pride.

When did he have the time to make that?!

"I've been working on it, but haven't had a chance to show it to Parker yet."

I had to shield my eyes, nearly blinded by the neon glare of multiple Post-it notes. My column was all pink.

"I don't need a chart to know what my job is," Sophie said, crossing her arms over her chest, clearly not impressed.

Francesca glided by the door and peered in, her eyes sliding over the poster board. "Nice chart," she said, then made a pouty face. "Where's Angelo?"

"In the studio where he belongs," said Kevin kindly. "You need to stay at the front desk. I'm waiting to hear from Serena."

She sighed heavily before melting back into the hallway. He followed her with his eyes before returning to his chart of Domination and Distress.

"I think we're done here," Sophie said and moved to leave, but that only snapped Kevin's attention back to us. He went over our assigned duties in painful detail. My glamorous Italian adventure— reduced to a poster board of pink sticky notes.

I knew what Kevin was up to. When Serena came back to the office and Parker eventually returned, he'd show both of them how well he kept things running while they were out. He had to be sucking up for a promotion or a raise. Maybe his name on the masthead?

In the end I did none of Kevin's assigned chores. To keep the issue on schedule, I was recruited by Aldo to set up for the morning and afternoon shoots, call the models to confirm their sessions, and of course make uncountable cappuccinos. As Parker had said, other parts of the September issue were being tended to: bit columns on accessories, a double-page spread on the upcoming trends for eyeliner. While Parker and Kevin claimed everyone did a little of everything, it felt like I did most of the work reserved for people on the bottom rung of the ladder.

Sophie and I passed each other on the stairs, each time with a grim "I can't wait for this day to be over" smile. But even in all the chaos, there was a sort of restraint in the atmosphere. Every time the phone rang everyone froze and quieted. When, after a few moments, no message came from Francesca with news on Parker, everyone reluctantly went back to work. It was hard to concentrate, but staying busy helped me not to focus on "What if . . ."

At the end of the day, there was still no word.

Back at the hotel, I ordered room service for dinner. Between forkfuls of pesto-soaked gnocchi, I trolled the Internet for area hospitals. I called the closest ones, trying to locate Parker or even an African-American woman who had been admitted. Between their poor English and my worse Italian, I had no luck. Finally my body begged to go into sleep mode.

Tomorrow, everything will be better, I promised myself.

But it wasn't.

In spite of being exhausted, I had a restless night and didn't sleep well. In the morning, I was disturbed to find that there was still no news about Parker's condition.

"Any word?" I asked Kevin as soon as I could get him alone.

"No. But Serena's here . . ." He didn't finish, and he sounded annoyed—at my question, or at his new boss?

I debated calling Mom. I didn't want to worry her, even though I'd gotten no clue about Parker's status, which directly affected my own. I had ways of finding things out. Serena had been with Parker before the accident. She might spill some valuable intel—if I asked the right questions. The problem was where and how to corner her.

At that moment she appeared on the balcony and clapped her hands for attention. She wore a serious frown, but there was a glint in her eye and a sharp edge to her lip that looked like she was almost fighting a smile. Parker told me that things would be a wreck without her. Was she pleased about being in charge now? She opened her mouth to speak, but at the same time there was a loud crash as the front door was flung open.

A statuesque blonde woman in sky-high alligator heels and a crisp navy suit with edges so sharp they could slice off a finger swept through the place with an entourage and on the arm of a man who looked like he'd arrived fresh from Fashion Week in Paris or Milan. His suit was a dark coppery color, set off by a pumpkin-colored shirt and striped tie. A coordinating paisley pocket square peeked out in two perfect points. His hair was wavy, not too long, and he had an exotic look to his eyes. Which didn't look kindly on any of us.

Behind them came Nelson, and then Ortiz, black-eyed and bandaged, and a new guy—tall, dark, and menacing.

It became instantly silent as everyone, myself included, stared. Serena still stood on the balcony, her mouth open, apparently awestruck. I knew the blonde woman—totally knew her—but couldn't immediately remember from where. Behind me, someone whispered, "It's Candace Worthington!" I had a name, but still couldn't place the face.

Her dishy companion unhooked himself from her arm and flipped a slim palm in introduction. "Candace Worthington will be taking over *Edge* for Parker Phillips," he said, looking down his nose and speaking in a posh British accent worthy of the stuffiest aristocrat.

"You," she pointed a danger-orange fingernail at Kevin, "must be Kevin."

"Managing editor," he said, stepping up with a hand out for her to shake, but she squashed him with a look.

"Come with me." Then she glanced at Mr. Dish, who acknowledged her with the barest of smiles. "You too, Varon," she said to him. "Everyone else," and she whirled around like a lethal ballerina, looking at each individual person, "you know what you need to do for the next half hour. Do it. And be quiet about it." She twirled a dismissive wrist jangly with golden bracelets and strode briskly up the steps. When she reached the top she paused to raise her large black sunglasses and glare directly at Kevin. "Coming?" He hurried after her to Parker's-temporarily-Serena's office. A moment later, I heard a door slam.

I couldn't decide if I liked her or hated her. Candace Worthington, Candace Worthington . . . *Who was Candace Worthington?*

All eyes turned to the new Suit. He glowered back, assessing everyone. When his critical eyes landed on me, taking in my pink-with-blonde-roots braids, he frowned. I smiled back brightly and turned to Sophie.

"This isn't going to be good."

"That's an understatement," she replied morosely, tugging me into the kitchen. Yes. Coffee. Now.

I chuckled. "Although Candace put Kevin in his place."

Sophie punched my arm. "*Ms.* Worthington!"

"Candace, Ms. Worthington, who cares?"

"Do you live under a rock? That's *Candace* Worthington. Super-model? Reality show host?"

Then it clicked.

Oh yeah.

Former supermodel. The bitchy cohost of such quality TV view-ing as *You Want Me to Wear That?* And, *Did You Get Dressed in the Dark?* Oh yeah. And the star of that scandal when she flipped out on a designer boutique owner who tried to sell her an imitation bag. She brought TV cameras, cops, and state and federal investigators and ended up uncovering a multibillion dollar counterfeiting oper-ation. No one crossed her.

And now she was my new boss.

No.

No no *no! No buona fortuna!*

"This *really* isn't going to be good," I said.

Sophie gave me a slow, sad nod. "You bet your Gucci."

When Kevin emerged from Candace's—no, Parker's— office, he was dazzled and frazzled—and called me over with a finger snap.

"Candace wants you to go to the hotel with agents Ortiz, Nelson, and Case, and show them where her room is, and then—"

"I don't know where Candace's room is," I cut him off. I didn't— and *no one* snapped their fingers at me.

"*Candace* is staying in Parker's suite. *Candace* is in charge of *Edge. Candace* is now your boss, so you'd best make her happy."

Candace had better not think *she* was going to be both boss and guardian. Not. Happening.

"What about Parker?"

Kevin's arrogant face went soft with worry. "She's still in the hospital."

"Which one?" I demanded.

Back came the sneer. "Candace didn't say."

Candace had all the answers, didn't she? Except the ones that I wanted. Mom and Dad would have something to say about this—

I didn't care how busy they were. I opened my mouth to protest, but Kevin had already waved over Ortiz and Nelson and the new Suit, Case.

I'd play along for now, but as soon as I got a second alone, Mom was getting an SOS call.

Varon stood close by, looking absolutely perfect; not a hair mussed, nor a wrinkle in his perfectly coordinated ensemble, not even a shiny nose, although it was warm.

"You coming too?" I asked him.

A patronizing smile. "Ms. Worthington needs me here," he said, as if I should have known better than to ask.

So much for trying to be friendly. Or helpful. As soon as I deposited the Skulking Suits at the Hotel Beatrici, they'd be on their own.

We drove the short distance in silence. When we pulled up, three porters hurried down to the car. They struggled to unload Candace's luggage—a dozen bloodred leather cases of varying sizes, each piece monogrammed with an oversized cream-colored C and secured with shiny gold locks. I watched them steer their unwieldy carts up a side ramp and into the lobby.

Case checked in at the desk while I waited off to the side, sneaking surreptitious looks at Ortiz and Nelson. Ortiz looked like she was in pretty rough shape. I guessed that she'd been driving the car. That meant that Parker was on the passenger side—the "Death Seat," my driver's ed teacher called it. Ortiz caught me looking at her and the corners of her mouth twitched, like she was fighting a small smile.

Finished with the concierge, Case motioned us over, but when I tried to follow, he held up a hand. "You can go back to the office. We're good on our own from here."

"You sure?" Not that I was really interested in helping them, but if Candace and I were sharing a suite and they were moving her in, I didn't want them touching any of my stuff.

"We're good," he said. "We need to clear the area for Mrs. Jennings's arrival. No one who isn't personally approved by us gets inside the perimeter."

Perimeter, checkpoints, surveillance—lots of security. I understood that. Theresa Jennings was the First Lady, and Parker, who was supposed to be hosting her, had been in an accident. That didn't look good. Still, my room was up there and I wasn't an outsider. "But—"

Case frowned so fiercely his eyebrows disappeared below his shades and the fight went out of me. I'd bide my time. I still had to locate Parker and tell Mom what happened. I'd never responded to her e-mail. As I left the hotel, I tapped her number into my new phone.

Ring . . . ring . . .

"Cici Jackson, leave me a message . . ."

Leave a message? Why wasn't her ear glued to the phone like it always was whenever I saw her? What should I say?

Hey, Mom, Parker got into a car accident. Have you heard from her? Because I haven't. I know I promised no hacking, but I may need to break that promise to find out what's going on. But no worries. Candace Worthington is looking after me. You know, Candace You-Want-Me-to-Wear-*That? Worthington. You must have seen her on TV once or twice. Well, gotta run! Have to escort the Secret Service around Rome! Ciao!*

Nope. That wasn't voice mail or text message material.

"Hey, Mom! Got your e-mail, my new number should show up on your phone. Call me when you have a sec!"

End call.

Around the city, bells tolled. It was noon and I was starved. I passed shop after shop, searching for a place to snag some food, ducking into what looked like a deli.

When it was my turn to order at the counter, I pulled out my wallet, still full of American dollars. Damn. I hadn't exchanged them for euros yet. Looking up into the eyes of a rotund man with a kindly face, I held up a $20.

"No euros," I said. God, did I sound pathetic.

"*Sì.* Dollars."

Yep, those were American dollars. One last, longing look at the scrumptious buffet behind the counter, then dropping my head down in disappointment, I turned to go, but he tapped the glass with his huge fingers to get my attention.

"What you want, *bella*?"

My stomach growled, not afraid to embarrass me. "Um . . ." I scanned the case and pointed to a puffy, shiny topped bun.

He nodded. *"Carla! Una brioche!"*

Carla bustled behind him and handed him the brioche, nestled in waxed paper. She'd split it in half and stuffed it with something that looked like ice cream.

Reaching under the counter, he pulled two small cookies from the showcase and stuck them into the ice cream. It was almost too pretty to eat. Seeing my surprise, he put a finger to his lips.

"Shhh!" He winked at me, handing over the bounty.

"Grazie!"

As I walked, I savored first the delicate crumble of the cookies as they melted on my tongue, then the ice cream as it burst out of the flaky brioche. I licked my fingers, not wanting to waste a precious morsel.

My sweet reprieve didn't last long. When I got back to the office, it was as if I'd stepped into one of the lower circles of hell. My pit stop had given Case ample time to get back ahead of me, and now he had everyone in the office lined up.

Kevin saw me, scowled, and gave me a dressing-down glare. "And where have *you* been?"

"I was at the hotel with Ortiz, Nelson, and Case, remember?" Well, I *was*. I didn't think that stopping to eat counted as blowing off work. Just because the majority of the staff counted every calorie didn't mean I was going to follow their example. I smiled sweetly and directed my attention to Case. At least I knew his attitude came from being official.

"Agent Case said you left before he did," came a voice from above. Candace peered stiffly from the balcony, Varon behind her with an open tablet, tapping away. "From now on, you're to report straight back here when you're given a task."

You're not in charge of me, whatever Kevin says, I thought mutinously. I wouldn't accept that I had to go hungry because it wasn't on anyone's schedule. Thankfully she dropped it and turned her attention to Kevin.

"Bring water, espressos, and some crudités," she said to him, and then to Case, "You can use Kevin and Serena's office." She looked up and down as if she was examining everyone's face. "Everyone needs to speak with Agent Case." Then with a curt nod, she spun smartly in her alligator heels, and on her long legs glided back to her borrowed office, faithful Varon in tow.

"She's not going to let anyone leave, not even to eat, until we've all been 'talked to,'" Sophie whispered, annoyed—and probably hungry. I was glad I'd stopped at that bakery.

"Don't just stand there. Get everything together," Kevin ordered, his voice low and tight—and through clenched teeth. I wanted to refuse—she'd ordered *him* to get the food—but I didn't need any more trouble. I rounded up water, coffee, and chopped veggies on a dish—and Kevin snatched them from me.

"I'll take that," he snapped, spilling some steaming coffee on his hands. With a stare that promised ill for me, although I wondered how that could've been *my* fault, he stomped out, muttering under his breath about stupid interns. I suddenly missed uptight deans and shallow prep-schoolers.

Case peered over the balcony and called to me. "Rebecca Jackson?" I moved into view and he waved me up.

Agent Case ran through a mini-documentary on my life, which didn't sound so good, even to me. There was no detail that seemed to have escaped him. So why the inquisition? He even knew what flight I'd been on, but the questions were relentless and I was losing patience.

"Did you talk to anyone at any of the airports?"

"No."

"Did anyone approach you on the planes or at the hotel?"

"Only the old man who drove the taxi like we were on the Daytona Speedway, Parker, and the woman at the hotel who brought up my breakfast, saving me from starvation." His tightly knit brow told me that he didn't appreciate my witty repartee.

"Have you talked to anyone about the First Lady's visit?"

"I didn't even know about it until I got here, but no, I haven't talked about it to anyone."

"When was the last time you saw Ms. Phillips?"

My voice cracked a little when I answered. It seemed like everyone had forgotten about Parker. "The night before last we walked back to the hotel. We had dinner, then I went to bed. Is she . . . is she okay?"

He paused as if he was thinking—debating on what he should say. Finally he said, "Stable but critical."

Critical? That wasn't good.

I swallowed my fear. "Where is she? I want to see her. She's my guardian while I'm here."

"Yes, we're aware of that. Ms. Worthington will be responsible for you until other arrangements can be made."

Responsible for me? Other arrangements? How . . . caring.

"Unfortunately, Ms. Phillips is unable to have visitors and I'm not authorized to give out any information." He looked genuinely apologetic. "I'm sorry."

It's okay, Bec. You've dealt with worse. Well, not really. But this was no different from any other set of problems to work out. Case might not have been able to tell me where Parker was, but I knew I could find out and go see her on my own. No one, not even the Secret Service or Candace I-Eat-Nails-for-Breakfast Worthington, would be able to stop me.

I emerged from my interrogation to find Ortiz and Nelson bustling about in a cool but determined matter. Ortiz had an electronic device and was scanning everything as if it had a bar code. I knew what she was doing—looking for listening devices. I guessed frequent security sweeps would be the new norm around here, probably until the First Lady left. But I was still wondering about Parker, what injuries she had. Where she was. Serena and Ortiz were the last people with her before the accident. One of them had to know something. I was pretty sure I could talk my way around Serena if she would give me a moment—and why not? It wasn't like she had much say anymore. Candace had stepped on, and into, those editor's shoes. Ortiz, on the other hand, was a trained Secret Service agent and so more of a challenge—but hey, I was up to one if it came to that.

I slipped downstairs and into the bathroom that was right off the kitchen, checked my makeup and my braids. And then I heard Serena's voice.

"I can't believe how bad it was!"

"You did what you had to." That sounded like Ortiz. "Stop worrying about it."

It was nice of Ortiz to comfort Serena, I thought.

"How long do you think she'll be in the hospital?"

"I don't know. Her injuries . . . were extensive," Ortiz trailed off. Was she unwilling to say any more? Agent Case did say the information was classified.

"And Candace? How long will she be here?"

"Her being here is as much of a surprise to me as to you."

Ortiz didn't sound too happy. And Serena . . . there was no mistaking the anxiousness in her voice.

Then it hit me.

She wanted to run the magazine.

She was Parker's second in command and would have been running the show if Candace hadn't shown up. They stopped talking, but I waited a long time before coming out. I wanted to be sure that they were both gone. When I opened the bathroom door, there was Ortiz standing by the espresso machine. The squeal of the hinge made her start and turn around.

"Bec?"

I nodded, trying to keep a straight face, as if I hadn't heard anything private.

She scrutinized me closely. "I didn't know you were in the bathroom."

"The one upstairs was occupied." I scrunched up my face. "The men use this one. So it's almost always free."

A short laugh, and then, thankfully, she turned away.

I spent the rest of the afternoon fetching accessories, food, and water and getting yelled at in Italian by Angelo. When he wasn't manning his camera, he was eating. Aldo, who usually doubled up as Angelo's personal waiter, was AWOL on a long lunch. Aldo's surrogate—me—had been busy being interrogated, and Angelo was hungry.

What kept me going was that whenever Sophie and I crossed paths, we smiled and mouthed, "Four thirty!"

Dante time!

But the magic hour came and went with no deliveries. And I really *really* needed one happy moment after all I'd been through in the last two days.

Sophie shrugged at me when we packed up to leave for the night. "I probably should have told you he doesn't come every day."

"Maybe tomorrow," I said, feeling let down.

Before any of us could go home, Candace insisted we all had to have staff photo IDs taken. I wasn't taking a picture without a little sprucing up; my school ID card was scary enough. For once, I counted myself lucky that we were stuck behind the primping models, giving Sophie and me valuable time to improve whatever we could. I sidled up to her as Ugi "fixed" her already perfect complexion. I leaned over to borrow a brush from Joe but he pushed me into the chair.

"The braids," he said as he unraveled my hair, "too young for you." A few pulls of his brush and a spritz of something that smelled like plums, and he handed me a mirror.

"Ooooo!" was all I could get out. I loved my braids, but this . . .

"Nice color, *bambina*. But no need to look like a little girl." He wiggled his fingers at the model behind me. "Next!"

Dismissed, I moved into Ugi's chair.

Ugi rolled his eyes in Joe's direction. "It's nice," he said offhandedly, as if he didn't want to admit it.

"Office romance gone bad," Sophie said under her breath next to my ear as he sorted through his array of skin-toned powders. "I'll have to fill you in later."

Ugi gave me a dab of foundation and a swipe of lip gloss and mascara. "Don't go overboard, you don't need much," he said sternly as I stood.

"It's not a beauty contest," said Case, tapping his arm.

Ugi shook his head and shooed me away with a grumpy "You're welcome" to my "Thanks."

It took over an hour to get my badge. I said good-bye to Sophie and started making my way back to the hotel. It felt so good to get out of the office.

A cool breeze played with my hair, sliding it across my face. I brushed it out of my eyes. A few steps ahead of me, a guy with his back to me sat on his Vespa. Two girls smiled and played shy, batting their lashes at him.

I knew who owned those broad shoulders, that golden mane—Dante!

Maybe it was being in Rome, or the new hairdo, or hearing the heartbeat bass of his voice that made my breath flutter in my chest, but I found myself walking right by him.

Close enough for him to see me.

"Bec!"

I stopped short and turned, a totally believable look of surprise on my face.

"Dante! *Come sta?*"

"*Ciao*," he said to the two girls, who looked miffed that he pushed his scooter over to where I stood.

I win!

"Your hair, it looks *bella*, beautiful. I like it very much."

A little shiver ran down my spine. "*Grazie.*"

"Want to take a ride? I can show you around town."

I winced. I oh so wanted to, but wasn't sure if it was a good idea with Candace monitoring my movements.

"How about we grab a drink instead?" I pointed to a café few yards away.

"Okay." He grinned and rolled his Vespa down the side of the street. "So, you like Roma?"

"I like it more every day," I answered truthfully. Sure, I'd been shipped here without my consent, but I was discovering so many amazing things, like the breathtaking sight of Dante in front of me.

The Vespa parked, Dante chose an outdoor table under a large canvas umbrella. All around us, waiters bustled, people chattered, plates clinked. He pulled out a chair for me.

And a gentleman too.

"It's better here, we can watch the people go by." He waved to someone. "You know," he said, leaning closer and whispering conspiratorially, "you can tell all the Americans. They wear jeans and sneakers." He shook his head sadly, then smiled. "But not you. Ever since I saw you, you are different. I like that. And today, you are different again."

I smiled at the unexpected compliment. "So, what's good to drink here?" I asked.

"Forget the drink. Get a limoncello gelato."

"Dessert before dinner? I'm in!" Rome was so decadent!

He ordered, and soon the waiter brought a single plate stacked with scoops of pale yellow gelato—with two spoons. As we savored the tangy-sweet dish, Dante asked, "Are you an exchange student, like Sophia?"

It sounded so cute, the way he called her So-fee-ah, rather than So-fee. I shook my head. "No. I'm still in high school."

He waved his spoon energetically. "I finished last year. Now I am saving up to study in America. I have cousins who moved to New York City. Tell me about Broadway! Times Square!"

I smiled apologetically. "I live in California."

His eyes lit up. "Hollywood! Have you seen any movie stars? I would like to visit there."

Again I had to disappoint him. "Sorry, I don't live near Hollywood or L.A. I live farther north and I'm usually in boarding school because my parents travel."

He looked a bit sad. "My parents never traveled out of Italy. I want to see the world. First, study in the United States to make a fortune."

We spent the next hour discussing places around the world we wanted to see. At the moment, he was working two jobs. Soon, his sister would finish school and get a job and he would be free to travel.

When it was time to go, Dante paid the bill before I could offer to chip in, and then he walked me back to the hotel, pausing in front of the doors. I knew one of the agents was probably watching.

He sweetly kissed my cheek and grinned. "I see you again, no?"

I nodded—hopefully not too eagerly. "Yes, I'd like that."

"*Buono.*" He waved and walked back toward the café and his ride.

Happy, I strolled into the lobby. Inside, Nelson stood by the elevator looking deceptively relaxed; I could see his fingers twitch as I approached. Bet he had a gun under all that black.

"Rebecca," he said, and stood aside so I could go up.

In the suite there were clothes and boxes piled everywhere. Gingerly stepping around the stacks, I headed toward my room. Parker's bedroom door was open, and I caught glimpses of a coat, a hand, and a sensible shoe. There was a flash of silk, maybe an evening gown. And then someone staggered past, hidden behind a stack of monster electronics. Varon spotted me and kicked the door closed with his foot. Totally rude.

Were all those cases full of clothes? What did a model-turned-reality-show-star-turned-temporary-editor need with so many high-grade laptops and electronics equipment? Why would Secret Service agents be unpacking for Candace? If that was part of the security detail for the First Lady, why was it in Candace's bedroom? And where had they put Parker's things?

My room, on the other hand, was exactly the way I'd left it.

Or was it?

Having had more roommates than most people have in a lifetime, I'd figured out ways to protect my privacy. A single hair draped across my laptop, pens aimed at some focal point, money hidden in smelly shoes. Only I hadn't had time to set up my usual safeguards. Anyway, a strand of my neon pink locks would be too bright and noticeable lying on the black cover of my laptop—and I'd had that with me all day, so it was safe. Was I paranoid? A little. I'd had my share of privacy invasions.

Still, something didn't feel right. I had nothing anyone would want, but something was out of place. I scanned the room. On the desk was the homework packet from Dean Harding.

I'd left it with the text facing the window; now it faced the door.

My room had been searched.

7

I banged on the door of Candace's room. The talk on the other side went silent, and after a long moment, it opened. Varon stared back at me, his eyes narrowed in annoyance.

"What can I do for you, Miss Jackson?" he said.

"I want to see Candace. Now." I tried to peer around him, but somehow he managed to take up all the available space the doorway had to offer.

"Ms. Worthington is busy."

"I. Don't. Care."

Suddenly Candace materialized behind him, towering head, neck, and shoulders over her proper PA. "What is it, Varon?" she asked. Catching sight of me, she wrinkled her brow—someone skipped a Botox session. "What do you want?"

"Someone was in my room," I said.

I thought I heard Varon huff. Candace definitely did. "I doubt—"

I crossed my arms over my chest. I wanted to show them I meant business, and I wasn't leaving until I was taken seriously.

Candace stared at me but eventually Her Highness gave an impatient sigh. "No one searched your room. Why would we?"

I fixed her with a stare. "I never said you did. And I don't know why, all I know is that someone, not me, was in there. My homework packet was moved. The address on the envelope was pointing toward the window when I left. After I came back from the office, it was pointed in the opposite direction, toward the door."

"The maid service—"

"I was here when they were. My stuff was moved after."

Her face gave me no clue to what she was thinking. She tapped her fingers against her elbow; 1, 2, 3, 4. . . . "I'm sure with all the excitement, the First Lady's upcoming visit, the Secret Service asking questions—"

"It's true!"

Her tone was even and sure. "No one was in your room. We know everything about you. Unless there's something new . . . ?"

"No." My reply was a bit surly, but at least it wasn't offensive. Yet.

She nodded. "I thought so. Now, I don't want to be bothered with nonsense like this again. I don't have time for it." She held up a broad palm when I opened my mouth to argue. "No one touched your things, Rebecca. Go back to your room." She turned away. "Varon," she called, and the door was slammed in my face.

WTF just happened?!

I felt like banging on the door again, but I was smart enough to know when I'd been dismissed.

No—dissed.

And I wouldn't be getting any further information.

Right there I made a holy vow to get even with Candace. No one—and I mean *no one*—touched my stuff and got away with it. It was probably one of the agents who did it—before they returned to the office, when I'd stopped at the bakery. Or it could just as easily have been Blondie herself. Or her little minion. They were both here before I was, thanks to the ID photography session. I stomped back to my room. Someone had been in there, and dammit, I was going to find out who and what he—or she—messed with.

I pulled my pencil case out of my backpack, retrieved my makeup kit from the bathroom, and took out my black eye shadow, blush brush, and some clear tape. I locked the door against someone coming in, then like a CSI investigator hunting a serial killer, I dusted the surface of the desk and the envelope from Dean Harding. Real detectives used a special black powder. I would have to make do with MAC Onyx Dust.

Using the brush, I gently swept the powder away and a number of fingerprints appeared. I took a picture of each with my phone, then using the clear tape, lifted the prints off. I didn't bother doing the entire room because between maids and former guests, I'd get too many prints to identify. The desk and the envelope were enough. I stuck the samples in a notebook. Now the only thing left to do was to get prints from Candace, Varon, and each agent and find who matched. If it was Candace, then my evidence would prove that she was a liar and I wouldn't believe anything she told me. If it was any of the agents, well, then I'd blame her for that too.

Satisfied with my plan of action, I moved on to the more important task of finding Parker. I'd already called the closest hospitals, but in addition to the language barrier, it was possible that an order not to disclose the fact that Parker might be there stood in my way. Time to go stealth digital. If the agents were watching—monitoring the Internet—they'd be able to see that someone at the hotel was trawling for Parker's name. Of course I would be the prime suspect. Couldn't have that! Bypassing the hotel's wi-fi, I tapped into a neighbor's connection and scrambled my IP address just to be safe before I launched a search of all the hospitals in the city. That done, one by one I coded myself into the patient databases.

Medical Nuovo Salario. Nothing.

Casa Di Cura Villa Salaria. No Parker Phillips.

Nothing came up in any hospital in Rome.

Case said he couldn't disclose where Parker was, but she couldn't have gone far if she was in serious condition. I had to dig deeper, but I knew I wouldn't have much time; I was sure Candace itched to get rid of me, so any excuse—like getting caught hacking in a foreign hospital's patients' private records—would do. Mom would be in Belize for the next two weeks. If I got sent back to the States, she would have to cut her business trip short and she'd be furious. I'd never managed to kill one of her deals. Or Dad's. What would they do to me if that happened? House arrest?

I ate dinner alone in my room and used the rest of the evening to try and dig up some dirt on Candace. I only found things that everyone already knew: temper like an unstable volcano, a penchant for five-inch heels, preferably in the skin of an exotic species like Komodo dragon, baby seal, or shark. And that infamous icy stare. Surprisingly, there wasn't much on the Web about her life before her glamorous career.

No one came looking for me even though I'd been quiet for hours, which just reinforced everything I'd heard and seen on TV: Candace Worthington was domineering, stone-hearted, and cutthroat—and didn't notice anyone she considered beneath her. I was unnecessary and unwanted baggage. And with my history, a potential security risk. I was pretty good at covering my tracks, but I'd have to be extra careful with the Secret Service sneaking and snooping about.

First I would locate Parker and find out exactly how and why she ended up in the hospital.

Then, I'd turn my attention—and talents—to Blondie.

The next morning I stopped by my new favorite panetteria for a coffee and pastry. Just about every place I passed reminded me of running into Dante. I was about to leave when my friend the baker came out of the back.

"*Come sta, signore?*" I waved to him.

He threw up his hands, a jovial expression on his face. "Eh! *Buono, buono!* Good!"

Candace hadn't given me an exact time to come in or specified that I had to be escorted, so I felt no guilt about taking my time and stopping for breakfast. I couldn't face Kevin and Candace on an empty stomach. This time I ordered—and paid for—an ice cream–stuffed brioche. There was only one way to walk and eat: S-l-o-w-l-y.

At the office I discovered Francesca holding Taliah captive halfway between the kitchen and the front desk. Kevin really should consider stapling her to the reception chair.

"I heard that Taj is coming!" Francesca gushed.

Taliah's eyes sparkled. "If you stay at your desk, you'll be the first one to see him! Oh, I'm *so* jealous!" From her pinched smile I could tell Taliah didn't mean a word about being jealous, but Francesca let out a breathy gasp and practically ran back up front.

I strolled past, trying not to laugh. Taj was probably some model, photographer, or designer they both had their claws out for. Big deal. I had more important things to think about: like keeping a sharp eye on what Candace, Varon, and the agents touched.

I offered to take Case's cup to the kitchen when he finished his coffee—and stuffed it behind my backpack. First item to be dusted for prints—acquired. There were plenty of powders and brushes around, so no one would notice if I borrowed what I needed. The problem was the actual dusting without getting caught. That would really raise eyebrows and questions.

When Nelson, the agent with the buzz cut and itchy trigger finger, threw away his water bottle, I noted which one it was and began to collect the trash around the room as soon as he was gone. I was about to lift his bottle and dump the rest when—

"What are you doing?" said Kevin over my left shoulder, making me jump.

"Straightening up." Well, I *was* collecting the trash, but only to get Nelson's prints.

He nodded. "Initiative. Keep it up."

After he turned away, I made sure no one saw that I stole Nelson's bottle and dumped the rest. Holding it by the cap, I quickly stuffed it behind my backpack with Case's cup. No one was paying any attention to me as I organized the makeup tables upstairs and pocketed the dark setting powder and brush used on Taliah.

Trying to play it James Bond–smooth, I headed toward the bathroom, bulging backpack and all—and almost ran into Candace coming out.

"Hey," I said and kept walking. She didn't react and didn't seem to see me watching her out of my peripheral vision. She headed downstairs, not back to her office. Opportunity! I nipped across the hall. Praying no one would spy me, I snuck into her office.

It was a good thing Candace saw herself as something special. No water bottles for her. Crystal glass only—and she'd left one on her desk. The morning sun shining through the windows highlighted her bloodred lipstick and several nice, clear prints. I swiped it, turned to leave, and there was Varon standing in the doorway in another exquisitely fitted, expensive-looking suit. He leaned with one slender palm pressed on the inside of the door frame. When would I be able to dust that? Probably never.

"What are you doing?" he said.

I lifted up the glass boldly. "My job. Collecting dishes and trash. Haven't you seen Kevin's chart?"

"With a backpack?"

"Multitasking," I said, not missing a beat. "Kevin says I can't stash my stuff up here anymore. Figured I'd stop in to see if there was anything to clear away. And look." I shook the glass at him.

He deliberated a moment. "Fine. Go."

I pushed past him and ran downstairs to the kitchen, not stopping until I was safely locked in the bathroom. Only then did I exhale. *Close call!* I held the bottle, the cup, and last, Candace's glass up to the light for closer inspection. The glass had three glorious prints. My guess: index, middle, and thumb.

Priceless.

I dusted and photographed the glass, then ran them through the Compare/Contrast app on my phone. Who knew an app designed to compare designer handbags to see if you bought the real thing or a fake could also be used for comparing other things—like fingerprints. The result—no matches.

Somehow I felt deflated that it wasn't Candace who'd searched my room. But that just meant she'd had one of the agents do it. When I found a match, she was going to hear about it.

I dusted the bottle and cup. No match on Case or Nelson either, clearing them. That left Agent Ortiz and Varon. I took a wet paper towel and wiped away the powdered prints. Ducking out of the bathroom, I stashed my backpack under a couch in the common room.

With the agents about, I was more determined than ever to keep their prying fingers off my laptop. If they found out about my hospital trawl and confiscated it, a search might reveal things that would set me up for another round of questioning—and maybe a red-eye flight back home. And I wasn't leaving without finding out about Parker.

All that was left was to return the borrowed brush and powder to the makeup station, put the water bottle in the recycling bin, and wash the cup and glass—which I did without anyone having a clue. I joined Sophie, who was helping Francesca stamp and address envelopes at the front desk.

"Should I have Joe cut my hair? Taj is really into bangs now," Francesca said.

Sophie shrugged in response.

"Who is Ta—" I began to ask, when Kevin interrupted me.

"Bec. Angelo needs you in the studio."

"I'll go!" Francesca jumped up, smoothing her hair. Kevin shook his head and crooked a finger at me. "Now."

I spent the remainder of the morning as Angelo's second assistant, which meant tilting lights by the millimeter, learning which camera he wanted next, and adjusting Taliah's clothes seam by seam. When the day crept past noon, people started trickling out of the office. Sophie found me helping Aldo dismantle the gigantic green screen.

"Let's go out for lunch," she suggested. "You look like you need to get out of here."

"We'll have to sneak out," I whispered, "Candace hasn't given me permission to leave."

Sophie laughed. "No need. She's already gone." Downstairs, she grabbed her purse from a desk drawer and I quickly snagged my backpack from under the couch.

First we stopped off at a bank where I exchanged more of my money. Apparently we got lucky because the clerk behind the desk was about to shut down for his own lunch.

"Who closes up at one in the afternoon?" I asked.

"Around here? That's normal. Everyone takes a long lunch, except at *Edge*." She made a face. "But even we can take a breather once in a while."

My greenbacks swapped for colorful euros, I stuffed them into my wallet as we stepped outside. From out of the corner of my eye, I noticed Agent Ortiz, but she got lost when a group of tourists passed by. She seemed to be looking for something or someone. Deliberately, I turned away. She was part of Candace's crew, and I didn't want to risk meeting her eyes and giving her the opportunity to tell me that I wasn't allowed out of the office.

"Let's go," I said, urging Sophie ahead. We walked down a street to a little sidewalk café and I didn't look back to see if Ortiz had seen us or followed us.

"You'll love this place," Sophie gushed, "they have the best *pranzo* in town."

"*Pranzo?*"

"Lunch! Hope you're hungry!"

The meal was long and languorous. Sautéed chicken, fresh tomatoes, and basil tucked into tiny nests of angel-hair pasta came first, followed by a pile of zucchini flowers, golden, crispy, and stuffed with cheese. Mom would love the fact that I was dining out and not holed up in the hotel room in front of my computer with a bag of chips and a can of Red Bull. I glanced at my watch more than once. Candace had us all on a short leash, and I did *not* want to get on her bad side.

"Don't worry," said Sophie. "She's lunching with some Italian journalists, and you can't hurry them through a meal. I promise we'll be back before them." She sipped her lemon water. "So, how do you like working at *Edge?*"

"It's okay," I said, not wanting to sound critical or admit even to myself that despite my initial resentment, I was starting to like being here. "But it's not what I would have chosen for a summer job. What about you?"

Sophie pushed her mostly empty plate aside and leaned back. "I thought I'd be able to write more, even if it was small sidebars and fillers, anything that could make an editor say, 'You're fabulous!' The most writing I've done is photo captions."

The waiter brought the check. Ten euros each—not bad for all that food. We pulled out our wallets and paid.

"So, is that what you want to do? Write for a fashion magazine?" Inwardly I shuddered at the thought, but hey, not everyone could be a techno geek.

"I've been writing since I was five and pulling outfits together since I was seven."

I could believe it. Sophie always looked good—in the way that you didn't notice her outfit so much as her. Today she had on a simple white linen skirt, tee, and brown jacket, all perfectly fitted and accented with an ethnic-looking belt and gold earrings. Nude-toned pumps with a chunky heel made her long legs seem endless.

"Fashion is in the sky, the street." She went on, "It has to do with ideas, the way we live, what's happening. It's the ultimate form of personal self-expression."

I nodded, considering. "That's deep."

She smiled. "That's Coco Chanel—paraphrased, of course. I love finding the connection she and so many other designers see between fashion and life."

I stood. "Come on, we have to get back. I'm sure Kevin is in the process of finding new ways to torture me, like assigning me to help Francesca do her job."

On the way back to the office, I spotted Ortiz again on the opposite side of the street. Where had she been? Not in our little café, but there were plenty of them all through the neighborhood.

As soon as we walked in, Sophie was sent to run errands, and I got to take care of all the models' clothes. Of course the skinny darlings dropped them all over the floor, turned inside out.

Kevin pointed to a heap of sweaters I'd dumped in a pile with one of his pointed two-tone brogues. "What's this?"

It seemed obvious to me. "Those are the dirty clothes. Is there a laundry basket or bag to put them in?"

He nudged the offending pile. "These are very expensive, one-off *loaners*. You don't *dump them on the floor.*"

Then you shouldn't be touching them with your shoes.

"So what do I do with them?" Me, intern, new here, *capisce*?

"You. Hang. Them. Up. On a rack, with notes saying to which designer they have to be returned." He sighed. "I can't believe Parker, Candace—and now I—got stuck with you. Serena doesn't know how lucky she is."

My cheeks burned while everyone paused to listen to my dressing down.

"Kevin!" called Serena.

He stalked away to join her. She was sulking in a corner with "the Book"—the infamous *Devil Wears Prada* binder that was the ever-evolving draft of the current issue. I didn't see why she was so upset. Apart from the official title and the nameplate on the door, Serena had gotten what she wanted. Candace seemed too busy to concern herself with running *Edge*. I hadn't seen her do a single work-related task for the magazine since she arrived. Serena made all the decisions—which models wore what clothes, what copy would be used. Everything.

I hoped that she'd keep Kevin busy for a while, but of course I would never be so lucky. He came back a few moments later and shoved a USB drive and a stack of marked-up papers at me.

"Serena needs you to enter these corrections."

He jerked his head at a table set up with laptops and printers for me to use. A model whose name I couldn't remember was parked in front of one and playing solitaire. She was killing time while she waited for Angelo to call her to do the photo shoot for the half-dozen pages dedicated to new fall footwear. All the others were occupied by people doing real work—photo editing, page design, and e-mailing.

"Sorry, but I have to use this computer," I said to her.

She huffed and strutted to the kitchen like she was walking a runway.

Shaking my head, I exited the game and got to work on an article about some new designer they were featuring. Kevin's résumé was shoved between the last two pages. It definitely wasn't meant for my eyes, but I looked it over anyway. He was updating it to include a freelance article he wrote on menswear for Italian *Vogue*. If I didn't know better, I would say that he was gunning to ditch *Edge* soon.

Actually, that could be a good thing for me. I made a mental note to look into his e-mail to see where he'd be sending this. Maybe I could give him a little extra help, a shove out the door. Yeah, technically it was breaking my promise to Mom—but I was helping him, right? That had to count for something.

"Wonderful. You *can* follow directions," he said when he reviewed the fresh copy I handed to him. Then, turning to answer his phone, he waved me out. I slipped his résumé onto a corner of the desk facedown and gave him my best Botticelli angel smile. I couldn't move fast enough.

When the clock struck 4:30—delivery time—Sophie and I staked out a window on the second floor behind a stack of boxes, perfect for peering out onto the street below without Kevin, Serena, or Candace stalking us. The window was open, and we leaned out, waiting. . . .

There it was—the buzz of Dante's Vespa. He parked, kicked the stand down, and cut off the motor. He took off two packages and paused to look up. Seeing us, he smiled and waved.

With a happy sigh, I waved back. "Let's go downstairs!"

When he came in, I could hear Agent Case demanding to see ID and examine the parcels. Dante complied, giving him no trouble. Case made him open everything so he could check the contents. When he was done, he had Ortiz hustle Dante out the door before we could even say good-bye. I went back upstairs, following Sophie and grumbling that the one thing I'd been looking forward to all day was cut short.

I was helping Ugi set up when my phone buzzed with the arrival of a new e-mail. Three new e-mails, actually. Mom's itinerary, Dad's travel schedule (which didn't include any slots for me coming home yet), and a cautionary reminder that my credit card was not to be abused. I'd barely even used it! I wondered if Mom sent a copy to Parker's e-mail as a heads up in case I started bringing lots of shopping bags back to the hotel. She had to have sent Parker their schedules at the least. Since there was no mention of Parker, my parents probably didn't know about her situation. I wasn't going to say anything—yet. Things were going on as planned.

The credit card warning had me thinking there were going to be a lot of "necessities" I'd need while in Rome. I wasn't just a student anymore; I was an employee at a world-famous fashion magazine by day, and by night, secret techno-detective with an expanding social life. And I was about to meet the First Lady—tomorrow! Certain wardrobe standards had to be maintained—after all, I worked with Candace. Not even Mom could argue about a few style updates. It might even thrill her that I was dressing up.

Candace came out of Parker's office—it was still Parker's office—bristling in another power suit, this one khaki with gold buttons and tailored pants. Did she ever wear flats? She had to be near six feet, four inches tall barefoot—did she really need the extra height?

She strutted about, her sharp gaze taking in everything. "Francesca, put those files away. Sophie, if you're done with that copy, send it to the layout designer. Kevin, check on the status of the payroll. Bec!"

"Yes?"

She looked around then waved her hands. "Is the whiteboard current? Everything has a place, let's get it there, people!"

Yes, ma'am!

While Sophie rushed to finish the pile of edits, I updated the whiteboard schedule, returned messages, and filed everything within sight. The last chore was to put away the outfit Taliah was wearing as soon as Angelo finished his shoot. Thumbing through the countless dresses, I took a slinky, clingy neon green sheath off the waiting wardrobe rack and held it against me.

"What do you think?" I asked Sophie.

She made an amused face. "It's . . . colorful. Especially with your hair."

"Taj will hate it, and I have to be seen in it!" Taliah snapped.

"Okay. Who's this Taj everyone's talking about?" I asked. Maybe I would finally get an answer.

Taliah's jaw hung slack and her head jutted back. "Of course *you* wouldn't know." Then she cat-walked away.

I turned to Sophie.

"I don't want to spoil it for you," she said with a sly grin. "Google him."

Snagging one of the office laptops, I searched. There were thousands of pages of results, and they told me all pretty much the same thing: he was a guy who traveled the world blogging about fashion. And he was one of those "single name" people. Madonna. Bono. Ke$ha.

Taj.

Dark eyes, bronzed skin, and great clothes, he was eighteen, the same age as Dante. Judging from the cocky grin he wore in most of the photos I saw, he looked like a typical rich kid, probably with an attitude to match. I knew enough guys like him from my various schools to spot his type instantly—without hearing a snide insult.

Not impressed.

Sophie sighed. "That's Taj,"

"Uh-huh."

"I've heard that he only dates models. Francesca's pathetically desperate to snag him, but he doesn't like pushy divas," she confided.

"Then at least he has some brains."

"Wait till you see him in person," she whispered breathily in my ear before she sauntered away, an infatuated look on her face. "There's just something about him."

It was after six when Candace was finally satisfied enough to dismiss us.

"Wanna get dinner?" I asked Sophie when we were safely outside.

She pouted. "Wish I could, but Kevin has me taking this outfit"— she shook the garment bag in her hand—"back to the designer to be altered. I have to drop it off before seven. Tomorrow, okay?"

I shrugged, feeling more alone than ever. Then I thought guiltily of Parker. Could she even eat dinner, or was she being fed through tubes? I shook my head to shatter the thought.

"All right. See you."

With a little wave, she flung the obscenely expensive and definitely-sized-for-a-double-zero outfit over her shoulder, and disappeared into the evening crowd.

I started making my way back to the hotel. It would be room service again for me. I would try to collect the other prints that I needed and worm my way into the *polizia* database for accident reports. . . . They'd be in Italian, but flagging key words like *Parker Phillips*, *Edge*, *editor in chief*, and *American* would narrow the search and I'd get some hits pretty fast. My mind whirled with what else I could do.

Glancing around I could see that the traffic and tourist crowds were a bit lighter now, but a number of scooters and cars whizzed by. Shop windows were stuffed with handmade leather goods, sugared confections in a rainbow of pastel colors, baroque jewelry in gold and silver, and religious trinkets.

Then I saw Candace.

She passed by on the opposite side of the street. I ducked behind a fruit cart. Thankfully, she didn't see me. Even though I was heading there, I didn't want her to order me back to the hotel. And I didn't like her. She came in and took Parker's place a little too quickly for me to be comfortable, and I was willing to bet that *she* knew where Parker was but refused to say anything, just because she could. She crossed the street up ahead. Where was she going now, alone, without even Varon?

I kept to the narrow sidewalk, following her, when I heard the familiar purring of a small engine. The yellow Vespa rolled to a stop beside me, and Dante pulled off his helmet and flashed his billion-dollar smile.

"*Ciao*, Bec!"

He held out an extra helmet to me. The invitation was clear—but I hesitated. I wanted to go.

Could I? Yes.

Should I? Don't know.

Would I? Then an idea came to me that convinced me I had to.

"Can you follow Candace? The woman in the beige suit?" I said, looking left and right to see if any of the agents were around. I saw none. "I don't want her to see me."

His mouth opened but suddenly he grinned. "Like bad guys in the movies?"

"Yep!" I hopped onto the back of the Vespa, tugged on the helmet—making sure my pink hair was tucked in, just in case Candace turned around—and wrapped my arms around him. Leaning on his strong back, I felt his muscled, trim, solid middle. This could be a good thing.

"You ready?" he asked over his shoulder.

"Yes!"

We took off and joined the snaking train of traffic behind Candace and skirted down a side street. If anyone was following *me*, it wouldn't be for long.

9

With a reckless confidence, Dante wound through traffic down Via Borghese. I strained to keep an eye on Candace as she wove in and out of foot traffic, but while we waited at a light and then for two drivers who cut each other off to stop arguing, we lost her. Dante drove around a bit, but we couldn't find her again.

He pulled over and half turned on the seat. "She's gone. Why did you want to follow her and not be seen?"

I looked around. Still no agents in sight. Then I met Dante's eyes. I didn't want to lie, but I couldn't tell him the truth—that would be given out on a need-to-know basis, and right now he didn't need to know why I wanted to follow Candace. I took a deep breath. "She's my boss. Don't tell anyone, but I heard that she's on her way to have dinner with Beyoncé."

Dante's eyes widened.

I shrugged. "Guess we blew our chance to get some autographs."

I was about to ask him for a ride back to the hotel when he said, "You hungry? My cousin Adriano has a nice *ristorante*. . . ."

My stomach grumbled, making the decision. "Let's go!"

He drove onto Via della Lupa past a number of churches, some with simple but elegant stonework, others more ornate with stained-glass windows, the light behind them bringing virgins and saints to life.

He took a sharp left turn down an alleyway, too narrow for cars to follow us, even the tiny Fiats. Terra-cotta pots filled with flowers and leafy herbs squatted next to narrow doorways, and homes sat squished next to each other in varying shades of sand and clay. My teeth knocked against each other as the Vespa bumped over the uneven cobbles. When I looked down I caught flashes of squared granite and worn river stones; roads past and present meshing and tangling together.

We rolled to a stop near a building with cracked plaster walls. Long black shutters framed the windows, the thick layers of paint peeling and curling from them like eyelashes. Bright fuchsia flowers hung down from baskets on the upper floors. A blown-glass lamp hanging from a scrolled wrought-iron sconce swung slightly in the small breeze that wended its way through the labyrinth of streets. It was like time had hopscotched over this place.

I pulled off my helmet and was assaulted with the scents of fragrant herbs and roasting meat. Dante took off his helmet and raked his hair back with a strong hand. I hopped off, and he swung a leg over and pushed the Vespa into a corral of others parked near the curb. I waited for him, smoothing down my pink waves.

Dante held the heavy wooden door open for me, then followed me in. There were a few scattered rustic tables where people were eating and drinking and a small bar over against one wall.

"*Eh, Dante! Come sta?*" someone called from the bar: a sweaty, muscular guy who needed a shave, wearing a stained apron.

Dante grabbed my hand and pulled me along as he wound his way through the tables.

"*Adriano! Come sta?*" he said, and a warp-speed conversation in

Italian followed. Adriano nodded at Dante and then at me and disappeared into the back. Dante's hand slipped out of mine and found
its way to my shoulder to guide me to a table.

"I ordered for both—okay?" he asked.

"Sure." I took my seat. The table was small, and once he sat down,
we were close. If he leaned on his elbows, and if I did too, we'd be
close enough to . . .

Kiss?

Slow down, cowgirl! I scolded myself. But it didn't stop me from
thinking about it. A lot. And when he smiled at me, I thought about
it even more.

A flash of fire came from the back, followed by a sizzle. And
then the smell of fresh, hot garlic and shrimp wafted right to my
nose, making me hungrier.

A number of people waved or called hello to Dante, and by the
time he talked to all of them, Adriano came out of the kitchen and
plunked a plate on the table. On it, a small pile of golden triangles
nested in a tangle of shredded basil leaves.

We decimated the polenta as more small dishes were brought
out: paper-thin meats, and then a huge seashell piled with shrimp
and scallops decorated with fresh herbs.

"This is so much food."

He raised a hand. "This is my cousin's place." Dante patted his
chest. "He takes care of family."

Between bites, I learned about Dante's family and heard funny
stories about when he was little. I told him about my various
schools, skimming over the unfavorable reasons why I left each one.
He didn't question why there were so many, and the conversation
drifted to music we liked.

At one point I glanced at my watch. Two hours gone?! Somehow the laws of time weren't behaving; the night was moving too
quickly. While there wasn't an official curfew, it wouldn't do to
draw the attention of Candace or the agents by strolling in late.
When the last plate was cleared away, I searched my bag for my

wallet. Those euros were itching to be spent. But Dante shook his head.

"No, Bec," he said, ignoring my protests and refusing to let me leave anything. I felt bad; as Taliah pointed out, how much could a delivery guy make?

"Adriano would be insulted if I paid. And if *you* paid?" He looked horrified. "*I* would be insulted!"

I gave in and closed my pack. When we got up to leave, Adriano called, "*Buonasera, Dante! Riportare la tua capelli bella rosa amica!*" He had a twinkle in his eye.

Dante made a goofy face at Adriano, making me laugh again as he led me outside. "You have nice time, yes?"

"Yes! *Sì!*" I smiled. "What did Adriano say?"

He laughed and turned a dark shade of pink. "He tells me to bring back my friend with the pretty, rose-colored hair."

It was my turn to blush. I headed for the Vespa, but Dante grabbed hold of my hand. "You have to go back so soon?"

I thought about it. Did I have to go back yet? If Parker weren't in the hospital, I'd probably be out on the town with her right now—it wasn't *that* late. Candace might not notice I wasn't in the hotel—if she was even back. I shook my head. "No. Not yet."

That heart-melting grin again. "Good. I'll show you *my* Roma."

The restaurant sat in a tiny courtyard with a plain-looking marble cube in the middle.

"The big piazzas have fancy fountains, but even the little ones have something to look at. This one used to be a well," said Dante, walking me over to it.

Close up, it wasn't so plain. The stone was marble with gray and white veins streaking through it. Unlike the street, it was pristine, as if it was regularly cleaned. Blurred words and figures of people in togas had been carved into it a long time ago. Now the details were softened by weather and time.

Holding hands, we walked around the piazza. Every time he paused and looked at me, I felt almost breathless, as if I were suspended on the top of a roller coaster, in that dizzying moment before the fall. At last we stopped, and we faced each other.

"How long are you staying in Italy?" he asked.

"I don't know," I said, and I stared into his eyes, so blue, like pooled water in a fountain. "I'm supposed to stay with a friend of my mom's who worked for the magazine, but she was in an accident, so I'm not sure what will happen."

His face fell. "I'm so sorry."

"No one will tell me what happened or where she is because—" I stopped. Probably because the First Lady was coming. Now that I thought about it, it seemed like suspicious timing. Was that why I thought I saw agents everywhere? Did they think that someone would try to get to the First Lady through one of us? Did they think *I* was a security risk? Was my record actually coming back to haunt me, as Dean Harding threatened?

Dante's brow wrinkled. "When did this happen?"

Coming out of my paranoid reverie, I shook my head. "The day before yesterday."

"Morning?"

I tilted my head. "I think so, why?"

"Was it a car accident?"

The skin on the back of my neck prickled. "Yes."

He looked back at the café. "Adriano's brother Nunzio drives the *ambulanza*. They cleared an accident not far from your office yesterday morning." He shook his head. "Americans. They don't know how to drive in Roma. They think the roads are bigger than they are."

My heart lunged into my throat. It *had* to be her. What were the odds? American, a car accident near the hotel, and on the same day that Parker didn't show up for work?

"Do you know where she is?"

"I'll ask Nunzio and he'll find out for you."

I threw my arms around him in a tight hug. "Thank you!" I felt better with the thought that I had a good chance of finding Parker now. So much for the Secret Service and their protocols—I had friends with connections on the local level. For the first time since Parker disappeared, I felt . . . hopeful.

We pulled apart. The lights around the piazza glowed like little moons in the deepening blue velvet dusk. Dante's gaze held mine. *Closer . . .*

And as if on cue, music started to play—but not a romantic, a "Bec is in Rome, about to enjoy the most romantic kiss of her life" music. It was a twangy melody with a reggae beat, cutting into the night, the mood, and my brain. Total buzzkill.

It was the phone Parker gave me before she went AWOL.

Who dared to interrupt my Juliet moment?

I sighed, reluctantly backed away from Dante, and fished in my pack for the phone. The screen glowed out with a number I didn't recognize. If it was Sophie . . . *that* might be awkward. I hadn't gotten around to finding out how she felt about Dante. I slid my finger across the screen to unlock it and answered the call.

"Hello?" I said.

Nothing.

"Hello?"

There was a bit of a crackle on the line, and then, at last, a voice practically blared out of the speaker.

"It's about time," a man growled. The words came out deep and gravelly, and with a bit of an accent I couldn't place. Not like Dante's. It wasn't Aldo, Ugi, or the designer Gianni either.

I opened my mouth to speak, but he interrupted my chance.

"What went wrong?" he demanded.

"You tell me."

That was Candace.

"I gave you all the information I had," he said.

I pulled the phone away from my ear and looked at it. The call was live, but clearly it wasn't meant for me. *I should hang up—*

"Ortiz is a good agent," Candace answered him sharply, "and there's no reason for anyone to believe it was a hit. It's too soon."

A hit?

As in an *assassination* attempt? My hand gripped the phone tighter.

The man let out a short harsh laugh. "I have good reason to believe what happened to Parker Phillips was definitely no accident, timing aside."

I felt my knees tremble at the mention of Parker's name. My breath caught and I pressed the phone tighter to my ear. I must've looked upset because Dante frowned at me, a wrinkle of concern on his brow. I held up a finger, motioning for him to wait.

"Tell me how you know," Candace demanded. "From the initial evidence I saw, it was unavoidable."

"I can't discuss this over the phone. Meet me at the warehouse on the river at Passeggiata di Ripetta. Look for the Arturo i Fredo Transporto sign. Nine thirty."

"See you then."

And the call ended.

Passeggiata di Ripetta.

I repeated it over and over in my head to commit it to memory. Then I looked at Dante. "That was Candace," I said with a nervous laugh. "I have to get back."

"It's too late for work. She's *pazza*. Crazy." He made little circles next to his temple with a finger.

I might have found that funny if I hadn't overheard that call. Was Candace crazy—or crazy dangerous? Why did the stony-voiced man say that Parker's accident wasn't one? Who would want to hurt her?

There was Serena. She seemed more pleased about taking over *Edge* than concerned about Parker's condition—until Candace's surprise appearance.

And Ortiz—but would she hurt—almost *kill*—Parker and put her own life at risk just to help Candace be in charge of *Edge*? Would Secret Service agents do that? It seemed so over the top . . .

. . . unless they weren't really Secret Service agents.

But they had badges!

I had no way of checking if they were real without raising a lot of suspicion. Could it be a deeper conspiracy of some type? Either way, I'd find out more by going to that meeting.

I questioned my sanity, but someone hurt Parker and they needed to pay. And if that someone was Candace, I was going to make sure she got taken down, alligator pumps and all. I looked at the phone. The meeting was at 9:30—that gave me forty-five minutes to get there. I dragged Dante back to the waiting Vespa.

"I can't be late, Dante, we have to go. Can you take me to the Hotel Beatrici?" I didn't want him to drop me off at the warehouse because there would be questions I couldn't, and wouldn't, answer. I knew that Dante would insist on staying with me, and I didn't want to involve him in what could be a dangerous situation, or put him in a position to rat me out. And how could I be stealthy with a gorgeous hunk driving a noisy electric yellow Vespa?

"*Si.*" He looked a little downcast that our date was over. Hopefully there'd be another one soon.

The ride back to the hotel was chilly, and I snuggled against his broad back for warmth. The city was no quieter than it'd been when I'd left the office; people were still everywhere, walking, chatting, and sipping espresso from tiny cups or dark wine in deep goblets on sidewalk tables.

When he skidded to a stop near but not in front of the hotel, I jumped off and strapped his extra helmet onto the Vespa, then stepped back.

"*Arrivederci*, Bec," he said softly, his eyes shining in the lamp-light.

"*Ciao*, Dante."

With a smile, he buzzed out of sight.

No kiss, but still, a *bella notte*—while it lasted.

Quickly I walked a block away from the hotel to find a cab, not wanting to bump into the agents, or even any hotel staff who could run to Candace tattling about my comings and goings.

I hailed a taxi.

"Passeggiata di Ripetta by the river," I said to the driver. Scanning around, I was pretty sure no one saw me.

As soon as I shut the door, the cab took off with a squeal and a lurch that slammed me into the back seat. The old guy who picked me up at the airport was agile; this woman was a lunatic on a suicide mission. She took a hard right that sent me sliding across the seat so that I almost hit the door. I gripped the seat belt and tried hard not to think about car accidents—with Parker on my mind and this daredevil, that was pretty much impossible.

She slowed only when we reached the river; I could see the lapping water between the buildings as we rolled past warehouse after warehouse. I waved my hand for her to go a little farther in case she didn't understand. I didn't want to get out too near the meeting place.

"I got you," she said in English, then looked over her shoulder at me. "Interesting tourist site."

I met her eyes in the rearview mirror. Her lips pressed into a thin line, a disapproving look on her face.

"Be careful, *bambina*," she said. "You want I wait for you?"

There were no people or cars or cabs out here. And who knew what was lurking in that warehouse besides Candace and whomever she was meeting?

"*Sì*," I said. "I won't be long."

I hoped.

She nodded, cutting the engine and shutting off the lights as I slid out. I heard the click of the door locks.

Staying in the shadows, I walked around the warehouse, and spying the faded Fredo Transporto sign, I knew I was in the right place. Around the corner of the building, I passed cracked windows grimed over with soot and dirt and eventually found a door. After a quick glance to make sure no one was around, I ran up to it and stopped in dismay. It had an electronic keypad lock. Cracking this would cost me extra time that I didn't have. Lucky for me, it was a cheap setup. I didn't have the equipment for disabling a more sophisticated system. Carrying the necessary tool in my luggage, even if I had it, would have instantly gotten me yanked out of the security check into a room for a full body search and interrogation.

Sliding my backpack off, I pulled out my penlight. A swift look up assured me I was still alone. Using my hand to shield the light, I turned it on and searched the ground near the door.

Not too far from the walkway was a patch of dirt, bare of grass, dried and hard packed. I ground it with my foot, creating a powdery dust. I scooped up a small handful, went back to the door, and gently blew dirt onto the keypad. It was almost like dusting for fingerprints. The penlight showed it stuck to four numbers: 3, 5, 6, and 8, where residual skin oils remained from repeated pressing on the pad.

That meant only twenty-four possible combinations if it was a four-digit code string. It wasn't a high-end lock, so it probably had a shorter sequence of numbers and wouldn't freeze up with too many wrong combos, like a computer would after three incorrect passwords.

I began with 3, 5, 6, 8.

Then 3, 6, 5, 8.

Sweating, I rushed. Being caught picking a lock on a warehouse would be the most legitimately jail-worthy thing I'd done to date, taking me from hobbyist-hacker to criminal-cracker.

Focus! If Candace or the man shows up early . . .

5, 6, 3, 8.

Click!

I slipped in and closed the door behind me. A dim bulb hung from a rusted metal beam cast a weak circle of light. Stacks of boxes lined the walls. I peeked into one; it was empty except for some straw packing, old newspapers, and splinters of wood.

A garage-type door on the far side of the building began to slide open, and I quickly slunk around a stack of smaller crates, careful not to bump into them. First one, then another dark car drove through. I moved a bit farther back; I didn't know who or what I was dealing with, and at the moment I couldn't think of a plausible lie as to why I was in this section of town, in a locked warehouse, at this time of night. Oh yeah—and uninvited.

I gulped. I knew Candace had some sort of martial arts training; I saw her demolish a huge rolling wardrobe rack with a well-placed side kick when a designer tried to make her wear his reworked polyester leisure suit on an episode of *You Want Me to Wear That?* The expression on his face told me and the other four million viewers that it was for real.

Before the engines shut off, I dashed into a box that had fallen onto its side and eased the lid closed. There was a small crevice where the wood had cracked, leaving me a slit to see through. Out of the first car, nearer to the feeble light and me, stepped Candace. Gone were her couture suit and coordinating bag. Even the alligator pumps got the night off. Now she wore dark pants, a dark jacket, and dark shoes.

From the second car, which was farther back and swathed in darkness, two figures emerged. The bulkier one stood off to the side. The other was tall, but I couldn't see either of their faces. All I could dimly make out was the profile of the second man; slouchy, with a big nose. He loped farther back into the dark with an uneven gait, probably maneuvering around the debris that lay all over the floor.

Bec, you are stupid. If something goes wrong, no one knows you're here except the cabdriver—if she hasn't left. What if Candace and company check to make sure the place is empty?

"What happened to your information?" she demanded, interrupting my mini panic attack.

"Beautiful as always, Candace." It was the gravelly voice of the man on the phone.

She huffed, then gave a grudging nod. "Thanks."

"Come now," he tsk-tsked. "You need to relax, slow down. It's the way things are done in Italy."

"I can't afford to 'relax,'" Candace said hotly. "That hit—"

"—clearly missed its intended mark," he finished for her. "It put a glitch in my plans too. I shared what information I had. It should have been enough. Obviously someone didn't use it."

"It was more than a glitch," Candace grumbled.

What was the "glitch"? That Parker was hurt instead of killed? It was becoming clearer to me that Parker wasn't simply in the wrong place at the wrong time, an innocent person in an everyday car accident. She'd been in someone's way.

The Man continued, "It won't be the last problem, I'm sure. If you can't do your job, then there's no sense in wasting my time with future meetings or exchanging information. I can't afford any more unexpected surprises and neither can you."

"Don't worry. I can do my job, whatever it takes," she said, her tone quiet and menacing.

I inhaled sharply. What kind of people was I mixed up with? Candace was starting to scare me. I prayed, like the good sisters at St. Xavier's taught me, to not sneeze, breathe too loud, or do anything that would draw attention to my presence. Panic urged me to run. *Now.* But slow shallow breaths helped calm my nerves enough to realize that would be the worst thing I could do. Before, I'd always felt safe behind my hacks: I was anonymous, faceless. That would not be the case here.

Candace rubbed her temple as she paced a step or two to the

side. Her footsteps were silent—she must've been wearing rubber soled shoes. How convenient for running away from bad guys or sneaking up on good ones. My wedges wouldn't be as forgiving if I had to dash away. Fashion could be a killer—literally.

She jammed her hands on her hips, and when she spoke again, her voice took on a worried tone. "I didn't expect things to start so soon. I need better information next time or you can forget getting any information from me."

The Man laughed. "If I remember right, I'm doing you a favor."

"That favor backfired," she shot back.

"Not my fault," he said in his grating voice. "Nothing in this business is absolute, you know that. Maybe if you'd done some checking, you would have discovered that. You have to do your own snooping. I don't have all the answers."

Anger bubbled in my throat. I hated how they were talking about Parker as if what happened to her were nothing more than a screwup.

"I can and will only give you details that won't disrupt my own plans," he went on. "Unfortunately, timing is never an exact science—"

Candace glared at him. "I can't have a dead First Lady."

Dead?!

Then what *did* she want?

Oh. God.

Did Candace want to kidnap Theresa Jennings? And what part did the Man play in this horrific scene? Was he just selling information, or was he more of a coconspirator or a terrorist? Paid assassin? Foreign spy?

He said the timing wasn't exact. . . .

Could Parker have been mistaken for Mrs. Jennings? She did look like her, I'd said as much when we met. If that was the case, then whoever caused the accident put Parker in the hospital thinking it was Mrs. Jennings. The First Lady wasn't supposed to be here until tomorrow—but the culprit might not have known that. Candace said the timing was off. Maybe they saw Parker and assumed the First Lady arrived early. *That* explained why we didn't hear anything about the accident. Was Parker still in danger now that they knew they'd gotten the wrong person? I really needed Dante and his cousin Nunzio to come through with her location—so I could warn her.

My heart pounded so loud in my ears I was surprised no one else heard the hammering. My foot was starting to go numb from my being crouched down. I shifted my weight—

—and the box squeaked.

Damn!

I held my breath when Candace glanced in my direction. I froze and tried to calm my panic. This could be serious—deadly, maybe. Thankfully, she turned away.

I had to warn the Secret Service—the real ones—about the threat to Mrs. Jennings. I had intel and they needed to hear it. But first I had to get out of here alive.

Pack your red leather suitcases, Candace, I thought. *You're going down.*

11

The Man's partner, who'd been standing still by the driver's-side door mostly out of sight, moved slowly forward. I'd been so intent on listening to the deadly plot that I hadn't paid him much attention. Now he was heading where Candace glanced—my direction. What would he do if he found me?

I looked around for a weapon. Next to the crate on the cement floor was a long, sharp sliver of wood. I could count on a million splinters in my palm if I had to use it, but a stab to his calf would put him out of commission—maybe long enough for me to get away. It was too late to take off the wedges if I had to make a run for it. Hopefully Candace and the Man wouldn't get in on the chase. Gingerly, and oh so carefully, I picked it up without making any noise.

He shuffled closer and against the pounding of my heart, I tried to inhale silently through my nose. . . . My eye to the crack, I could see his shoes, highly buffed, pause next to my box. One false move . . . The blood thrummed in my ears. How could he *not* hear it? It was only moments, but it felt like hours that I sat and he stood, only inches apart.

"Let's go," said the Man, and blessedly, the menacing black feet moved off. My breath escaped slowly in relief.

Doors slammed and I heard the crunching of wheels on gravel. I didn't move until both cars were gone and the garage door closed.

I crawled out of my hiding box and ran out of the warehouse by the side door where I'd come in. The cabdriver was waiting for me right where I left her.

"Where to, *bambina*?" she asked.

"The Hotel Beatrici, please. No rush," I said. Candace and the Man were gone, but the sound of peeling tires could draw attention if they were still close by.

The driver had to know I shouldn't have been there; she rolled the taxi down the narrow road, lights out at first. She skirted around corner after corner through the warehouse district. It seemed to take forever, and I kept checking to make sure no cars were following us, but we were the only ones on the empty roads. Only when we were back in a populated area did I allow myself to relax a little bit.

My mind raced. If I ever told my parents about this, would they believe me? While I was a screwup in school, I'd always been honest with them, at least when confronted. It would take every bit of faith they had in me, which at the moment wasn't at a high point, for them to buy this. I couldn't tell them anyway, this was too big.

Who could I tell? Who would believe me? Candace was a world-famous model, actress, and now head of a fashion magazine—who went to meetings in dark, deserted warehouses to talk about assassinations and the First Lady. Would the Secret Service believe me, a sixteen-year-old hacker recently expelled from her sixth boarding school? The agents here had come with Candace and might be in on this with her.

No, going to them would definitely get me shipped off to a place where I couldn't make any noise. And what about the First Lady? No one was going to take out Theresa Jennings if *I* could help it.

A plan formed in my head as I groped in my purse to pay the fare.

I couldn't let Candace get away with treason, trying to kidnap the First Lady, and in the process, almost killing Parker. Even if I got sent home in handcuffs, I was going to stop her.

The car rolled to a halt in front of the hotel. I handed the driver a fistful of money. What were a few extra euros when I was saving America? And she'd kept her promise, waiting in a questionable area. Even Mom would've given her an extra-large tip for that.

"*Grazie*," I said, and shot out of the cab and into the hotel, praying Candace hadn't returned yet. I still had to get through the agent at the door.

Act naturally. Nothing's wrong. You didn't just hear that Candace is involved in a treasonous plot to kidnap the First Lady, I told myself as I went up the front steps. None of the Secret Service that came in with Candace were to be trusted except maybe Ortiz. She'd been hurt too. If she could have avoided an accident, which I was sure she was trained to do, she would have. Today her bruises had been dark purple with a green tinge. In a day they'd probably look worse. Until proven otherwise, the rest of the agents were all under the same suspicion as Candace.

Agent Nelson was standing outside trying to look casual, reading a magazine through dark shades. I couldn't tell if our eyes met, but he seemed to nod at me. I didn't return it. And there was my friend, Agent Case, at the elevator.

He held up a hand. "I need to check your bag, Miss Jackson."

Trying to look cool and unsuspicious—like I wasn't about to school Candace Bec-style—I handed it to him. He rummaged around, felt the lining, then handed it back. "Thank you." He pushed the elevator button for me. I slumped against the wall when the doors bumped shut.

My adrenaline was skyrocketing when I got out. The hall was empty, but for how long? With the arrival of Theresa Jennings tomorrow, I expected Secret Service agents around every corner. As I walked to my room I swiped my hands on my pants. My palms were sweaty and my underarms damp as I thought about how close the Man's partner had come to discovering me. If he'd found me, would Candace have stepped in and protected me? That was something I was glad I didn't have to test. People went missing all the time, never to be found. It would probably be no big deal to ship me off to a foreign country or hide my body somewhere. Whoever was bold enough to plan to kidnap the First Lady of the United States wouldn't let a sixteen-year-old "glitch" interfere in their plans. I hurried; Candace and her posse might be back at any moment, if they weren't there already.

I knocked on the door to see if Candace was in; no answer. Sliding my key card through the lock and opening the door, I tiptoed into the little vestibule that led into the room. I had to keep the door open, but at least I didn't have to be out in the hallway. How would I explain myself if one of the agents or Varon went for a stroll and saw me? I had to work fast. Holding the door open with my foot, I pulled out my laptop and powered up.

It took two seconds to find the power socket under the door lock. Using an innocent-looking phone charger, I plugged my laptop into it. A "New Hardware Found" icon popped up. I clicked it and bingo-bango—access to the hotel's identification, locking ciphers, and safety features were mine, no password required. I would just make some adjustments with a few lines of code: *Let next swipe in*—that would be Candace. *When door shuts, bypass safety protocols*—the door would lock and she wouldn't be able to open it. So much for hotel security. How fun would it be to do this on every lock in the hotel? I wondered where Kevin's room was.

I unplugged the laptop then shut the door behind me. The trap in place, I ran to the window, waiting like a spider for Candace as I tapped some helpful phrases into the translator. I listened to them over and over until a black Mercedes pulled up. Candace got out; she'd changed out of her spy-worthy clothes too; she was all blonde locks, khaki suit, and alligator heels again. That's probably why I got back first. Lucky for me. Her vanity was going to be her undoing.

An agent—it looked like Nelson—jogged down the steps to meet her.

My stomach twisted on itself as I went over the plan in my head. Yes, I did everything right: one-time access, then bypass security. I didn't understand why people got so frustrated with technology; it was only a matter of telling the thing exactly what to do.

Picking up the phone, I dialed 113, and recited the line I'd listened to over and over on the translator.

"Please come! I have an emergency. Hotel Beatrici. Room 24. *Pronto!*" I didn't have to fake the anxiousness in my voice. I was so nervous now that I really felt queasy. Turning on the lights, I found a magazine and started leafing through it aimlessly, thinking of what to say to Candace when she walked in and shut the door. I wanted it to be perfect.

I heard movement outside.

This is it.

I tried to look casual and relaxed, flipping through the magazine on my lap.

The key-swipe in the door: Step 1. The knob turned and Candace walked in, and—*yes!* Step 2—closed it behind her.

She breezed by and said nothing as she walked to her room. I was being ignored.

Oh, I don't think so.

I looked up. "So, how was your meeting?" I said.

She stopped, turned. "Oh. You."

I stared back at her, hard. "How was your meeting?"

"I've had meetings all day. All boring and too long."

"Really? I thought that one in the warehouse by the river was *very* interesting. Kinda short too."

She stopped dead, glaring at me, then took a tentative step closer. "Excuse me?" Her voice was deadly soft.

I closed the magazine and placed it on the small table next to me. "And talking to mysterious shadowy men? That's so *Spy Kids*. Not what I'd expect from a celebrity like you."

Another silent step.

I stood, but she towered over me.

"What did you see and hear?" she growled.

"Enough," I shot back. *Where were the police? Having a late-night espresso?* "What really happened to Parker?"

Her face scrunched up—not her most attractive look. I knew she wasn't going to answer.

"'I need better information'? 'I can't have a dead First Lady'?" I said to refresh her memory. "Did you get rid of Parker to take her place at *Edge* so you could get closer to Mrs. Jennings?"

Her expression was inscrutable. Was she so surprised that she was speechless? Then she laughed—that scary maniacal kind of laugh that a movie villain does before she starts monologuing, revealing her evil plan to do away with meddling kids—like me. It sent shivers down my spine thinking that a lot could happen to me before the police got here. I backed into the wall until I was out of real estate.

She stepped yet closer. "I don't know exactly what you think you saw or heard, but you're wrong, Miss Jackson," she said, trying too hard to play it formal and cool. "I have a magazine to run and the First Lady will be here tomorrow—"

"Yeah, the First Lady. Got any accidents planned for her too?"

"Watch it, young lady. You've got everything all wrong."

Gee, the bad guys always say that.

And you can show up anytime, polizia.

"I think it's you who has to watch it. *Candy.*"

Her lips curled into a furious scowl. I guess *that* didn't go over well.

She shook a threatening finger at me. "That's enough! I don't care what inconvenience it'll cause, you're finished. I'm shipping you back to Mommy and Daddy." Then she turned on her heel and stomped to the door.

The moment of truth.

She put her hand on the knob and turned.

Nothing.

She tried the opposite direction.

Nothing.

Shook it.

No-thing.

An exasperated sigh. "Great," I heard her mutter.

I smiled. *Candace, you have been* pwn3d—*or, to put it in non-tech-speak, poned. Owned. Beaten.* She was right where I wanted her—no escape, unless the *polizia* came and broke her out.

She tapped a text into her cell phone. In a few moments I could hear someone in the hall.

"Case!" she called. "Open this, please."

He rattled the handle, swiped a card. None of it worked. The door remained locked.

"Problems?" I asked sweetly.

Candace spun around. That's what I was going for—that shocked look. Score one for team Parker.

"What did you do?" she snarled.

Flashing lights of police cars splashed across the windows. I folded my arms across my chest and tried not to smirk.

"Just initializing a little thing called karma."

12

Bam! Bam! Bam!

"We have a problem!" yelled Case.

"*Polizia!*"

"They say they're responding to an emergency call. Our jurisdiction—"

"*Polizia! Aprire la porta!*"

"*Dovete buttare giù la porta!*" Candace shouted back. "The door is stuck! You have to break it down!"

So Candace was bilingual too? Her accent's not as good as Parker's.

More Italian I couldn't understand came from the other side of the door.

Candace stomped over to where I stood. "Now you've done it!"

Yep, I trapped her. No escape for you, Candace!

With a splintering crack, the door burst open and the police rushed in, followed by Ortiz, Case, Nelson, and Varon. The *polizia* had drawn their weapons. I slipped behind Candace. She was slim, but there was a lot of muscle on that six-foot-plus frame of hers. She'd make a good barrier between me and any stray bullets.

"Worthington!" Case slid into the room, his hand hovering near the gun that I knew was hidden under his jacket.

"Everything's fine, Agent Case," Candace said calmly and smiled broadly at the police who were flicking nervous glances around the suite. "Everyone calm down, let's not do anything we will regret." She made a lowering motion with her hands. The agents, still tense and ready to draw, exchanged looks that seemed to be a mutual agreement. They lowered their arms a fraction, away from their guns but still close enough to grab. She carefully held her hand out to the nearest officer. "Candace Worthington, Central Intelligence Agency. These are Special Agents Case, Nelson, and Ortiz, and this is Varon, my personal assistant." The agents slowly produced their badges. Candace very carefully pulled a similar one out of her jacket pocket, close enough for me to confirm.

Candace was really CIA?

No. Freaking. Way.

This wasn't going to be good on an epic scale. I felt my face flush as everyone pocketed their IDs.

"Who's in charge here?" she asked.

"*Sergente!*" the nearest officer called behind him.

A stern-looking older man in a police uniform strolled in.

"*Signore,*" Candace said warmly, but definitely all business. "I'm sure you know that our First Lady, Mrs. Theresa Jennings, will be arriving in town tomorrow," she said. "We're testing security measures and couldn't inform you ahead of time that this was a drill. My apologies." Her head slowly turned around to me, a frigid you're-so-dead smile on her face. "Agent Case, please escort Rebecca into the hall while I speak with the officers. I'll deal with her in a few minutes."

It was shades of Mom—full name and the scary-calm Quiet Voice.

Case held out an arm, motioning for me to go first out the door. With a last look back at Candace, whose expression was unreadable, I walked out of the room. The rest of Team Secret Service filed out into the hallway behind me.

They closed the door as best they could, but with the frame splintered, it remained partly open. I heard Candace continue the conversation in fluent Italian and saw a glimpse of the officer she was speaking with visibly relax. I tried to slink back so I could get to my room, but with a slight shake of his head and a warning glare, Case pinned me to the spot. Would Candace even give me time to pack or just shuffle me off on the first available flight and ship my things later?

Just like the way I got here.

Then I began to worry. Where would I be shipped off *to* until—*crap!*—Mom and Dad would have to come claim me for interfering with the protection of the First Lady? Was that treason? *Jeez, Bec, you* really *did it this time.*

"*Grazie, grazie,*" said Candace as she ushered the police out through the broken door. I had to give the woman credit: when she wanted to, she could charm the smile off the Cheshire cat. As soon as the officers were in the elevator and the doors closed, the smile disappeared and the snake eyes came back.

"You. In here. Sit. *Now.*" She pointed to one of the charming little chairs that I'd sat in that first night with Parker. Now it looked foreboding because I'd be cornered.

"I don't want to," I said in a small voice.

She arched a perfect brow. "I could send you to the airport right now without your parents' consent. I'm guessing they wouldn't be too happy about having to drop everything to fetch you from federal custody. Or maybe I'll send you back to that fancy prep school—St. Xavier's, wasn't it?" She paused, scratching her temple with a manicured nail that looked lethal. "Oh, wait. You're not welcome there anymore."

I cringed. That hurt.

"Maybe juvenile detention?" she mused, tapping her cheek. "You'd have to be charged with an infraction to end up there, and you've certainly given me plenty of choices: breaking and entering, trespassing, fraudulent calls to foreign police, interfering with a federal agency. . . . As it is, your résumé has enough marks of *distinction*. That leaves me only one option."

I held my breath.

"With your 'technical expertise' and getting-into-trouble skills, I want you right where I can keep you in my sights. For the time being, you're too much of a security risk to be set loose."

She was already supposed to be keeping me in her sights, though she wasn't doing it very well if I could sneak out at night with someone I barely knew, roam around a foreign city on my own, follow her to a secret meeting, and lock her in her own room. But that was before she knew whom she was dealing with. I had everything to fear, but I didn't let that show. If she sent me home, I'd never find out what happened to Parker.

"Fine," I said with a dejection I didn't really feel. I hoped my acting skills were good enough. "Do whatever you want to me. I'm guessing the First Lady needed extra security so you needed to take Parker's place? But did you have to put her in the hospital? Couldn't you just ask her to leave—or would that take the 'secret' out of the Secret Service?"

To my surprise, Candace's chiseled features softened—just a bit. "So that's what this is all about." She studied my face long and hard and in spite of myself, I squirmed under her scrutiny.

She sat down on the couch and inclined her head at a chair opposite. I knew the time was right to make a concession, so I sank down into it.

"Not that I have to, or should, explain anything to you, but I'm going to. Like me, Parker Phillips is a CIA agent first, magazine editor second. It makes for good cover, especially in these high-profile cases. When she was injured—"

"Don't you mean taken out?" I said. "Or almost murdered—"

"We don't know that. And I can't and won't go into more specifics," she said, cutting me off when I made to interrupt her. "When we got the call that Parker was no longer able to carry out this assignment, I was called in to take over and make sure there are no threats to Mrs. Jennings while she's Rome."

Candace crossed her magnificent legs, looking down her long patrician nose at me. "Parker was standing at spots where the First Lady would be photographed while Ortiz did a security check. Only Parker, Agent Ortiz, Serena, and Serena's driver were at the location. Serena was there making notes for the staff. She and her driver were supposed to meet up with Ortiz and Parker at the next site, but the accident happened."

"So you really didn't know about it?" I asked, still uncertain.

She sat up straight. "Of course not! I have to play editor *and* oversee security. This is a nightmare! I desperately need Parker now." She rubbed her forehead as if she had a headache.

"How is she?" I didn't care about Candace, the CIA, or their preparations and plans. I just wanted to know if Parker was going to be okay.

"Stable," she said, "but serious."

"Oh good." I breathed out, relieved that she hadn't used the word *critical*. Parker must have improved. Then I sat forward. "Where is she? Can I see her?"

Candace shook her head. "That's not possible."

"Why?" I demanded. "She's my guardian here, so that practically makes me family, doesn't it?" That was stretching our relationship, but I had to try.

"The questions never end with you, do they?" she said with the barest hint of a smile, but one that said she was reaching the end of her patience. "I can't tell you any more. I've already told you too much."

I plopped back against the chair. Couldn't, or *wouldn't*?

"We need to move forward. No more drama. Your theatrics have already put this mission in jeopardy. Now that you know everything you need to, I trust you won't question or impede my directives."

Me know everything I needed? Hardly. But don't worry, Candace, I'll find out, and I'm not waiting around until someone throws me a scrap of info. "Who was the guy in the warehouse?"

She shook her head vehemently. "I'm not going to answer any more questions, and forget about him. He's dangerous to nosy girls, got it?"

"Okay," I agreed, even though I didn't mean a syllable of it.

Candace held up her palms. "Good. As I have to step into Parker's shoes, my identity as CIA is *not* to be discussed with anyone. Parker's status as an operative was only known to a few people for security. And now you'll explain how you knew about my meeting and managed to get into a locked warehouse."

Thankfully a knock on the door interrupted us before that could happen.

"Come in," Candace called in the modulated voice she used when she was schmoozing someone.

Varon came in holding a tray with two macchiatos and a plate of delicate-looking anisette cookies.

"Varon, Rebecca will continue to stay at the hotel, report to the office, and accompany us to the various photo shoot locations. Inform the rest of the team."

He peered at me from under dark lashes. "Do you think that's—" he started, but she cut him off with a slash of her hand.

"How do you think it would look if word of tonight's little police raid made its way into the press, and then back home? Don't you think it's better to make sure she doesn't have free time to instigate any more problems?"

She was right. Bad press was something none of us wanted.

Varon fixed an already perfect tie. "Right as usual, Candace. I'm sure that Bec and I will get along just fine—if she behaves." Great. Another "personal" supervisor.

"And please get someone to fix my door."

"Consider it done," he said as he left.

I watched Candace. She sipped her drink, closed her eyes briefly in pleasure before they popped open suddenly and stared directly at me with a calculating appraisal. Something bad my way was coming.

"I know how people like you think. We need to set some ground rules and restrictions so you can never say you weren't told what not to do."

Story of my life. I'd just done this with Parker. This second time wasn't going to be nearly as pleasant.

"The First Lady is arriving in Italy tomorrow. Besides attending the gala she'll meet with the pope, dine with the prime minister, and spend time promoting her charity against hunger. There's no sense canceling or postponing the magazine's plans. Everything has to go on as normal. I will be acting editor in chief, and the issue will be produced as usual, with no indication of anything out of the ordinary. You will keep quiet about schedules and places we'll be and cooperate with the restrictions we impose on your movements." She eyed me. "No security breaches."

Like I was going to agree to sit by and not find Parker and who put her in the hospital. Or who messed around with my stuff. Or who the Man was—and answers to a thousand other questions. I'd already broken the law—several times—and I was not going to stop now. I'd just be more careful.

"Absolutely," I lied.

Begin *Operation Screw Candace and Find Parker.*

"What do you think she's like?" I asked Sophie.

Not much work was getting done. Even Kevin slacked off and joined us on the balcony; not that I thought he liked my company—he stood next to Sophie. And it was *the* primo spot to get a good look at First Lady Theresa Jennings when she came in.

"From everything I've read, she seems pretty down-to-earth," Sophie said.

Candace, Varon, and Agent Case had gone to the airport to meet the First Lady's private jet. Ortiz and Nelson stayed behind to check and recheck all entrances and make sure no one came in or out until the group returned. The only one who seemed unsatisfied with the plan was Serena. As executive editor, she had a right to go to the airport too—or so she tried to tell Candace.

"With Parker out of commission, you're needed here, and the car's crowded enough." Serena clenched her fists and her furious eyes looked like they wanted to kill Candace, but Candace either didn't see or didn't care about Serena's reaction, because she had walked away without another word.

After that battle of the bosses, everything seemed relatively calm, and I guessed Candace managed to keep the First Lady's quick stop at *Edge* before going to the Hotel Beatrici a secret from everyone, even the *polizia*—in spite of me. Even the models had the day off, to keep as many people away as possible. I wondered how long the quiet would last.

I craned my neck to see outside and spotted the top of a black car glide past. "They're here!" I said excitedly.

The staff crowded around the door and Nelson moved in to shepherd them away. Serena stood her ground. Nelson shook his head, but stayed close to her.

I ran a hand over my freshly coifed locks. Sophie had bribed Joe to do our hair. Leaving the blonde roots alone, he deepened the pink at the ends, then twisted my reverse ombréd locks into loose curls. I didn't know if it was the fresh color or the springy coils, but the updated look gave me a new confidence. Braids were *so* yesterday.

And my clothes arrived too. Today I wore my favorite electric blue shift dress with black tights and silver Doc Martens, and with a few bits borrowed from wardrobe—a pewter fitted jacket and a pair of crystal bobby pins—it all seemed new, and would be forever known as my "meeting the First Lady outfit."

Downstairs, the door opened.

Candace swept in with her usual flair, immediately scouring the place with her sharp eyes. She was followed by Mrs. Jennings, escorted closely by Case, two new guys, and then Varon, who walked next to a plump Asian woman in a smart navy suit and matching flats. The sharp edges of her bob haircut made a stark frame around her bright moon-shaped face. They stopped right in front of Serena, blocking her view. She would have to plow past them *and* Nelson if she wanted to be in the front row, but a look from Nelson squashed that idea if she was thinking about it. She stood still, frowning between their shoulders.

Theresa Jennings looked smaller than she seemed in magazines and on TV. She was petite with smooth ebony skin like Parker's and walked easily in sky-high heels. Her flared skirt swished around her knees, and her matching fitted jacket made her look like she'd walked off the set of *Mad Men*. Guess that bit of gossip about her having a thing for vintage style was true. Like Parker, her super-short dark hair accentuated her face, making her large eyes look doelike and bright. She glanced around the room and up to the balcony, smiling gracefully. When her gaze caught mine, I inadvertently gave a little wave, which she returned.

"We welcome you, Mrs. Jennings," said Candace in the most human voice I'd ever heard her use, "to Italy and to *Edge*."

"Thank you, everyone," Mrs. Jennings said. "These are Agents Stephen Collins and Sal Mignone, and this is my personal secretary, Lidia Chay." Ms. Navy Suit gave a curt nod. Mrs. Jennings turned to Candace, her eyes sparkling with excitement. "The next few days should be fun."

"Yes, ma'am," replied Candace as she guided her and the entourage upstairs. "We'll do your hair and makeup in the studio. The indoor photos will be taken in there as well."

I didn't have anything urgent to do, so I thought I'd sneak a peek at the shoot. Mrs. Jennings was ushered into the large studio and right into Ugi's chair. He was so excited I thought he was going to hyperventilate.

"If I was American, I would have voted for your husband!" he gushed. "This is *such* an honor!" His hands shook as he tried to match powders to her skin.

"Don't spill anything on her dress!" hissed Joe. "And *pronto*! I need to do her hair. She can't be photographed without my taking care of her!"

Everyone wanted to get their hands on the First Lady.

"Play nice," warned Candace.

"Please! I have several styling products I want to show her—"

Varon placed a hand on his shoulder and magically, Joe calmed. "You will. Patience, she just got here."

Mrs. Jennings laughed and everyone seemed to relax. Joe got

his opportunity fifteen minutes later, and then it was going to be Angelo's and Aldo's turn to be nervous. She rose out of Joe's chair and started walking toward the white background.

Bang!

Screams erupted, people started running.

Case and Mignone pulled guns and threw themselves in front of Mrs. Jennings, bringing her to the floor.

I dropped down, my heart racing. Was that what gunfire sounded like? *This is not a drill . . . this is not a drill. . . .*

When I dared to look up, I saw Collins tackle a screaming Aldo. Sophie and Kevin were on the floor next to me, arms over their heads. Ortiz and Nelson came running up the stairs, guns drawn.

"It was an accident!" shrieked Angelo.

"Quiet!" Candace's voice boomed through the studio, and everyone froze. "One of the lights fell over and exploded. It's okay."

Someone hiccupped as Mrs. Jennings was helped to her feet by a furious-looking Mignone. Case and Nelson dragged Aldo against the far wall.

Mrs. Jennings laughed anxiously. "I'm fine, I'm fine. It was an accident, no harm done." She insisted on going over to Aldo—escorted by Case—to try and comfort the hysterical photographer's assistant.

Slowly Sophie, Kevin, and I stood. My legs shook, my pulse pounded.

I wasn't cut out for the in-your-face guns and death-threat stuff. First the warehouse with the guy in black shoes so close to finding me, then the standoff between the agents and armed Italian police, and now this? Tapping into a neighbor's Internet and covering my tracks—in my jammies and surrounded by junk food—was as close to danger as I wanted to get. Even when I got caught I'd only been slapped with a warning—okay, and expulsion from school—but that didn't happen with screaming at the end of a gun.

Everyone was too shaken for the shoot to continue. Collins, Case, Nelson, and Mignone hustled Mrs. Jennings out, and Candace sent Angelo, Aldo, Ugi, and Joe home, saying that she'd reschedule the session. So much for going on as normal. It wasn't a good day to be in Candy-land—but at least the disaster wasn't my fault.

"Let's do something constructive," Kevin mumbled, and he gave me a stack of filing to do. I headed down to the common area, away from the mess upstairs. At least I was near the kitchen. With trembling hands, I made myself a double espresso. After last night's adventure, then the drama so far today, I was drained.

Walking over to a desk, I settled down to sip and file. Ortiz sat nearby, working on a laptop.

"Don't I get one?" she asked.

Her bruises looked even darker, the purple deepened to almost black, and they looked painful. She probably didn't want to talk about the accident, but I had to find out what happened. Maybe a little caffeine and kindness would get her to open up.

"Sure," I said, and headed to the kitchen again.

As I switched on the monster machine, I heard Nelson open the front door and then talk to someone. A guy. I saw Ortiz go over, hand on her gun. Everyone was still jumpy.

It was hard for me to see because the espresso machine was in a far corner of the kitchen. Now all three were talking. I wanted to know who it was. Leaning over to peek around the corner, I caught my breath.

It was him.

Taj.

Sunlight streaming through the huge front windows highlighted the glossiness of his short, black hair. His eyes were dark and framed by thick black lashes, his cheekbones were high, his chin sharp. He did look better in person than in pictures. Not Adonis-beautiful like Dante, but there was something about him, in the way he talked and held himself. Dressed casually, he had a slight swagger. Too bad that smirk said "arrogant jerk."

Candace must have heard his arrival because she hurried out of her office and down the stairs.

"Taj! I'm so glad you made it!"

I moved farther into the common area across from the stairs for a better view.

Serena, who'd been talking to one of the photo editors and had started to make her way over to where Taj stood, was nearly trampled by Candace. Kevin and Sophie came down the stairs together, discussing something, but they stopped when they caught sight of the new arrival. Kevin frowned, Sophie grinned. They skirted around to where I stood.

"What did I tell you?" said Sophie.

I turned to stare at her in disbelief. Was she *drooling*?

"Huh" was all Kevin offered.

"Kevin likes to be the style–alpha male around here," she whispered, fighting a grin. "I think he's jealous of all the females hot for Taj."

Candace steered Taj away from the door, past us. Her head snapped in our direction. "Kevin, standing there gawking is *not* on my schedule or yours." She jabbed a pink nail at Sophie and me. "And not on theirs either. I'm sure there's work for all of you to do, especially since we're already behind schedule. Do it."

Kevin's face flushed. "Of course," he stuttered.

Gee, was it only yesterday that he was treating *me* that way? Sucks, right?

Taj's eyes roamed over each of us. "Do I need to know them?" he asked in an aside to Candace. He sounded vaguely British. Thanks to my off-grid buddy DR#4, I knew Taj of the single name was from a nice, rich Indian family, which meant UK-run schools and private tutors for when he was globe-trotting. Only the best for T-bone, the code name DR#4 had given Taj. That was all we could dig up.

Looking exasperated, with her lips pursed Candace said, "This is Kevin Clayton, *Edge*'s managing editor, Sophie Gaston, copyeditor intern, and Bec Jackson, short-term probationary intern, of sorts."

Ouch. It stung more with every additional adjective.

"And I'm Francesca," said the receptionist. She had that ability to materialize out of nowhere when she was least wanted. Francesca stepped in front of Sophie and struck a pose, putting one of her slim perfect hands on her chest. Taj gave her a curt nod, then turned to me.

Why didn't I have my phone ready to capture that moment: Francesca's expression caught between snooty—and shot down.

"Hi." I couldn't resist thrusting a hand at him—he deserved a handshake for that. But he didn't take it, and only stared at my empty, open palm.

"How American." One side of his mouth quirked up. "Nice hair," he added. I couldn't tell whether his tone was was praising or mocking. People were usually easy for me to read, but not this Taj. Dropping my hand, I felt unsettled and didn't like it.

Or him. No matter how . . . *intriguing* he was.

Candace led him upstairs to her office. Kevin turned to me, one hand on his hip, and started to open his mouth.

"I have stuff to do!" I rushed. I knew exactly what he was thinking: Candace yelled at him, so he had to pass it on to me. I retrieved Ortiz's coffee from the kitchen and delivered it to her.

"Me too!" Sophie scooted over to a table and buried her nose in a stack of copy.

Without a word, Kevin retreated to his office and quiet returned. I worked hard to get through all the filing, finishing just before lunch. I retrieved my backpack from its hiding place underneath the couch in the common room and was about to leave when—

"Bec!" Candace called.

Groaning, I hiked up the stairs.

Parker's desk nameplate was gone. Did Candace have to obliterate her presence completely? I shifted uncomfortably as I waited for her to say something. She scrutinized me from roots to boots, all the while keeping a bland expression. She tapped an uncoordinated staccato on the desk with her long pink nails, then grabbed a folder and thrust it at me. Receipts spilled out of it.

"I think you're underutilized. I want you to feel challenged," she said.

Ugh. I could see where this was going; she was trying to keep me busy—too busy to get into trouble, but close enough to keep me under her pointy heel.

"Expense reports," she said in explanation. "I'm sure you can figure it out. Every expense needs to be verified with its proper receipt. For *everyone*, no exception." Her emphasis sounded a little overdone, and I had my suspicions that she was hoping to distract me from thinking about Parker—or from doing some investigating on my own. There had been no updates today.

"Sure," I said. What else could I say?

Clutching the folders to my chest, I stole down into the kitchen. I opened the fridge to get a bottle of water and when I turned around, Taj stood there.

"May I have one?" he asked, eyeing the bottle.

I handed him the one I'd just retrieved, grabbed another for myself, and then went out into the common area. Finding a large table where I could spread out, I sat and started sorting through the receipts. Serena's were up first. I sorted the papers into piles: travel, tips, food . . . One caught my eye. Primo Electronica for ninety-eight euros.

Serena bought some cables, ports, and other equipment. Not much, and not very significant—although I could think of a few unconventional uses for most of the things she'd picked up. What would she need with them—especially since she wasn't exactly known for her technical expertise? She had trouble retrieving her voice mail.

I felt eyes on me. Head down, I peered through my bangs—and was surprised to see that Taj had joined me. Why was he staring at me? I could see him looking in my direction but our eyes didn't meet. It was a bit unnerving, but I tried to ignore him.

"Do you have a thing against Candace?" he asked finally, his voice deep and smooth.

I lifted my head and looked him in the eye. "Excuse me?"

"You looked almost angry talking to her." He slowly spun the mostly empty water bottle in his hands, his elbows on the table.

I had to be careful; he was very friendly with Candace and I was an outsider. The last thing I needed was for him to have a good long sit-down with her about "what Bec said." And I didn't like the idea that he was able to read me and I couldn't do the same to him.

"She pops up when I least expect it. Takes me by surprise. Bosses do that."

His eyes were directed right into mine. "And you don't like surprises."

I stared right back. "No."

He smiled, easing the tension a bit. "I don't either. And Candace is full of surprises."

Tell me.

I merely nodded. Finished with his water bottle, he crushed it— and put it in his courier bag. What was he, a hoarder? Or maybe he thought someone would take it and sell it on eBay for a small fortune—him being who he was. Ha! If there was one thing I had already learned in my few days abroad, it was that these fashion types were crazily delusional when it came to their own importance.

Odder still was the twinge and flutter I felt in my stomach when he glanced my way with those intense brown eyes. *Okay, it's just a normal reaction to a guy you find intriguing, even if he is strange. Get over it, Bec.*

"Are you doing an article on one of the designers in the shoot?" I asked before I said something stupid.

He leaned back, casually crossing his arms over his chest. "I'm doing a three-part post on the First Lady: her style, her favorite designers, and finally, what she hopes to contribute to Fashion Fights Famine. I'd made arrangements with Parker to talk to her between the shoots and interviews for *Edge*. I'm lucky Candace agreed to honor that request—all things considered."

I nodded grimly. "You really like all that? Fashion, I mean." I couldn't imagine spending day in, day out thinking about clothes.

He smiled faintly. "It's nonstop drama, controversy, and excitement." He tilted his head. "It's true that 'clothes make the man.' Or the woman. Take a guy who works with his hands, like a plumber. Give him a custom-made suit, a designer tie, and thousand-dollar shoes, and people look at and treat him differently. Anyone can be anything with the right clothes, and fashion is accessible to almost everyone." He looked me up and down, his eyes lingering on my pink hair and then on my eyes. "You have a . . . unique sense of style. Betsey Johnson meets Alexander McQueen."

"How'd you get started in this business?" I asked.

"I wrote an essay about a designer for my tutor and he entered it in a magazine contest."

"And you won," I cut in. Guys like him always did.

He made a wry face. "Actually, no. But the magazine editor sent me an e-mail saying that I had a good eye for style and I should follow it—when I got older. I decided not to wait and started my blog. Word got around. Boring story."

I was impressed, in spite of myself. Thankfully I was saved from keeping the conversation going by the sound of Dante's Vespa outside. I glanced at the clock. Almost exactly on time. A few seconds later Dante strolled to the front desk. I leapt up to meet him.

"Hi, Dante," I said.

"Hi, Bec!" He leaned over sideways to glance behind me. I turned to find that Taj had followed me. The two of them leveled measured glances at each other, then shifted their sights to me. Was it me, or was there a crackle of tension in the air? Francesca was just hurrying back to her desk, her face beaming at Taj.

Dante turned his attention to her. "*Ecco,*" and tapped on the envelope.

As she signed for it and handed back the receipt, Dante started to say, "I talked to—"

"So how are your cousins?" I blurted, and grabbing his hand, pulled him outside as he pocketed his pen. I didn't want Taj or any-one else listening in if Dante had info on Parker like he promised.

He looked confused. "My cousins?"

"I didn't want to talk inside, this is private," I explained in a low voice. "This isn't the time or place. Tell me later. Dinner, my treat. Pick me up when you finish work." Giving him a quick peck on the cheek, I hurried back inside, leaving him baffled and speechless.

14

Going 2 eat

At five p.m. I typed in the text and hit send. Candace had left the office shortly after Dante made his delivery, escorting Taj out. I didn't know her plans, but I assumed they would include the First Lady in some way.

Surprisingly, the message that came back was almost Momlike.

Fine. Back at hotel b 4 10

Really? Ten p.m.? A junior high curfew?

I *was* sixteen—almost seventeen—

—and in a foreign country *and* going out with a boy who hadn't met my parents. Gift horse—shutting up.

"Dante's here," said Francesca in a bored voice. He'd come back for me after his last delivery and was waiting patiently.

I gave him the thumbs-up. "Let's go!"

Taking the extra helmet he passed to me, I looked left and right before putting it on. No agents. Thankfully, Sophie was gone too, on some errand for Kevin, who was cloistered upstairs in a meeting with Serena. I hadn't told Sophie about my dates with Dante. I didn't know if she was interested in him, and I didn't want to find out by her catching me with him before I could talk to her about the situation. Then again, she seemed starry-eyed over Taj, more so than over Dante. Maybe I was stressing over this too much. If she was interested in him, wouldn't she have said something when she introduced me to him? Pushing it off my mental list of Things to Worry About, I slung my backpack over my shoulder and leaned over to whisper, "If you see any of the agents, or Candace, or Varon, we have to lose them."

"Easy," he said, his mouth crooking, making him look mischievous. He was up for some cat and mouse—Italian style.

Cinching the helmet straps, I hopped on the back of the scooter, ready for action. We zoomed away. No way could anyone catch us on foot.

Dante zipped through the streets, dodging traffic, pedestrians, potholes, and food carts. We flew over a pretty bridge into a newer part of the city, with broader avenues, more modern umbrella-decked cafés, small boutiques, and more cars. Every so often I'd glance in the sideview mirror, but I always saw a different car or motorbike. So far, so good.

The traffic thickened and the cars seemed to come within inches of the Vespa. More than once I held my breath, but Dante easily maneuvered us out of danger. Suddenly, over the buzz of traffic, I heard an engine rev. Hard. Peeking into the sideview mirror, I saw a small white car dodge in and out of traffic. Whoever was driving was in a hurry.

In seconds, the car was behind us, and I could see the driver more closely. He was tan, lean-faced, with dark hair and shades. He got dangerously close to the rear wheel, then unexpectedly zipped alongside of us. I clutched Dante's middle tighter. In the days since I'd arrived in Italy, I'd been with crazy drivers, but on the back of a motorbike, I felt exposed and vulnerable.

Dante glanced to the side, saw the car, then swerved between lanes of traffic as the white car slid into our space almost before we vacated it.

My heart leapt into my mouth as he steered the Vespa between moving cars as if they weren't lethal tons of metal and glass and rubber flying over the road, but eight-bit blocks in a video game. He sped up, then darted down a thankfully empty but narrow side street where no cars could follow. I was ready to drop down and kiss the ground when we putted to a stop.

He turned to me and flipped up the visor of his helmet. "*Pazzo* driver! He could have killed us!"

No kidding!

For the rest of the ride, we stuck to the less-traveled lanes, away from nut jobs with a license to kill.

The San Pietro Hospital was a sleek, modern building that stuck out in the middle of Rome's old-world charm.

Dante found a place to park and put the kickstand down. We locked the helmets onto the back and I followed him inside, smoothing down my dress. The place bustled with activity: nuns, nurses, visitors, and staff.

"I'll find Nunzio. He can sneak us in, but only for a few minutes, *sì?*"

"Okay."

We slipped through the crowds, Dante holding my hand. Good thing he knew his way around because I couldn't figure out what section of the hospital we were in or where we had to go. We passed little plaques screwed into the wall giving directions, but they were all in Italian. Maybe I should have spent more time with a copy of *Italian for Dummies* instead of trying to decipher menus and checking out delivery guys.

"*Cugino!*" A tall man, a little older than Dante, walked toward us.

"*Nunzio! Come sta?*" They hugged and back-slapped, grinning like they hadn't seen each other in a long time, even though Dante had to have talked to him to set this meeting up. They whispered in Italian, Nunzio giving me pointed looks. Dante pulled me closer.

"This, my cousin Nunzio. Nunzio, this is Bec."

I smiled at Nunzio gratefully. "*Grazie*, Nunzio."

"I'm happy to help you, but—" He quickly glanced around before pulling us over to a far wall, out of the way of passing people. His voice was hushed. "Before I take you up, I warn you . . ." He paused, and I felt needles of unease shoot up my spine. "If the *signora* upstairs is the person you're looking for, she's hurt. Very bad."

If? I suppose there was always the possibility that the person he'd found was someone else, but my gut told me it was Parker.

"She was conscious when we bring her in, but the doctors, they give her sedative. For her own good."

Nodding, I tried to choke back the heavy lump swelling in my throat. *Pull yourself together, Bec.*

Nunzio shook his head. "It make no sense. She was wearing her seat belt. The car, it was smashed from hitting a stone wall. I smelled smoke, but there was no fire. . . ." He looked at me grimly. "She looks very bad. Okay, we go. Follow me."

He led us to an elevator, waving and answering people's greetings as he passed.

Stuffed inside at first, we were the only ones left by the time it stopped on the fifth floor. The doors opened to a quiet hallway, but I heard hushed voices.

At the nurses' station, Nunzio stopped to smile and chat with the woman sitting behind the desk. He kept her totally distracted as he waved us on behind his back. Swiftly, and crouching low, we tiptoed by, Dante searching for a specific room number. With a furtive glance around, he opened the door to room 31, and we crept inside.

None of Nunzio's warnings prepared me for what I saw. I choked back the sob that had been growing inside me. On the bed, connected to tubes and wires and machines, lay Parker. Absolutely still, she looked like a wax figure: fragile, her beautiful skin lackluster, her brown eyes closed. Bandages swathed her head, starkly white against darkly bruised skin. I'd never seen anyone in such bad shape.

With trepidation, I moved closer. A chart hung next to the bed, and I picked it up.

"Don't touch anything!" Dante whispered, but I was too busy trying to read to listen to him. All of the information on it was in Italian, and here and there were the pen strokes of a doctor's scrawl. But the name at the top of the chart wasn't Parker's. It was Maria Castano.

I looked at her face again, just to make sure it was her. It was Parker, no mistaking it.

Leaning closer, I gulped hard, gripping the bed rail to steady myself. There were IV lines in her wrists and what looked like a drainage tube in her chest, held in place with surgical tape. Her hospital gown was open to accommodate the cyborglike equipment that snaked out of her body. Her chest was bruised and cut. I tried to look away, but I couldn't, my eyes drawn to a dark purple and mottled patch of skin unhidden by bandages or hospital gown. Checking it from different angles—as the bandages allowed—I almost swore it had a distinct shape. Like a shield, with a circle inside it. What *was* that?

I picked up her hand. It was cool to the touch, and I hated the way it felt so lifeless in mine. Fiddling with the plastic bracelet around her wrist, I caught sight of the name printed there. The same: Maria Castano.

Suddenly, she gasped, and I backed up a step just as every machine in the room started beeping and blaring. Lights flashed and a thunder of footsteps came from the hallway.

Three men and two women in scrubs burst into the room and crowded around Parker's bed.

"*Uscire!*" One of them shouted at us, then they all seemed to be barking orders to each other in Italian.

"They're telling us to get out," said Dante, taking hold of my hand.

I edged closer to him and stood fast. "What are they doing? What are they saying?"

He watched them warily, shaking his head. We were supposed to be leaving.

"They said something about her head."

One of the men pulled out a defibrillator and, tearing open Parker's gown, placed the pads on her chest. I clutched Dante's hand.

"And her chest, something with her chest . . ." said Dante.

I heard the hum of the defibrillator and then the buzz as the current jolted electricity into Parker. I saw her body jump.

Would she . . . *die*?

"Oh God!" I clamped my free hand over my mouth, and one of the nurses turned and saw us.

He squinted at me. "*Chi sei?*"

One of the women looked over. "*Cosa stai facendo qui?*"

"They want to know who we are and what we're doing here," said Dante. His hand felt tense on my back. He was ready to run out and push me along with him.

"Maurizio! Philomena!"

Nurses, doctors, and technicians rushed to Parker's bed.

"Quick!" Dante's breath was hot on my cheek as he pushed me out of the room. "Security is coming!"

The drone of the machines screamed in my ears and didn't die away until we were far down the hall. Then I stopped. I couldn't leave without knowing if Parker was okay.

"Bec, we go. Now!" Dante said firmly, grasping my hand.

I tried to wrangle free from his grip. "No! You don't understand. I won't go. Not until I know if she's—"

He held on tightly. "I *do* understand. But we have to leave before we get caught."

When he started walking away, I had no choice but to stumble after him. I didn't want either of us to get in trouble. Any publicity and Candace would definitely ship me back to the States, maybe in handcuffs, ending my investigation. Besides, now that I knew where Parker was, I'd find a way to come back. Then it would just be a matter of getting past the nurses.

Dante tugged me in the opposite direction of the nurses' station and into a stairwell. We raced to the ground floor and out into the lobby. All I could hear were fragments of Dante's words.

. . . *head injury* . . . *chest injury* . . .

And that bruise . . .

We barreled through the exit doors, out into the open air. I put my hands on my knees and bent over, breathing hard. When I straightened up, I saw Ortiz.

She blocked my path, hands on her hips—and she didn't look happy.

How did Ortiz find me?

Duh. She's Secret Service. Of course the team would be checking on Parker. This was probably Ortiz's shift, and when I set all the alarms off, she was notified.

She fixed a cold eye on Dante. "Time to go home, Romeo."

Romeo?

My cheeks burned with anger, but if she was letting him go, maybe it would end here and he wouldn't get in trouble. Me, on the other hand . . .

Nodding at him that it was okay, I gave his hand a quick squeeze. "See you tomorrow."

I followed Ortiz outside where a black sedan that screamed *Secret Service car!* waited.

"Get in," she snapped, pulling me by the elbow of my jacket. How much trouble was I in this time? I'd already bested the Suits once. They wouldn't take too kindly to it happening again.

We drove in silence for a while.

I was ninety-eight percent sure: Parker's accident was no accident.

Whatever Candace said afterward, I knew what I'd heard in that warehouse. And Parker had been admitted to the hospital under a different name and far from the hotel or the magazine offices; there were at least two hospitals that were closer.

Despite these precautionary measures, Dante and I had been able to find her and walk into her room without anyone even trying to stop us. It was a weak link in their security chain. But neither Candace nor her Secret Service sidekicks would ever admit to that. I was in the same situation as the hackers who got a bad rap and were punished for exposing the screwups of the powers that be. Blame the whistle-blower instead of the bad guy.

Ortiz expertly navigated through the chaotic streets. Finally, she spoke. "I hope this little adventure of yours doesn't put Parker in more danger."

Did this mean she wasn't going to turn me in? Why not—unless it would look bad, seeing as I slipped in to see Parker on her watch?

She sighed heavily and glanced in her rearview mirror before going into a traffic circle. "You know Parker well, don't you?"

I shrugged. "Not really. She was a friend of my mom's. I was supposed to stay with her for a while."

Ortiz nodded. "Until your parents sort out where you're going to school next—we've all seen your file."

I slumped in the seat.

"Relax," Ortiz said with a slight smile. "Look. What I'm about to tell you is classified. Need-to-know only. Really, I shouldn't be telling you anything."

Up went my feelers. When people said "I shouldn't tell you" but did anyway, it meant they wanted you to know—for a reason. But there was something in Ortiz's voice that gave me pause. What would she want me to know?

I said nothing, but stared straight ahead.

"See? You're smart. You know when to talk, and when to keep your mouth shut—but I can see you want to know, 'Why would

Ortiz tell me anything?' Am I right?" That made me look at her, and she nodded slowly. "I'll take a chance and trust you. Those skills of yours, they deserve respect—and the truth."

"Go on," I said, keeping my voice noncommittal and unimpressed. I was determined to check out everything she told me, in case she was trying out some reverse-psychology B.S. For all I knew, this was some sort of test. I wouldn't put that past Candace.

She narrowed her eyes as she looked over at me. "You are not to repeat a syllable of what I tell you now, understood?"

"I promise," I said, trying to portray an earnestness that was believable.

She scrutinized my face, probably wondering if I really meant it.

"Really, I won't say anything. I know I'm in enough trouble already."

"Good. I just wanted to hear you say it. Thinking it is one thing. You just gave me your word, and where I come from, your word is everything."

Word up, Ortiz. Now spill the beans.

She took a deep breath. "The morning of the crash we were doing a security run-through. An agent will stand where the First Lady will be, and we check for places where a shooter can hide, see if the perimeter can be breached, that kind of thing. Parker was the stand-in for Mrs. Jennings. We were headed to the next location."

Ortiz abruptly swerved out of the road and into a narrow, empty lane. My heart slammed into my throat as the car screeched to a stop. She clenched the wheel for a long moment before shutting the engine off. I heard her take a few long, deep breaths, then she cleared her throat.

"I was driving when the accident happened." Her voice and face were strained.

I'd wanted Ortiz to spill what she knew. So far, her story and Candace's matched exactly.

"I was trained in extreme defensive driving," Ortiz continued.

"I should've been able to judge that the road was too narrow and then compensated when that scooter passed us. . . . I walked away, but now Parker's laid up in the hospital."

"You were hurt too," I reminded her.

"Not like she was." She leaned back against the seat and, closing her eyes, let out a long breath. "She had her seat belt on, and I remember the car smelling like fire."

"Sounds like electronics," I ventured. "If something shorted, it could have fried the whole system to a crisp."

Ortiz turned sideways to face me. "These cars were thoroughly checked out before we arrived. Everything was working perfectly."

"Not if someone accessed the car's onboard port system after," I said before I could stop myself.

Ortiz's smile was grim. "I guess you'd know about things like that. Tell me, what did your dad say when he found out that you'd experimented with his Lamborghini?"

Ah, that infamous file of mine. . . . Was there anything they didn't know?! I thought Dad made a "donation" to have that hot-wiring incident disappear. "We're cool."

"Show me what you know," she said.

I laughed. "I can't just show you that here. Now. I mean—"

"Why not? Can't you do it?"

"I can," I said—again before common sense told me to keep my mouth shut. Ortiz's eyebrows lifted in doubt. I didn't have much of a choice now. Stupid pride.

But I was going to get something out of this in exchange.

"Okay, I'll do it. But only if I have your word that my visit to Parker stays between you and me."

She blew out a long breath, clearly debating with herself about my request.

"Come *on*. If anyone followed me here, wouldn't you have seen it? And she's my mom's friend, and . . . I don't want Dante to get into trouble." I didn't want to say that I wouldn't go see Parker again—I had a feeling that Ortiz would hold me to that. I willed her to just agree.

After a long moment, she regarded me with a searching look. "Deal," she said.

"Get out of the car," I ordered, stepping out myself. When she didn't, I shook my head. "I swear on my *life* that I won't drive away or do something stupid. I said I would show you—and it'll be a lot easier for you to see if you're standing next to me when I do it." I waited for her to make the decision about whether to trust me in the driver's seat.

Slowly, and grumbling under her breath, she got out of the car, but I could see that she was tense, ready to drag me out of the way and take over the wheel if she thought she had to. One little "borrowed car" episode and everyone freaks. Did they forget I brought Dad's Lambo back, undamaged? I inhaled deeply, praying for divine patience.

I took my laptop, a USB cable, and a flashlight out of my backpack. I plugged one end of the cable into my computer and held up the other end. "This goes here." I shone the light underneath the steering wheel. There was a plastic tab protecting an electronic port, which I pried open. I plugged in the cable, connecting laptop and car.

"That doesn't look like a normal computer cable," Ortiz observed.

"It isn't. I got it at the auto parts store, but electronics places carry them too. Dad's into racing, kind of a hobby. He makes tweaks to the Lambo himself."

"And you carry a car cable around in your backpack so you can . . . ?" She stared hard at me.

"I'm like the Boy Scouts—always prepared. I don't need much— a few pieces of equipment have a lot of uses, especially since electronic access ports have become standardized. One cable connects so many things."

"So I see," she said, sounding like she was sorry she'd trusted me.

As soon as the laptop booted up, the car computer synched and the diagnostic chart popped up on the screen.

"Now, watch." A tap and the car started without the key in the ignition. Then the headlights turned on and off. Another, and the windows rolled down.

"Once you're in, you have access to pretty much everything. I've done it with a cell phone too, but this is better. With an actual cable connection you get more details, have more control over the car. You can see how efficiently it's working, alter or shut off specific systems, bypass safeties." I looked up at her. "My guess is that if someone got access to the car's internal systems, then they could've messed with anything connected to it, then fried the electronics so no one would be able to figure out which system was tampered with. And there'd be no trace of the access."

"Son of a b—" Ortiz shook her head, astounded. "And you're *how* old?"

"Sixteen," I said. Still a minor. Still too young to be sent to Sing Sing.

I turned off the car, pulled out the wire, coiled it up, and stowed it and my laptop away. Ortiz's brow creased, her mouth turned down, then she pursed her lips. What was going through her mind? In mine, my ninety-eight-percent certainty jumped up to a hundred: Parker and Ortiz were doing security checks for one of Theresa Jennings's photo shoots. Parker looked like Theresa Jennings—and someone must have thought she *was* Theresa Jennings. But like Candace said, the timing was off; the First Lady's arrival was still two days off when the crash happened, and the person who did this, not being in the loop, sabotaged the car too early and got Parker, not the intended target. The next question was, *why?*

I thought there'd be an *aha* moment, when Ortiz belatedly should have realized that the accident wasn't her fault since someone hacked the car. Instead, her eyes became guarded.

"You keep your mouth shut about all of this and I'll keep mine shut about your unauthorized visit," she said.

Clearly, my need-to-know session with her was over. But I wasn't even close to being done with finding out the whole story. Without hesitation, I lied. Again.

"Deal."

"I'm out of the office for the rest of the day," Candace said the next morning. "Call me *only* if it's an emergency. Otherwise, *don't*." She paused in the frame of the front door for added drama—because the snakeskin stiletto boots, tight navy pencil skirt, and fitted jacket with silver braid detail weren't dramatic enough.

Theresa Jennings was already tucked safely into the waiting car, accompanied by Lidia and flanked by the other agents—except Ortiz. She got to stay behind and keep the office secure while the rest escorted the First Lady to Miuccia Prada's private showing of her new collection.

I regarded her gravely. "Yes, ma'am."

She clenched her teeth. "Don't call me that."

"Okay." I smiled. "Candy."

Did Ortiz snicker? Candace frowned at me. "You're pushing it, Bec."

"Fine. Candace."

Shaking her head and exhaling loudly, I heard her mutter something about Parker being insane. The door shuddered when she slammed it behind her. At least with Candace gone I would be able to take stock of the clues I'd collected about Parker, the accident, and the mess that had become my life—and maybe get Ortiz's prints, the last one on my list.

"Bec! Sophie!" Kevin shouted as he and Serena emerged from their shared office. "Serena wants the outfits for tomorrow's shoot inventoried—"

"Working on copy!" Sophie shouted from the couch where she was intent on her laptop. Kevin turned a demanding glare on me.

"Sorry!" I brandished the expense file. I hadn't done the actual report as I'd been too busy scrutinizing Serena's receipts. "Gonna have to find another minion. Candace ordered me to do these." Let Kevin try to one-up the Queen Bee on my list of people to appease.

Before he could argue, Taj walked in.

"Candace said I could work on my posts on Mrs. Jennings here. I'm using one of Angelo's tables," he said to me as he laid his laptop case down on one of them. "Keep this one clear for me."

Giving orders didn't work for Kevin; wasn't going to work for the fashionisto blogger.

"Speaking of Angelo, better call him. He's late. The models are waiting for him, and we're paying for it," said Kevin. "And I need espresso, *pronto!*"

"I want espresso too!" Francesca tottered out from her post at the front desk. Her heels were higher than usual today. Yesterday I heard Taliah telling her that *she'd* heard that *Angelo* said that if *only* Francesca was a *little* taller she'd be *perfect* for a shoot he was commissioned to do for Versace.

"Two espressos while you're at it," Kevin barked.

Francesca gave him a sultry smile that he awkwardly returned before he disappeared into his office.

Yup, I'll get right on that.

"I can't believe he falls for that act," said Sophie, not looking up from her copyediting. "She's just using him."

"I don't think he falls for anything," I replied as I waited for Angelo to pick up the phone, "but he eats up the attention with a gold demitasse spoon." The call went to voice mail. I hung up just as Ugi rushed in the door, out of breath.

"You're late," snapped Serena from the balcony, glancing at her watch.

"I just called Angelo," I volunteered. "He didn't answer so I guess he's on his way." Ugi shot me a look of thanks for the reprieve as he hustled upstairs. Serena huffed and waddled back to her shared office.

Determined not to be Kevin's personal barista, I jammed ground coffee into the metal filters. I'd make espresso—but not for Kevin or Francesca. I shot a glance back at Ortiz, looking comfortable on one of the couches flicking through a thick magazine. I knew she'd heard everything. I made four espresso shots, placing one before Sophie and another in the place next to her.

"Why so many?" Sophie asked before taking a careful sip.

"One for you, one for me, one for Ugi because he's bummed that Joe and Varon are a couple." I lowered my voice. "And one for Ortiz because she's still in recovery." The truth was that I still had to get her prints. As much as I'd warmed to Ortiz, I still wanted to know if she'd been in my room.

"What about Francesca and Kevin? Serena?" I saw the teasing light in her eyes.

I grinned. "Serena only drinks tea. I make espresso really hot and I wouldn't want to risk Francesca spilling anything on herself—she can barely walk in those heels. And Kevin didn't say please."

I was about to take a cup up to Ugi when Kevin came barreling down the stairs.

"I'll take that—" he started, but I pulled back, sloshing some onto his hand and the pristine white cuff of his shirt. "Look what you've done!" he shouted.

If I gritted my teeth any harder, they'd crack. "That wasn't for you—"

"Hello? I'm the one who ordered the espresso."

Ordered?

"Get the stain remover pen in my office!" he shouted, then added, *"Move,"* when I didn't bolt for the steps. I handed him the cup.

I gave myself credit for working hard, not complaining, and resisting the urge to tie up Kevin's e-mail account with thousands of spam messages to keep him too busy to bug me, but this time, he'd crossed the line. I waited a long moment before going up. Slowly. Did he really think he could shout at me like that and get away with it? Passing the studio room, I saw Serena talking to Joe while Taliah looked up at the ceiling as Ugi applied a layer of mascara.

Two tables faced each other in Kevin and Serena's shared office. It was easy enough to tell whose was whose. Serena's was a dumping ground of fabric swatches and photos. Kevin's was as neat as a boot camp barracks. The stain remover—one of several—was in the pen holder next to the printer, but something else caught my attention. Kevin had come downstairs after doing a little online shopping and wasn't done as he'd left his credit card out on the desk.

Not smart.

I pulled out my phone. If someone looked in, I could be responding to a text. But I wasn't—I was taking a quick snap of the abandoned Amex. Then I plucked a stain remover pen from the cup and went downstairs.

Kevin snatched it from me without so much as a thank-you and ran to the bathroom, dabbing at his coffee-stained cuff.

"He's just—" Sophie started, but I held up a hand. If this is what Kevin was like, I didn't want to get used to him. Taking a deep breath, I put my espresso and the remaining cup on a tray and took one up to Ugi, and then the other to Ortiz.

"Here," I said, offering it to her.

She grinned. "You kept your cool. Good job. And thanks." She took the cup—by the teeny, tiny handle.

Be an American! Put your whole hand around it! Her manners were suitable for tea with the queen, but not what I wanted for getting her prints. Hopefully she'd put her fingers on it by the time she finished. I'd have to come back later for the cup.

Cleaned up, Kevin left the office for an appointment. I went back to the common area and was happy to see that the laptop farthest away from everyone was free—no way would I use my own machine for what I was about to do and take the chance of anything being traced back to me.

I opened up a blank screen and started encoding a bot—a little computer program embedded with Kevin's credit card information and a few crucial criteria:

Make a purchase every forty-five minutes.

Make each purchase on a different continent.

Purchase multiple quantities of items with the following meta keywords: muscle building, bulk up, protein, steroid, herbal supplement, enhancing.

Set loose on the World Wide Web, it would raise enough red flags for American Express to shut Kevin down for a little while. Enough to be inconvenient—and embarrassing when he had to review the purchases—but not do any real damage. My guess was that the bot would get to a dozen or so charges before it was shut down and Kevin's hoop-jumping would begin. I only hoped I'd be around to see it.

Well, Kev, I thought as I put the finishing touches to the code, *let's see how you live* la dolce vita *when your Amex is as frozen as a woolly mammoth. Happiness is expensive . . . and so is trampling on Bec Jackson.*

"How petty," said a deep voice behind me.

I jumped. Taj stood at my shoulder, steely-eyed and silent. He must have snuck up on me—I would have heard him if he walked like a normal person.

"Couldn't think of anything better than interfering with his spending?"

"I don't want to go to prison just to teach Kevin a lesson in courtesy," I snapped.

There was that sultry—or was it sly?—smile. "Then you mustn't be very good. If you can program a bot, you should be able to do it without getting caught—or you shouldn't do it at all."

Did I ask for your opinion?

I couldn't say "I don't get caught." I'd gotten kicked out of St. Xavier's because I'd been impatient and stupid—I should have waited until the year was over to change my grades instead of trying to do it third quarter. Once the grades were posted, the teachers would have been gone and no one would have known—except me. And here I went and made the same mistake again. I should have waited until I was totally alone to take my revenge. But no, I had to do it *now*. Stupid stupid *stupid* me!

I'd have to think of something else, and I *would*, but it was probably best to just get back to work. Would Taj say something? I narrowed my eyes, trying to assess his trustfulness.

"I won't say anything," he said, as if he could read my thoughts, and left as silently as he'd come.

Taj could say whatever he wanted; I wouldn't be caught with any evidence if he changed his mind. I deleted the unfinished code and the photo of Kevin's Amex on my phone, then opened the expense spreadsheet to focus on the rows and columns. Candace expensed everything. *Wish I could do that.* I would have loved to get my hands on the latest Alienware laptop—the best for games and customization for my, *ahem*, questionable technical activities—but it was a bit out of my personal price range. I didn't dare put it on Mom's credit card. Even *she* would notice a purchase that expensive.

A couple of hours later, I heard Kevin's return before he actually came in.

"What do you mean my credit card has to be confiscated?!" I

heard him shout in the foyer. "Of course I've run up a bit of a bill, I'm in Italy! I wired money into my account just two days ago!"

Bam!

Did he just punch a wall?

"No, I did *not* order five cases of extra-bulking vanilla protein powder! Yes, I bought three pairs of Gucci shoes! Is it a crime to buy three pairs of shoes? Don't you *dare* cancel that custom order or I'll sue! I was on a waiting list for months!"

A string of colorful curses followed; even I was impressed with his creativity in pairing body parts and inanimate objects. Did he kiss his mother with that mouth?

He let out a bloodcurdling scream and I stood up, stretching to see him. Ortiz and Taj sat across from each other and he barely looked up from his laptop. Kevin looked around wildly, then stormed upstairs.

Taj didn't even flinch at Kevin's histrionics. His total lack of interest in the whole scene made me curious, and I decided to do another round of searches on him. I kept him in my sights as my fingers flew over the keyboard, but all I could find after searching countless databases and mentions of "Taj, fashion blogger" were copies of his posts, information about his blog, cities he'd visited. There was barely any personal information anywhere, except for the stuff I'd already found. No mention of a girlfriend, which for some stupid, insane, ridiculous reason, pleased me.

The only thing that was unordinary—because it was so ordinary—was a reference to him tagged in a picture taken only days before. The caption said it was at a place called the Forte Prenestino. The only clue was that he was standing in front of a wall covered with graffiti—but that could be anywhere. When there was that little information on a person, it was too suspicious and time to put out an alert. I sent an encrypted message to DR#4, R2Deterent, and haxorgrrrl: *Knowledge on T-bone raised from yellow to red*. Who was he really?

"Can you believe it?" Kevin rushed back in, a furious scowl on his face. "My Amex *and* my bank account are *frozen*. And I'm going to have to spend *all day* at the consulate tomorrow getting proof of my citizenship because they won't accept my passport!" He was practically pulling out his perfect hair. "What did I do to deserve this?"

A bunch of stuff, I thought, and wished that I was the cause of his grief. Still, this would do.

"Bummer," I offered, falsely sympathetic. Out of the corner of my eye, I could see Taj's lips curled up ever so slightly. My eyes widened as I looked at him; *he'd* done it! He nodded his head just a fraction, acknowledging my guess. I didn't know whether to congratulate him or be jealous. Kevin stormed into his shared office, slamming the door shut.

"Always have a plan B," Taj mouthed, and tossing his messenger bag onto his shoulder, he pointed a finger at me, smiled, and left.

*The following day gave me no opportunity to ana-*lyze my clues—how could I when I was expected to help out with the day's photo shoot, one of two that the First Lady would be doing off-site? Even though the insanity of the last session had been an accident, everyone's nerves, mine included, were still jittery, and now super fueled by a morning's worth of espresso. If nothing else, I would keep my eyes open for any new information.

Photographic equipment, wardrobe, and makeup were packed into a van that, once checked by Agent Mignone, took off for the Pantheon—Rome's best-preserved ancient building.

Mrs. Jennings, Lidia, Candace, and the agents got into the bullet-bomb-fire-everything-proof limousine on loan from the Italian government—after it was checked out. I doubted it was as secure as the president's huge monstrosity the agents called the Beast, but it looked pretty formidable. Last in, Ortiz slammed the door shut and the car zoomed away.

The rest of us piled into vans except Serena, whom Candace insisted stay at the office. Someone had to stay and deal with Gianni, who'd been overseeing the outfits and accessories for Mrs. Jennings to wear for the other two scheduled shoots: one at the Vatican, the other for the interview being done at the office. She might have been given free rein over the magazine, but Candace allowed few people near Theresa Jennings, and those few were closely supervised.

At the site, all the surrounding streets had been barricaded with wooden sawhorses one block deep to keep the curious crowds back. Word of the First Lady's visit had gotten out. The local police were hard at work keeping people from trying to sneak past. Some in the crowd held signs welcoming Mrs. Jennings. Only we were admitted into the narrow lane that opened into the large square in front of the Pantheon, a massive temple with a big portico and soaring columns. Mrs. Jennings traveled all over the world, and even though she lived in the White House, she looked as impressed as I felt, although I was sure she'd seen the Pantheon before. I stopped a moment to take it all in.

The supply van was waiting, and Sophie nudged me to help unload and cart cases and equipment up the shallow steps into the shady coolness of the colonnaded porch. We lugged and dragged, sweated and huffed, leaving everything in piles for the assistants to set up in the locations cased previously. Taliah and two other models, Marina and Adele, lounged on one of the crates out of the sun. They were background models today. Sophie told me the shoots at the Pantheon were going to be goddess-themed: Mrs. Jennings was going to play Ceres, the goddess of abundance—a tie-in to her charity work. Taliah, Marina, and Adele were her court, the Three Graces.

When the van was empty, I plopped down next to Sophie on the steps, trying to catch my breath. I leaned over, snagged two cold waters from the cooler, and handed one to her. As I savored that first cold swig, I wondered if she knew about Dante and me. Nothing seemed to have changed between us, and since today we would be crazy busy, I decided to hold off.

And where *was* Dante, anyway? I hadn't seen or spoken to him since he'd been dismissed at the hospital by Ortiz. Was he as mortified as I'd been when she called him "Romeo"? I should've gotten his phone number. I'd just have to wait for the next delivery to talk to him.

Theresa Jennings emerged from the dressing tent and was instantly flanked by Mignone and Collins with Nelson and Case close by. Everyone stared admiringly at her in her flowing toga-style dress. A sparkling band of emerald leaves circled her head.

"Wow," Sophie murmured.

Our First Lady really did look . . . divine.

"Water!" shouted Candace, snapping her fingers in our direction. Sophie had slipped her stilettos off—silly girl, knowing we'd be doing manual labor, to wear those.

"Could you get it? Please?" she pleaded, looking pathetic.

I grabbed as many bottles as I could and handed them out. I was about to give the last one to Mrs. Jennings when Case put out a hand to stop me, almost knocking me over.

"Hey, careful! I'm a loyal American, Mrs. Jennings is safe around me." *And you know me, remember? Your room is down the hall from mine? You've seen my ID so many times, you should have every freckle on my nose memorized.*

His expression didn't change. "Only agents or Ms. Chay get water for Mrs. Jennings."

Lidia, who'd been standing near Mrs. Jennings, came over to us. "I'll get some water bottles from the cooler in the car."

She walked off. Mrs. Jennings looked my way and then, giving a nod to Case, waved me over.

Somehow, I found my legs and moved to her side.

"Hi. What's your name?" she said.

My breath hitched. *I was about to chat with the First Lady!* And then I thought, *Wow, she really does look like Parker. They'd even have the same haircut.*

"Bec Jackson."

"It's very nice to meet you, Bec. Are you here on an internship?"

I smiled, with teeth. "It's kind of like a work-study program, but I don't think it's what I want to do for a career." It was the nicest way I could put it without saying the alternative might have been a detention center.

"Well, I'm sure you have lots of options. Just choose something that you're passionate about." She smiled at me and looked up at the ancient stonework. "This is quite a place."

"It is."

She nodded and looked around with regret. "I would love to be able to wander around on my own, but I have a very busy schedule."

And a short leash, I thought to myself. It wasn't easy being famous. What could I say to her? "You get to see all these cool places, meet important people, and wear amazing clothes." I wanted to add, *and people actually listen to what you have to say*, but I didn't think it was a good idea.

She nodded. "You're right. And those things are all wonderful. . . ."

It sounded like she wanted to say more, but didn't. I could guess what she was thinking: . . . *but it's hard, always being watched and guarded*. My eyes sought out Ortiz, who was strolling around the "perimeter," and the other agents, hovering like pesky biting flies.

Lidia returned with a bottle of water that looked exactly like the ones I'd been holding. She opened one, then handed it to Mrs. Jennings, who took a long drink.

"We're ready for the next setup, Mrs. Jennings," Candace said, striding over to us. She turned to me, her voice clipped, "Bec, stay out of the way until we call for you."

They went inside. I followed behind, secretly thrilled that I'd had a personal chat with one of the most powerful and influential women in the world. *This summer may end up being pretty cool, after all.*

The outside of the Pantheon barely hinted at what was on the inside. It was vast—and round. Marbled floors and alcoves and columns blazed in a thousand colors. And it felt ancient, despite the electric lights that glowed with artificial brightness from the galleries and nooks along the single, curving wall. And then, I saw it—a pale beam, like the blade of a sword coming down from a round opening above. It sliced through the cool dimness and ended in a puddle of light on the floor.

I barely noticed that the photographers had begun working, checking lights and backdrops for Mrs. Jennings in one of the alcoves. I wanted to watch, but my eyes wandered around the space, my gaze drawn upward to the light at the center of the coffered ceiling; the sun shining down like an eye in the sky. Looking for a nearby nook, I slipped in, took out my phone, and pulled up the Internet.

The Pantheon . . . now used as a church . . . the best-preserved ancient building in Rome . . . staircase to the top closed off in the nineteenth century . . . burial site of the painter Raphael and the fiancée he put off marrying so he could carry on an affair with a baker's daughter . . . Naughty!

A commotion erupted near the entrance.

"Scusi! Scusi!" someone called.

The click and whir of cameras stopped. Candace turned and glowered at the speaker, a young and now obviously nervous policeman.

"Scusi, madama—" and he started babbling in Italian, Candace nodding impatiently. When he stopped, she tilted her head back and yelled at the top of her voice. "Apparently we have a special rush delivery? Someone take care of that!"

Her words echoed around the dome and were answered by a squeak and, *"Bellissimo!"*

Ugi came running up. "Finally! The foundation I order for Mrs. Jennings! It matches her skin tone *perfetto—*" he gushed, but his enthusiasm faltered when he saw Candace frowning at him, stonefaced. "Much better than what she wear now, better for photos," he said in a small voice.

"Bec," she said through clenched teeth, "go get the special order so we can avoid any *further* delays, please."

Glad that her bad mood wasn't directed at me for once, I followed the policeman outside and down the steps—to where Dante waited beside his Vespa! Fluttering butterflies danced in my stomach. I guess Ortiz hadn't ruined my chances with him.

"Bec!" He waved to me and I hurried over, the giddiness from our almost-kiss at the fountain flooding back.

"Hi, Dante." I took the package from him and signed for it. He tucked the receipt into his back pocket and followed me as I started to cross the plaza. Mignone met us halfway and plucked the package out of my hands. Opening it, he rifled through the contents before handing it over to Ugi, who snatched it away. Then Mignone quickly frisked Dante.

"What's going on?" Dante whispered as we stood there. No one else was cleared to be any closer to the shoot. The agents gave him the Look.

I took his hand. "Come on." To avoid any trouble, as Nelson trained his eyes on him, I led Dante away from the immediate scene, but where he could still see the photo shoot in action.

He stared, openmouthed. Who wouldn't gawk at the First Lady being photographed in a place like *this*, and in a dress like *that*? Pointy satin heels peeked out from the draped hem of her gown as she posed.

Angelo shot from different angles, on the floor, and then up on a ladder. When he climbed down, he signaled for a change, and Aldo brought out a different piece of camera equipment. Ugi and Joe, accompanied by Ortiz, were allowed to fuss with Mrs. Jennings's hair and face.

"Everyone, take five minutes!" Candace shouted, then waved me over to where she stood with Taj.

"I'll be right back," I said to Dante, and ran to see what she wanted.

"Delivery boy is back," Taj said coolly, looking in Dante's direction. Their eyes locked, and that unfriendly aura that had simmered between them at the office made the vast space of the Pantheon interior feel small.

"Why is *he* here?" she said, flicking a hard eye at Dante.

"Dante delivered Ugi's makeup," I said.

"Get him out of here—I can't have any distractions!" Candace hissed in my face, "Stay in the vicinity—and out of trouble!"

Glad that Taj had nothing else to add, I passed water around, then went over to where Dante stood, waiting.

"We've been officially kicked out. We won't be able to see anything from here."

Winking, he grabbed my hand and tugged me away. We walked around the curved wall, toward the exit, away from the photographers, and then slipped through a small archway that led into a narrow hall ending in a small door banded with heavy rusting iron. Smiling at me over his shoulder, Dante pressed on it, and it cracked open just enough for us to squeeze through. Darkness and cool musty air flowed out. I wasn't sure I wanted to go in—it looked like spider territory. Dante disappeared through it, and soon all I saw was his tan hand, reaching out to me.

"Come, *bella*," he said.

A look back—we were alone. I took a deep breath, and then his hand, and passed through the opening, forcing myself not to think of creepy-crawly things. Dante reached over me with his free hand and gently pushed the door closed. We were in total darkness. I didn't like being cramped in the passageway, unable able to see, even with him.

"Watch the steps," he said. "There's no light. We'll go slow. Keep your hand on the wall."

I reached out and my fingertips met cold, damp stone. I shivered, fearing what I might touch, but started climbing up after him.

So many steps! The thud of our footfalls on the stone staircase and Dante's soft breathing were a steady cadence, encouraging me to go on. Just when I resolved that I couldn't climb another step we reached another door. Dante pushed it open and dazzling light flooded in. I blinked several times. When my eyes adjusted all I saw was blue sky and rooftops.

We'd taken the old staircase . . . to the top of the Pantheon!

I stepped outside. There was no better view. In the distance, over a sea of terra-cotta tiles, TV antennas, and power lines, I could see the Coliseum, broken and white, like a tiny crumbling cake. Church spires with glints of gold and copper pierced the sky. In the far distance, I was sure I saw the buildings of the Vatican. A flock of birds flew overhead. It was . . . magical.

"Here," Dante said, "we see everything. Careful, *bella*."

He stepped onto a precarious-looking walkway, the railings broken and rusted in spots. Eventually we came to another set of crumbling stairs, this one going straight up the dome. He went up a few steps before turning to me.

"At the top of the steps is the *occhio*."

"Huh?"

"The, how you say? The eye—where the light comes in."

Cautiously I scrambled over and looked down.

The photo shoot continued on below us. Everyone looked so tiny; there was Candace, in her bright red Dolce & Gabbana suit. There was Mrs. Jennings in another Roman-style gown. And Sophie, chatting with Kevin, standing very close and smiling at him. When had they gotten so chummy? Maybe she was trying to get her name off the chore chart; I couldn't blame her for that. I spied the Secret Service agents, and then Taj, Taliah, and the other models hovering close by. Taj ignored them, his eyes on a notebook in his hands. Every now and then he scribbled in it. What, no electronic tablet? Mr. "I can ruin anyone's life in keystrokes and not get caught" was going low-tech?

Suddenly, he looked up, right at me. Our eyes locked for a long moment. Did the corners of his mouth twitch upward into a smile? It was too far away for me to tell, and I backed away.

A few steps down from the opening, Dante took my hand, holding it loosely. I prayed that it wouldn't sweat. Nervously, I licked my lips, and hoped I didn't have coffee breath.

"Tell me more about where you live," he said.

I was a bit disappointed that he wanted to talk, but answered anyway. "It's just houses and stores and schools. Nothing exciting."

He shook his head. "I see pictures, videos, so many things to see and do, you have all kinds of people, and music. Here, everything's old. America is always changing, always new and exciting."

I didn't see how endless shopping malls and highways were exciting. "A great place to visit is—"

"No." He shook his head. "Not visit, I want to live there."

"But Rome is so beautiful," I protested. Why would he want to give up all this—and for what? Fast food, an overabundance of car dealerships, and suburbia?

Drawing one leg up so he could lean on his knee, he ran a hand through his hair, messing it up to look even better. I loved that he seemed to have no idea how . . . *delizioso* he was. He stared into the distance and I could tell he was gathering his thoughts. I waited, content to just sit there and be.

"My father, he died young, so as the only son, I must help my family. I have a younger sister and my mother. We all work together. It's a hard, but good life." He turned to me, his eyes somber. "But I want something more. I want to go to America, see everything."

I studied the stone under my feet, tracing the roughness of the weathered surface with my forefinger. "If you want to go to school, you can get a student visa. Then you could decide if you wanted to stay." I wondered if he wouldn't get homesick after living in this romantic city. At this point, I was pretty sure I could live in Rome forever. It would be easy to trade Starbucks for corner bakeries, traffic jams for walks to work, and mega-grocery stores for street vendors.

His voice was earnest. "I could visit you."

His assured smile broke my heart. I wanted to spend every moment I could with him, but I had no clue how long I'd be here. Would I be sent home as soon as they were finished with Mrs. Jennings's shoot, or would I stay here until Parker was well enough to fly back to New York? I had no assurances to offer him, so I stayed quiet.

He moved closer, a finger trailing down my cheek, tender and lingering. "I like you," he whispered. "You're kind, and . . . *bellissima* . . . so beautiful." He bent his head toward me.

His lips were soft, and nipped playfully at mine.

I didn't want playful. My hand delved into his hair and I urged him nearer, so that our chests touched. He deepened the kiss, exploring my mouth with his so slowly that I burned for more, and sighed in bliss.

We pulled apart, both reluctant. *This* was the place to be romanced by Dante—on top of the world—but it wasn't the time. I looked over my shoulder, half expecting to see Ortiz, or to hear my name being screeched by the blonde beast herself.

"They're going to come looking for you," Dante said with a last quick peck.

"Probably," I said. "But I don't care. This place is amazing."

"I don't want you to get in trouble. Take a few photos, then we go. We can come back another day."

I nodded and regretfully moved away from him. Pulling out my phone, I clicked a few shots of the view around me, then returned to the oculus and peered down. Right below me was the First Lady, in the beam of light. Then she really did look like a goddess.

What a great shot! I lowered myself so that I lay flat on the roof and adjusted my elbows on the lip of the oculus to get the right angle. . . .

I heard a crack, the gritty grind of stone on stone, and jerked my elbows back just in time to see a small chunk of the edge fall away— down to where Mrs. Jennings stood.

I screamed in warning. A second later, the sickening thud of stone dashing onto the marble floor below echoed up. Shouts of alarm rose up.

"Bec!" Dante's voice shattered my eardrum. And then his hands gripped me, dragging me back, away from the opening. I fought to get up, frantic to see what happened, but he wouldn't let go.

"No! It's dangerous! I shouldn't have let you go so close!"

Crash!

The stairwell door splintered open and Ortiz burst through, gun drawn—and pointed at us.

"You!" She waved her weapon at Dante. "Let her go and back up! Hands in the air!"

Dante nervously raised his arms.

"It was an accident!" I shouted, gaining my feet somewhat ungracefully. "The stone crumbled when I was on the edge. It's *not* his fault, it's mine!"

Ortiz didn't take her eyes off Dante, but with one hand, waved me over. "Bec, come here, *now.*"

I snatched a quick glance down the hole; Mrs. Jennings was safely surrounded by the agents off to the side. A sigh of relief escaped. I walked toward Ortiz. "It's my fault, Ortiz. I was trying to take a picture and then I heard this cracking. . . ."

She didn't look like she was buying it.

"Really! I swear!"

Bravely—or foolishly—I stood in front of Ortiz, forcing her to lower her gun. "Mignone already searched him, Dante can't and wouldn't harm Mrs. Jennings," I insisted.

Dante's formfitting tee and jeans made it obvious that he wasn't hiding any guns. Grudgingly, Ortiz reholstered her weapon.

"Whose bright idea was it to come up here?"

I stayed silent.

She glared back at him. "I thought so. No more secret rendezvous, Romeo. Clear?"

He nodded soberly, his arms still raised.

"C'mon, Juliet, let's go." She gave me a nudge toward the stairs.

I didn't know what Ortiz was thinking, but I knew that Dante wasn't a threat. Even if it had been his idea to come up here and take pictures.

At the bottom, Ortiz talked with the others, Candace sending a scathing glare in my direction. Both of them might end up hating me by the time the shoot was over—if they didn't already. Mrs. Jennings looked over at me and frowned. "I'm sorry!" I mouthed. Her mouth quirked into a comforting smile, letting me know she wasn't mad. But she was probably the only one.

The agents and Candace, then Mrs. Jennings seemed to be disagreeing over something. Everyone waited. When Mrs. Jennings moved to the steps and Angelo followed with his camera, I knew she must have convinced them to stay and finish. Another win for me. If they had gone, I'd be responsible for the cancellation. My record was really taking a beating.

Dante was escorted to the barriers none too gently by Case. Feebly, I waved good-bye. He shrugged and without putting on his helmet, got on his Vespa and sped away. My perfect afternoon—ruined by crumbling rocks and bad timing.

I stood there, not sure if I should move. Sophie and Kevin were closely huddled over a tablet, talking. Having nothing to do but try *not* to put Mrs. Jennings in mortal danger, I moved across the plaza, away from the lights and the people.

If anything fell, exploded, or crashed around the First Lady, I wasn't going to be the cause.

18

"I told you to stay out of the way—not disappear and then try to brain the First Lady of the United States with a piece of masonry!" Candace snapped, then added, "This is why I don't have kids. I'm not going to let you out of my sight when we're at St. Peter's Square. I'm beginning to feel sorry that I decided to keep you."

What was I? A dog?

My eye roved over the crowd as she made her way back to the First Lady, the photographers, and Taj. Lidia caught my eye and scowled. Angelo took a few more photos with Taliah, Adele, and Marina, now in different outfits, who posed like nymphs. Their long, flowing—and almost sheer—green dresses did not hide the fact that they were only wearing thongs underneath. It didn't seem to faze the First Lady, who smiled and posed elegantly.

A breeze seemed to come out of nowhere, pulling Mrs. Jennings's diaphanous silk scarf from her shoulders.

"Bec! Chase down that scarf!" Candace shouted.

Run, Bec. Fetch, Bec. Heel, Bec.

At first I didn't move. Candace glared at me.

"That's an Hermès, and you'll be paying for it if it goes AWOL!"

With my nonexistent intern paycheck? Knowing I was pushing Candace's patience—and considering that I'd almost killed the First Lady—I obeyed. But before I could sprint toward the fleeing scarf, a cyclist weaving through the crowd caught my attention. And Nelson's. The police shouted at him to stop but too late, the biker raced past the officer at the barrier and into the square.

Shouts rang in the air. A few police ran after the bike, but they weren't agile or fast enough to catch him. Mrs. Jennings was surrounded by a human cage of agents even though the biker wasn't near or heading toward her. In a flash he whizzed by me. I caught a flash of mirrored shades, long limbs, and tanned skin. Faster he went, head down, body straining forward, like he was aiming—for Taj.

"Look out!" I screamed, and forgetting the scarf, changed direction.

At the last moment, the bike rushed past Taj—so close!

Taj spun around and shouted something, angrily waving his hands at the departing cyclist as he whizzed around an unmanned wooden blockade and disappeared down a side street.

A local police officer, an older man with longish gray hair, a big nose, and a limp, hobbled over to Taj. The agents, seeing no threat, gave Mrs. Jennings some space, although they looked tense and on high alert. It seemed like ever since she'd arrived—or earlier, ever since she'd been expected—things had gone wrong. There'd been too many accidents.

Ortiz went over to Taj and put a hand on his shoulder. I stopped short, watching while they talked for a few moments. The policeman walked away, and finally Ortiz returned to her post, scanning the area. I managed to retrieve the scarf—thankfully unpulled and unstained—off the leg of a barricade, near where the policeman stood.

Something about him . . . He looked at Taj with . . . recognition? Taj didn't return it—but then most people gave him a double take.

Throwing her arms in the air, Candace shouted, "Pack it up!"

Hoping to redeem myself at least a little bit, I jogged back and started gathering and sorting and packing the accessories.

"Hey," said Sophie as she gave Aldo and Angelo a hand collapsing lights and screens.

I smiled back. "Hey." I folded the scarf and tucked it into a trunk.

"Some day, huh?"

You think?

"I think I topped my 'That was really stupid, Bec' benchmark today," I mumbled.

She punched my shoulder lightly. "It'll be okay, don't worry about it. No one thinks you tried to kill Mrs. Jennings."

It didn't take long to stow everything back in the trunks and pack up the vans. Candace strode over to me, stuck out a palm, and wiggled long fingers at me. "Before I go, give me your phone."

"Huh?"

The dark look on her face told me she wasn't about to ask twice. I pulled it out. She took it and tapped the screen a few times before handing it back.

"Now we're connected by GPS. Always leave it on, and no more surprises. Tomorrow I'm escorting Mrs. Jennings to lunch, and then she has an audience with the pope. I'll see you back at the hotel tonight, but I'll be keeping tabs on you in the meantime."

It wasn't a comforting thought. Candace strode back to Mrs. Jennings's tent, and Ortiz sauntered over to me.

"My advice to you?" she said with a pointed look. "Stay away from Romeo."

"His name is Dante," I shot back, peeved.

"Romeo, Casanova, Dante . . . Look what happened to girls involved with the likes of them. How did they end up?"

Not good, no happy ending.

"Look out for yourself so you won't get hurt."

That was awfully cryptic and sounded like my mother.

Ortiz took her cell from her pocket and frowned at it. She tapped furiously. "Damn."

"Problem? Maybe I can fix it," I offered.

"Stupid battery's dead. Can I borrow yours for a sec?"

I handed it over and Ortiz walked a short distance. "National security, I can't let you hear," she said.

I nodded impatiently and turned to watch Joe and Varon try not to make puppy eyes at each other. Ortiz returned my phone and joined the other agents.

Once Mrs. Jennings was back in her own clothes, the agents and Candace spirited her away. Much as I liked her, I was glad the shoot was done and she was off somewhere else—away from me. With her departure, the crowds had mostly dispersed. The police barricades were being removed and groups of tourists and locals filtered into the plaza again.

Unhindered by jittery agents, demanding photographers, and Candace's eagle eyes, all that was left to worry about was Kevin's detailed sweeps of the Pantheon to make sure we'd left nothing behind. That done, we were ready to head back to the office.

Kevin and Sophie sat in the middle row of the van. All the way in the back was an available seat—next to Taj.

"Taj is hitching a ride back to *Edge*," said Sophie.

"Sometime today would be good, Bec," added Kevin, turning toward the window.

Taj's smirk looked like a challenge, as if I might be afraid of him. I wasn't, and climbed in. He didn't say anything, and neither did I.

Sophie and Kevin were whispering. Suddenly she turned around, her eyes sparkling and her smile sly. She was up to no good.

"Candace will be busy for the rest of the day, and then with her dinner with the gala organizers, we won't see her until tomorrow. . . ." Her voice trailed off.

"So we're skipping out?" I was down with that.

Sophie nodded. I could see Kevin clenching his jaw, clearly not overly enthusiastic about the idea. Where ever we went, Candace could track me with the GPS on my phone, which I didn't dare disable. Even if I did, Taj was chummy with her and could report back everything I did. I'd have to be careful around him.

"Where to?" I asked.

"I don't know. Someplace fun. And nothing to do with fashion. I've had enough for one day," Sophie said.

Taj leaned forward. "How about the Forte Prenestino?"

Sophie's eyes lit up. Mine did too—we'd be going to the place from the photo! Maybe I could learn something more about him. But then my conscience scolded me. *Shouldn't you be trying to find out what happened to Parker? Too many things have been happening since Mrs. Jennings got here—accident or not.* I silenced my inner voice. There were other things I needed—no, wanted—to know. Like who Taj was. He was keeping secrets underneath all that couture and swagger, and I wanted to find out what they were. "What kind of place is it?" I said.

Taj's mouth quirked to one side. "An old prison turned art gallery and—"

Sophie put a finger to her lips. "Don't tell her any more! She can find out herself—*if* she comes." She grinned expectantly at me.

"I'm in." We just had to wait for the thumbs-up from Kevin. Technically, he could order us back to the office.

"Just this once," Sophie pleaded, linking her arm through his and leaning oh so close. "I need to have fun!"

Was she giving him *the pouty model look*? Things had really progressed between them while I was kissing Dante and almost crashing the Pantheon roof on the First Lady.

"We could find a quiet restaurant if it sounds like it'd be too much for you," Taj taunted—a straight-up dare.

"Fine." Kevin's lips couldn't have compressed any tighter. He was going to be a team player, but he wasn't going to like it.

The van deposited us in front of the office. We'd have to hail a taxi to get to the Forte.

We went inside, and I got my jacket and wallet, then checked my backpack, still safe in its hiding spot. Serena must have heard the door and appeared on the balcony. Her matching green bouclé pants and jacket made her look like a Chanel elf.

"Where is Candace? Mrs. Jennings?" she asked.

Kevin shrugged. "Dinner with the gala organizers, I think."

Serena's lips puckered into a bitter frown. "Did she say when she'd be back?" Her voice was tight.

Oops. Someone didn't get an invite.

Kevin shook his head and suddenly looked desperate to leave. "Hurry up!" he said to Sophie, then hustled us all toward the door.

"At least I want to see the proofs from the shoot!" Serena sounded pathetically desperate.

"I think Angelo is coming back with them," said Kevin, shutting the door behind us and flagging down the first taxi he saw. This time Taj sat next to the driver and I squeezed in the back with Sophie and Kevin.

"Forte Prenestino," said Taj, sitting back with a grin.

The taxi took off, zipping through narrow streets and then onto a broad avenue. We passed a colossal statue of a Roman soldier planted solidly amongst rustic brick-fronted buildings. Suddenly the Coliseum loomed in front of us, and I scrambled for my phone to take a picture. The scenery quickly turned from ancient to modern: a few sleek office buildings, and then a vast train yard that turned into a somewhat residential neighborhood. The taxi swung into a cul-de-sac.

This was the cool place?

The crumbling brick and cement walls were covered with graffiti and topped with rusted iron railings. Tree branches overhung in the few places where they could grow. The Forte was underwhelming, looking sadly similar to the boxlike buildings that surrounded it.

Taj led the way through a heavy archway crowned with a flashing red light and then down a long narrow tunnel lit by a spine of fluorescent lights and lined with benches on either side. Large-scale paintings hung at angles on the curved walls, covering the graffiti underneath. We came to an open area, cool and stark white. A twisty, modern-looking sculpture dominated the center.

A woman walked toward us in no hurry—until her gaze landed on Taj.

"Wait here," he ordered us, and he went to meet her in the middle of the room. They talked a few moments, and then with a curt nod, she gestured for him to proceed. He turned to us and jerked his head for us to follow him. Sophie grabbed Kevin's hand, and feeling a little awkward, I joined up with Taj.

"We still have some time before the club opens, so let's have a look at the gallery. Some of it's interactive. I think you'll like it," he told me.

I read a small plaque next to the first display, a collage of kites, made from old newspapers, recycled brown paper, and scraps.

Divertimento-non-Materialistica

"Nonmaterialistic fun," said Taj, and he guided me to the next piece, photos of people on a beach.

Summer would be here soon, and I . . . where would I be? New York, as Parker said, or back home in Cali, back to my "normal" life?

Taj stared at the photos, a contemplative look on his face.

"Did you ever go to the beach as a kid?" I asked.

He nodded.

"The Pacific Ocean isn't too far from where I live. I've spent a lot of time there. What's the beach like in India?"

He shook his head. "My favorite memories of the beach are in Alter do Chão."

"Where is that? I never heard of it."

"Not many people have. It's in Brazil. At the edge of the rain forest."

Sophie ran ahead to the next display, playfully dragging Kevin with her. It featured a lone guitar on a stand. Next to it was a box with a large red button and a placard, explaining the exhibit. She pushed the button and a lively salsa tune blared out of hidden speakers.

"Let's dance!"

Kevin shook his head, but he was smiling, and soon they were whirling around and around, laughing until I thought they'd fall over, dizzy.

Taj grabbed my hand, and pulled me close.

"I don't dance—"

"Relax, follow my lead, and stay on the balls of your feet." His arm around me, we spun and I crashed into his chest when I should have twirled away. The breath whooshed out of me, but before I could recover, he dipped me over backward. His face was close to mine, his eyes unfathomable, but they darted to my lips. I was suddenly nervous that he wanted to kiss me.

Would that be so bad?

But no kiss came. Taj's smile only widened before he swung me back up and onto my feet. When I looked around, Sophie and Kevin were MIA.

"Where did they go?"

"We'll catch up with them later. Why don't we find out who's playing tonight?" He guided me down another tunnel where the walls, ceiling, and floor were painted with intersecting lines of black and white, like a swirling giant Zen-doodle. "Your attempts to dig up information about me were entertaining," he said when I paused to take a photo with my phone.

I tried to appear nonchalant even though the statement surprised me. How did he know? It was a challenge not to look at him and let my pulse run wicked. I kept my voice cool.

"Well, at least you're entertained. Since I'm constantly reminded that I know nothing about fashion or style, who better to learn it from than you, the world-famous fashionisto himself?"

"Actually, I think you're much more fashion-savvy than the

people here give you credit for. So many who work in the business are contrived." He looked me up and down. "You have your own sense of style."

I gave a demure, hopefully unreadable smile. Compliments were a signal to throw up the security net. We came to a large courtyard, the sky turning a darker blue as the sun went down. More graffiti decorated the walls, and sculptures made of car tires were tucked into the corners. At one end was a stage where three or four guys were busy setting up a drum kit and amps.

"No tablet today?" I asked casually. He quirked a dark brow. "I saw you at the Pantheon scribbling in a notebook."

He smiled. "It's never a good idea to rely on technology too much. Machines break. I like to be able to work things out myself. You know, math without calculators, being able to read a map and have a sense of direction instead of just blindly following a GPS."

I nodded, understanding—but I liked my gadgets.

"And it's a pain to haul all that stuff around sometimes. A notebook and pen weigh nothing. Did you bring all your gear up to the top of the Pantheon?"

Right. I'd seen him—and he'd seen me.

"I only had my phone," I said. "And by the way, thanks for alerting the troops that I was up there."

"Agent Ortiz?" he asked, incredulous. "I saw you come down with her. I don't know how she found out where you were, but it wasn't from me. I wouldn't give you away to any of Candace's security detail."

I wanted to believe him.

But I didn't. He was too close to her.

"Are you all right?" I asked, seeming to change the subject—but not really.

"Why wouldn't I be?"

"I mean, after what happened at the Pantheon. That biker nearly took you out."

"Oh, that," he laughed. "It was probably just some maniac messenger. Maybe he was watching the shoot, realized he was running late, and took off. He was going so fast I didn't notice him until he was practically on top of me. That kind of thing happens all the time in cities."

That was true. Maybe I was so jumpy that I was starting to read into everything. "I guess. . . ."

"Look, I'm fine," he said, sliding his hand onto the small of my back. I felt a flush of warmth as goosebumps tickled my spine. His fingers curled around my side. Should I put my arm around him? Did I look afraid or stuck-up? If I did put my arm around him, would he think I was like all the girls in the office, chasing him?

"When I'm working, I don't lose focus. Since I got here I've been working on my blog nonstop. I have to be ready to interview Mrs. Jennings."

His palm rubbed my waist, slowly up. And down. Our shoulders touched. His head tilted down as he watched me. For a moment, we stared at each other. I swear we both held our breaths.

The moment passed, and he let his arm fall. "Are you hungry? Or did messenger boy bring you some treats up on the dome?"

I didn't like his tone. "He's a good guy. Be nice." I hoped that didn't sound sharp, but Taj didn't know Dante's story and I was protective of my friends. "I'm starving. This place has food?" I said, my voice softer.

"They have antipasto. And a bar."

We left the courtyard and entered a room with a vaulted ceiling. One wall was paneled with mottled and spotted mirrors, and in front of that was a huge ornately carved wooden bar with leather stools in front of it. Behind were shelves crammed with bottles. Round tables with pairs of chairs were scattered throughout the rest of the space.

"Drink?" he asked.

Why not? A sip of something might loosen his lips, and I'd find out more about him. Like how he managed to freeze Kevin's accounts so quickly.

Taj exchanged a few words with the heavily tattooed bartender and slipped a euro note into the tip jar. A few seconds later, we were each holding a glass filled with something icy and red. I sniffed mine.

Whoa! Strawberry . . . and something *strong*.

"What is this?"

Taj lifted his glass like he was toasting me. "*Strega dolce*. Sweet witch."

I took a small sip—and was under the spell as a delicious heat spread through me. Wine was way overrated.

I took another taste. I liked this, but I was in a foreign country with someone I didn't know at all, and Sophie and Kevin weren't around. It was better to exercise caution and not suck it down like a mocha Frappuccino with extra whipped cream.

"How come you're not in school?" he asked.

"How come *you're* not?" I countered. It was becoming a sensitive subject.

"I was homeschooled for the past few years."

"By a British tutor," I guessed.

"Very good. And you . . ." He stroked his chin. "You were kicked out of school. For hacking."

I tried to hide my shock. Would someone please raise their hand if they *did not* know my history? "Guess you've been talking to Candace."

He ran a long finger down the side of his glass, leaving a clear trail through the condensation. "No. Just a guess, but from what I've seen, you could really use some pointers."

I frowned at him. "Not on the tech part, maybe on the execution."

"When it comes to that kind of activity, you need the whole package if you're not going to get caught."

"True," I said, taking a big sip of my drink. Now I felt warm and bold. "How come you can just travel anywhere in the world? No parents? No chaperones?"

"I'm staying with friends."

Vague.

"What about you?"

"I was staying with a family friend while I sorted out my school situation." I could do vague too. Just watch me.

"Parker Phillips." He frowned and swirled his glass. Its swirling movement was mesmerizing. "I heard what happened. Is she okay?"

I hesitated a moment as I felt a fleeting flash of sadness—and determination. I had to get back on track finding out who hurt her. I didn't know how much time I had left, and I'd made little progress. A waiter came and brought a heavy ceramic dish layered with sliced meats and cheeses. I was too hungry to be shy, and I plucked a chunk of soft, herbed cheese from the pile with my fingers.

"Will you be there when the First Lady comes in for her interview?" Taj asked, helping himself to a paper-thin slice of ham.

"Who knows where Candace'll put me? She practically threatened a leash."

He took a deep breath, swirling the dregs of his drink. "I don't know where they're going to do the interview. I'm guessing either the office or the hotel."

I wished we could talk about something other than fashion and the First Lady. Besides, I'd made a promise to both Parker and Candace about keeping anything I knew about Theresa Jennings zipped. Even Ortiz told me as much. "No one tells me anything, not even when it's quitting time."

He nodded, a sympathetic glisten in his dark eyes. "I know Candace. It must be tough to work for her." He drained his glass.

Enough about Candace, *Edge*, and haute couture.

"Got any brothers or sisters?" I asked, hoping to take the conversation back to our cat and mouse game of "You tell me something, I tell you something."

He paused for a moment, as if he was considering. "A brother." he said. "You?"

"Only child."

"My turn. What outfit will the First Lady be wearing for the pictures in St. Peter's Square?"

This guy has a one-track mind.

Maybe it was the *strega* talking, but I shot back, "You sure ask a lot of questions."

He let out a long breath. "I'm sorry. I guess I'm nervous about this post with Mrs. Jennings."

"Taj? Nervous?"

He laughed. "I've talked with plenty of celebrities, but never a wife of a head of state."

I nodded, understanding his nerves. I felt them too. "You'll be fine. Tell me why a blogger needs to be such a good hacker."

Both dark brows arched up. "I wouldn't call myself a hacker; too many bad connotations."

Didn't I know that! "How about 'information retrieval manager'?"

"That's better," he agreed with a smile that brightened his face. "I can't tell you how many people have tried to hijack my Web site and e-mail accounts. The last thing I need is to run into problems with people claiming to be me. I've worked very hard on my image. I don't need someone stealing it—or destroying it."

In a low voice, I asked, "Then why did you lock up all Kevin's accounts? I was just going to put on a security alert and inconvenience him for a day or two."

Taj rubbed his lips with a finger in a way that made me think he was deciding whether and how to answer. I'd bet those lips were soft. And could make my heart stand still if they touched mine.

Stop that! Pay attention! I scolded myself, moving my gaze up to his eyes.

He pushed the plate forward and crossed his arms, leaning on the table closer to me. "He shouldn't have spoken to you the way he did. My parents taught me to always be a gentleman."

I felt myself warm, and it wasn't the cocktail. Taj didn't like the way Kevin treated me—and he did something about it.

"Thank you. That was sweet. But"—I grimaced—"if it goes on too long, everyone in the office will suffer from his rotten mood. If Sophie or I so much as look at him wrong, we might get stuck cleaning the bathroom with a toothbrush."

His laughter was lighthearted and appealing. "I doubt Kevin would make Sophie do anything like that."

"You're right. I'll be doing the scrubbing."

He raised his hand in oath. "I promise I won't make him suffer too long." His eyes sparkled with mischievous glee. "Only a day. Or maybe two."

I smiled back, enjoying the shared moment of conspiracy. "I guess that sounds reasonable. So where's home?"

A crocodile smile. "I travel a lot for my blog. I've learned to see wherever I am as home."

His mouth was sexy and I wondered about those lips again. Mentally I shook myself to avoid staring at him like the models and all those other girls we passed everywhere. Music wafted in from the courtyard. The band was playing.

"What's your favorite place in the whole world?"

"Right here, right now. I like the present. Before you know it, it's gone." He stood and held out a hand to me. "Want to dance?"

Back in the courtyard, the band was playing a danceable techno song. Lights flashed from the stage, cutting into the sky overhead, now a deep, velvety blue. The grassy center was full of spinning, gyrating people. Some of the girls had taken their shoes off to dance.

Taj's fingers found mine, and a tingling thrill raced up my arm that made me catch my breath as he pulled me into the writhing crush of people.

"That's Taj," I heard someone say. A girl in a dress that was probably meant to be a tank top stepped right up to him and boldly put her hand on his shoulder. He dodged her with a "Sorry, not interested" smile and skimmed around her, pulling me after him. I didn't get to see her reaction; I wished I did. Other girls and guys looked him up and down—and at me with envy. Taj didn't seem to notice any of them.

Part of me wanted to pull out a camera to document this on Facebook for all time. Another part wanted to take it slower, but I pushed that thought away and decided to enjoy the present. Just being here with a boy like Taj would have been impossible not more than a week ago. Funny how my life in Cali and at St. Xavier's seemed so far away.

The dance area was crowded, pushing us together. With every move I couldn't help but brush up against him, an arm, a thigh, his chest. It got hotter and hotter and beads of sweat dripped down my forehead.

He leaned in close to my ear. "I thought you didn't dance."

I pressed my cheek against his and whispered back, "I lied."

He laughed, and grabbing my hand, whirled me around.

The music changed to something decidedly slower. Some of the people around us stood and swayed to the music, a slow rhythmic beat like a pulse. Others paired off. Taj pulled me so close that I was pressed against him, my head on his shoulder. Peering between the rippling bodies, I spotted Kevin and Sophie, dancing close. Kevin moved his head so that he looked into Sophie's eyes. Then he moved closer.

I buried my face in Taj's neck, not wanting to spy on them. I breathed deep. The spice and woodsy scent of his cologne filled my head, and I ran my hand across his shoulder and down his back. He turned me around. Hoping I wouldn't see Kevin and Sophie again, I opened my eyes and found I was facing the exit. Two men who looked like security guards stood to either side of the arched opening. Both were tall, one dark-haired, one silver-haired—

"It's hot out here with all these people so close." His lips barely brushed my neck but I felt like I had a fever.

We were on the move again. I let Taj lead me out of the courtyard and into one of the decidedly cooler and sparsely populated tunnels, unmanned by any guards.

In the center, built into the curved wall, was a large porcelain drinking fountain. It had been reworked into a piece of art with hundreds of iridescent shards of glass cemented to it like mosaic tile. Water shot up and fell back down into a pool that spilled onto the ground and disappeared into a drain in the floor. The basin was filled with coins.

"Here." Taj pressed a coin into my palm. I looked at it: a silver center ringed with bronze. On one side, the number one, on the other, a relief of Leonardo's *Vitruvian Man*. It glittered under the fluorescent lights like a diamond.

"What's this for?"

He inclined his head at the fountain. "Make a wish. All fountains in Italy are magical."

I didn't do wishes. Wishes weren't real.

Even so . . .

I want Parker to recover—and I want to know who hurt her, and how, and why.

Four wishes, technically, and real or not, it was what I wanted more than anything. I flipped the coin into the water and watched the ripples cross the surface. I was so intent on staring at the coins lying on the bottom that I didn't notice Taj had moved closer to me. I felt the warm weight of his arm on my shoulders as he turned me, the pressure of his slim, soft fingers as they nudged my chin up.

I saw only his eyes, dark and glittering.

Closer . . .

His lips met mine.

So . . . soft . . .

His mouth tasted of strawberries and licorice. I raised my hands to his face, the backs of my fingers brushing his smooth cheek. He pulled me closer and the kiss deepened. His body felt solid against mine, and the heat I'd felt dancing in the courtyard flooded through me again. I stroked my hands over his shoulders and clasped them at the back of his neck.

"I thought I saw you come this way!"

Sophie's voice.

Taj and I pulled apart. When I glanced Sophie's way she flashed a mischievous grin. I thought Kevin looked pleased. Was that be-

cause of his night out with Sophie or because Taj was paying attention to me and not her?

"It's late," Kevin said. "You have to get back to the hotel before
Candace thinks we've kidnapped you. Let's go."

As soon as their backs were turned, there were more quick
kisses—on my temple, my cheek, and then oh-too-briefly my lips—
and then we were following, hand in hand.

Outside, the cul-de-sac was no longer empty. Cars lined up,
jammed into every available space. To one side, scooters and Vespas
were lined up on the sidewalk. A block away we were able to wave
down a taxi, which took us back to the office in silence, all of us
preoccupied with our own thoughts. Mine danced between Dante
and Taj.

Dante was fair, Taj, dark. Smiling came easily to Dante, smirk-
ing to Taj. Dante was solid, muscular, and golden, like a lion. Taj
was lithe and sleek and so quiet you didn't know he was there—
until he wanted you to. Dante was warm and safe. Taj was a jaguar.
He felt dangerous.

And I like them both.

We arrived at the office and Kevin let us in. Taj and I collected
our backpacks.

"I don't have to go home yet," I heard Sophie say to Kevin when
we joined up with them in the common room. He turned to us.

"Taj, will you make sure she gets back to the hotel?"

Taj nodded, and we got back into the cab—both of us in the back
seat this time.

"See you tomorrow!" Sophie gave me a little wave as she shut
the door.

"Where?" asked the driver. Taj turned to me, brows raised.

"Hotel Beatrici," I said, and the driver nodded and took off.

I wondered briefly who those friends were that Taj mentioned—
the ones he was staying with. Did they have a villa, or were they
traveling together and staying at one of the many luxurious hotels
in the city? Should I ask? Would it be too aggressive? Or suggestive?

When we pulled up to the colonnaded porch of the hotel, Taj pushed my hair away from my face and leaned his lithe body across mine.

"Tomorrow, Bec." His lips moved against my cheek, then trailed to my lips and lingered in a last kiss.

I pretty much floated up the steps of the hotel, waving to Nelson on duty at the front door and happily opening up my bag for Case to search at the elevator. I was about to swipe my key card to let myself into the suite when the door was swung wide open by Varon. His smile was smug.

"Good evening, Miss Jackson."

"Juliet's back at last!" Varon called over his shoul- der.

Was that my code name?

Candace was waiting for me, her perfectly manicured feet propped up on a footstool, her poppy red–suited arms resting in her lap. It was after midnight, and even barefoot she looked as poised and polished as ever.

"Juliet only had one Romeo," quipped Ortiz, leaning over a chair. She was here too. Fabulous. "Our girl has two guys falling in love with her."

I felt my face flame.

"Interesting. So where did you go?" Candace asked.

"I thought you'd already know, since I'm being tracked." I pulled my phone out of my pocket and waved it at her. "But I have nothing to hide. I went out with Kevin and Sophie—"

"And Taj," said Ortiz before I could.

"And Taj," I said, shooting her a cold stare. "To the Forte Prenestino."

Candace fixed me with a hard stare. "I should have told you to come back to the hotel when Kevin was finished with you."

"But you didn't."

"A mistake I won't make again. No partying, Bec. Leave that to the models."

I wasn't about to argue that I'd come home when things were just getting started. I slid my backpack off my shoulder, then slipped off my shoes, wanting nothing more than to take a hot shower and slip between my soft linen sheets.

"Have you said anything to Taj?"

I looked at her, confused. "About what?"

"About the First Lady."

"He asked about her outfits—for his blog." I didn't add anything else because he hadn't asked any invasive questions, and he deduced where the interview would be. But I had to be at least mostly truthful to Candace. She ranked higher than Taj on the scale of people able to ruin my life forever. "But I told him that no one tells me anything. Which they don't."

"And that was it? You were quiet for the rest of the time?" Her eyes narrowed. "What were you doing?"

"Chatting. Dancing." I left out the kissing. National security wouldn't be compromised if I didn't spill on that.

"Did he ask you about her schedule?"

"No."

"Did he ask you what room she was in?"

"No."

"Did he ask you to give her a note or a present?"

I exhaled dramatically. "No and no." My legs were ready to give out from standing. "Can I go now? I'm tired."

She tapped a fingernail against her lips as if she was contemplating my answers.

I shook my head and shrugged. "We talked about the places he visited, his blog. That's it. Really, Candace, I know how important it is for me not to say anything about Mrs. Jennings. You can trust me." I had tons of secrets in my brain more important that what the First Lady was wearing and I kept them quiet.

Candace finally smiled. "Good. And Mrs. Jennings wanted me to tell you not to worry about almost knocking chunks of cement on her head. She understands it was an accident."

"It really was!" I stuttered. "I would never do anything to hurt her!"

She held up that imperious hand. "Relax. You might have to convince Lidia, but the agents and I believe you too." Ortiz nodded, and Candace continued, "But we will be keeping a closer eye on Dante."

I could feel the heat of anger rising in my face.

Candace looked from Varon to Ortiz.

"Good night, Candace," said Varon. Then he and Ortiz left.

"You need to be careful, Bec," said Candace after the door clicked shut.

"I was," I said, and I thought I really had been. I'd been aware of my surroundings. Nothing and no one raised my suspicions. Parker and Mrs. Jennings and who was trying to hurt them were on my mind. Constantly. The why seemed obvious: whoever it was wanted Theresa Jennings but jumped the gun and got Parker instead. For anyone not looped in to the First Lady's coming and goings, it looked like she'd arrived earlier than expected, and that was understandable since the Secret Service was being as vague about her schedule as possible. As a famous and important person, Mrs. Jennings had to have her share of threats from the nut jobs out there. But I felt like I was missing something. There were still questions about Serena and her cables, why my things were touched, and by whom.

"The Forte is on an international watch list—"

"So is half of Rome," I argued. "So is San Francisco—only ten miles from where I grew up. Any big city where important people go—"

"I know you're smart," said Candace in her version of my mom's scary Quiet Voice. She leaned back again, but I didn't think she was in the least bit relaxed; it was more like a pose a viper makes before it strikes. "Terrorists, drug and arms dealers, and others just as un-savory go to places on watch lists. They go there to do business be-cause they think they're safe, that they blend into the crowd—and they will exploit anything and anyone to get an advantage. These people go for the weakest link." Her smile was grim, her pointed finger, accusing. "That would be you." Before I could object, she held up her hand. "I'm not saying you'd purposefully betray the First Lady, Bec." Her eyes held mine. "These people are smooth and know how to manipulate anyone, even agents and police. That's why I activated the GPS in your phone. It's a precautionary measure not just for your safety, but for Mrs. Jennings's too." Like my mother's could, Candace's eyes were soft and asking for my cooperation. "Now, did anyone ask you for a favor or suggest any-thing to you?"

I looked at her earnestly. "No."

She examined me long and hard before nodding. "Okay, we're done here. Good night, Bec."

I grabbed my backpack and went to my room. I appreciated Candace's honesty, but I was still aggravated. I had absolutely no privacy here. This was worse than that cloistered mountaintop con-vent school where Mom and Dad sent me before St. Xavier's.

After a shower, I felt calmer. *Candace and Ortiz are only doing their jobs*, I told myself, but I still didn't feel comfortable living like a bug under glass. A girl couldn't get a kiss without someone inter-rupting!

Too wired to sleep after the interrogation, I booted up my lap-top. Finding an innocent and secure wi-fi, I clicked myself in and entered a private chat room.

Cap'nCrunch: Any news on T-bone?
haxorgrrrl: Still in the package.

In other words, nothing.

Cap'nCrunch: Anything on his fam? Mom? Dad? Bro?
R2Deterent: Thought he was an only child.

That wasn't true, he said he had a brother. I started typing a new message: *Keep digging*—but then deleted it.

Taj was practically a celebrity—and even the biggest couldn't keep everything a secret. He was trying to stay off the grid as much as he could. *Why?* He couldn't go anywhere without being recognized. People threw themselves at him, like Francesca and that girl at the Forte. Some of his admirers had to be head cases. I'd read too many stories of celebrity stalkers and the things they did; they didn't just go after the person but also went after people related or close to them. He mentioned his brother to me; was he worried about his brother's safety? Was he trying to protect his family? It wasn't unlike the Secret Service's protection of Parker by keeping her hidden.

He'd told me about himself.

Because he must trust me.

Taj was starting to open up to me—not a wise move on his part. I didn't expect the guilt to weigh as heavily on me as it did. He didn't know about my life as an almost-secret-agent—and he never could.

21

*The next morning, Ortiz escorted me, like a pris-*oner, straight to the office—no stop at the bakery. Mrs. Jennings, with Lidia and the agents in tow, was off to visit some soup kitchens and then have lunch with the prime minister. Lucky Serena finally got some alone time with Candace to review the plans for the upcoming shoots and interview, which left me under Kevin's thumb—and I was feeling the pressure.

He snapped at everyone. It seemed like Taj's little prank was taking more of a toll on Kevin's sanity than I thought—not that I could blame him. Stuck in Rome with no funds? It really sucked to be him—and anyone within a ten-mile radius. The prediction I'd made about him taking his wrath out on me was coming true, but no way could I say anything to him. That would break every hacker code of honor in existence, and I didn't want to be connected to this anyway. I'd tried myself to reverse what Taj had done, but I was locked out each time. Because of the shooting schedule, Kevin hadn't had time to go to the bank and the consulate to straighten this out in person. Taj had to fix this. Today.

I was looking forward to a long *pranzo*. At last, I'd managed to get Ortiz's prints from a discarded espresso cup. I planned on waiting until I was utterly alone to check for a match, but right before lunch, a delivery came and everyone in the office went crazy. Not delivered by Dante—this was too big and too important to be carted through the city on the back of a Vespa. The contents: Theresa Jennings's couture wardrobe for her shoot at St. Peter's Square and her interview with *Edge*. It was a gift from the prime minister and a group of debut Italian designers. Gianni and Serena coordinated the effort. Theresa Jennings was, in addition to being the First Lady, an international style icon. The feature in *Edge* would bring attention to the new Italian faces on the fashion front.

Kevin signed for the delivery. "Hang all the clothes and catalog them," he ordered.

I didn't need the extra work—I was hoping to do a bit of surveillance around the office, particularly Kevin and Serena's shared space. I had yet to check out why Serena needed those cables. She knew when the First Lady was arriving, so she didn't quite fit the profile that was forming in my head of the person who almost took out Parker—but I still wanted to know why she was buying electronic equipment that was more advanced than she'd need.

"Then everything gets locked up!" Kevin shouted after me as he ran upstairs at Serena's call. "Even the accessories!"

"Yes, Kevin." It was best just to nod and smile at this point.

"And wash your hands before you touch anything!"

Grrr! I sort of felt bad about Kevin's situation, but I'd had enough. I wanted to text Taj about fixing his credit problem now, but it was better to tell him in person so our talk didn't leave a trail.

I took the box upstairs to the studio, where the empty racks were, and unpacked the clothing piece by piece.

Taliah came rushing in. "Let me see!"

"Don't touch!" I warned, spreading my arms to keep her back.

She was followed by the photo editor, a couple of copywriters, and of course, Francesca.

Everyone loved the mod-looking, Jackie-O-type dress suit in blue with a little cape and matching hat. That was for the shoot on the Square. When I pulled out the acid green sheath they would put her in for the *Edge* interview, it got some gasps. The color and cut would look fantastic on her.

"Can I take a few pictures?"

I nearly jumped out of my skin, and whirling around, saw Taj standing right behind me, hands in his pockets, looking very *GQ*. Was he here all the time now?

"Kevin would kill me," I said, "and speaking of him, we should probably—"

"Please?"

I considered. It wasn't like he hadn't already gotten a glimpse of the clothes. I'd been hanging and fluffing them where the entire staff oohed over them. Plus Sophie had learned that the designers had already leaked rough drawings. Taj came and went through the *Edge* offices with little supervision, courtesy of Candace. If Parker were here, I couldn't imagine that it would have been any different.

Mrs. Jennings would be seen at the Vatican, photographed by the world press, paparazzi, and tourists, so it would probably be all right, but considering the previous evening's interrogation, I wasn't taking any chances. Caution won out.

"Sorry."

"Bec." He put a hand on my arm, practically pleading.

I tugged him toward the hall to get away from everyone. I kept my voice low but tried not to look like I was. People's ears pricked up if they even thought you were whispering. "It's not that I don't trust you—well, actually, I don't. Not completely."

"Smart girl," he said with a one of those rare smiles that made my heart skip.

"Seriously, I got the third degree from Candace last night because I was out late. With you. At the Forte." I hoped the meaning was clear.

He raised his brows at me, but his face registered no shock or panic. I was anxious to lock the ridiculously expensive clothes up immediately so the subject would be dropped.

"Just one picture. Please." His dark eyes were magnetic.

Stay strong, Bec. . . .

It was nice to know I had some sort of advantage, even if it was small and silly. I gave him a firm "No," then turned to get the belt and earrings that went with the green dress. When I turned back, Taj was rearranging the blue suit on its hanger.

"Don't touch! It's silk!" I hissed. "Are your hands clean?" I rushed over to examine the cape. No damage. I exhaled in relief.

He laughed dryly. "Come on, Bec. I know not to have dirty, sweaty, or wet hands when touching silk."

"You're going to get me in trouble if Kevin finds out I let you near the clothes. And I asked you not to touch them. I'm putting them away." I rolled the rack into the newly cleared storage room and locked the door. After delivering the key to Kevin I went downstairs. Taj had seated himself on one of the couches in the common room with a thoughtful look. Was he sorry?

The front door flew open and Case barreled in, stone-faced. Mignone and Ortiz followed, one on each side of Mrs. Jennings. She looked all right, until she turned and I could see red dripping off the side of her beautiful face. I felt myself go numb until I realized it was too bright and too orange to be blood. It was caked in her hair and splattered all over her shoes. Lidia came next, her face and the pastel suit she was wearing smudged with pulpy red-orange muck.

"Mrs. Jennings!" Candace flew down the steps. "What happened?!"

"There was a crowd waiting outside the prime minister's office," Case explained. "They started shouting and throwing things as soon as she walked out the door."

"I'm *fine*," Mrs. Jennings said firmly. "Poor Lidia got the worst of it." She looked at her secretary and shook her head. "I'm so sorry—"

Lidia drew herself up. "I'm all right, Mrs. Jennings. A few tomatoes won't kill me."

Everyone, but especially Candace, looked worried. I moved closer to Ortiz.

"Protesters?" I whispered.

She nodded grimly, her jaw set. "You come to expect these things. Not everyone is happy with our government's policies, and frustrated people are looking for someone to blame."

"I'm glad no one got hurt," I started, but then Ortiz turned to me, her gaze fierce—so much so that it made me back up a step.

"The police arrested four armed men in that crowd. If they'd decided to use their guns—"

"Let's get you cleaned up," Candace said to Mrs. Jennings, guiding her to the studio. "I hope you won't bruise where you were hit."

"Thank you." Mrs. Jennings climbed up the steps next to Candace. Ortiz and the other agents trailed after.

Taj watched them go, then turned and gathered his things. "I've gotta go make a call."

"I'll see—" I never got the rest of my sentence out, he was gone that fast.

Okay.

It was quiet again. All the important people had gone up to the studio to fuss over Mrs. Jennings and Lidia.

Opportunity . . .

I crept upstairs. The studio room door was ajar. Murmuring voices rippled out. They'd be busy with Mrs. Jennings for a little while, but still, I probably didn't have much time, and who knew when I'd get this chance again. I slipped into Serena and Kevin's shared office.

There was no unusual equipment on or near Serena's desk. Crouching, I examined the cables connected to her computer. There was one connected to the printer, another to the wall outlet. And all dusty, as if they'd been there a while, not recently replaced, as the date on her receipt would suggest.

But maybe she'd bought them for someone else. I checked Kevin's computer. No new cables. Noiselessly, I padded over to Parker/

Candace's empty office, noting the studio room door. People were still talking. So far, so good.

I found the same thing in Candace's office—dust-covered cables connecting the computer tower to a printer and scanner. Nothing new.

"Miss Jackson?"

I whipped around. There was Varon standing in the door. Didn't they need him in the studio to fuss over Mrs. Jennings? Hold Candace's train?

"Hi, Varon."

He narrowed his dark eyes at me. "I don't need to ask you—"

"What I'm doing here?" I said overly cheerful.

What do I say, what do I say, *what do I say*? I spied one of Candace's crystal glasses, but I'd already used that excuse. Would the truth be better than a lie at this point? I took a deep breath.

"There were these cables on Serena's expense report."

He cocked a skeptical brow.

"And I was checking to see it if was legit."

"You were conducting a forensic investigation?" he said doubtfully.

I shrugged. "Guess so. Believe it or not, Varon, that's the truth."

Varon sighed and shook his head. I don't know if he believed me, but that was my story and I was sticking to it. If it stuck in his head, he might mention it to Candace. And if she gave any credence to my suspicions, she might give Serena a closer look, but I doubted it. More likely, she'd be convinced that I was up to no good. Nothing had been touched, so there really wasn't anything she could do to me.

"Varon," Candace called.

Motioning me out of the office, he waited for me to leave before closing the door and trotting back to the studio.

On my way down to the kitchen, I tried to work out what I'd discovered. The cables Serena bought could definitely have been used to tap into the internal systems on a car—but nothing indicated she was capable of that. Even if she somehow managed it, I didn't think she'd want to do away with the First Lady. But I could see why she'd want Parker out of the way. With the biggest photo shoot in the magazine's history coming up, Serena would have been top Chihuahua—if Candace hadn't leapfrogged over her into the big chair. And it was obvious to everyone that she and Candace were not simpatico, although maybe she was playing all of us: after all, the best disguise for intelligence was to feign ignorance.

Before I could accuse her, I had to be sure.

Somewhat cleaned up, Mrs. Jennings was hustled out by the agents, probably back to the hotel. Once they were gone, the office settled down again. I retrieved my laptop and took advantage of the quiet to do a quick background search on Serena: education, jobs, hobbies. There was no indication that she had the know-how to break into a car's computer system and take control.

Then why the cables?

I combed through the expense report I'd done for her, but nothing else seemed suspicious. Alone, buying new cables wasn't enough evidence. I'd have to keep my eye on her.

In the meantime, I reluctantly dragged out Dean Harding's package—and a notebook and pen. I hadn't put much of a dent in my assignments—that was the Dean's fault. He should've let me use my computer. Who hand-wrote papers anymore? I might as well *be* in ancient Rome, using papyrus and a feather quill.

Sighing, I closed the file and put my laptop aside. I had to get some work done. I made myself a latte and went back to the dreaded packet. After about two hours, I'd gotten a good chunk of math done and had just switched to World Civ when I saw Dante step into the foyer, stopping at Francesca's desk with several envelopes. As she wordlessly signed for them, he glanced around and spied me. He waved and smiled, which I returned. I was glad to know he wasn't upset over the Pantheon incident. After Francesca returned his clipboard, he strode over and dragged a chair next to me.

"Homework?" he asked.

"Yep."

"American history?"

"Huh? Oh. No. World Civ." I tried to focus on history, but all I could think of was, did ancient Romans have such beautiful faces? Maybe all those flawless statues were accurate and everyone was gorgeous.

"World history!" he scoffed. "Boring. Just wars and generals. American history is more interesting. I memorize everything *importante* about American history. Ask me, I will tell you anything." He crossed his arms and smiled broadly at me. It was infectious.

"Okay," I said, playing along. "Who was the fourth president?"

"James Madison."

"Correct."

Dante huffed at my surprised look. "Too easy. Ask another question."

I Googled James Madison and scrolled through his biography. "What is he known for?"

"He is the father of the Constitution, good friend of Thomas Jefferson. His wife, Dolly, saved George Washington's portrait from the British when they invaded and burned the White House. In 1812."

"History's dead. Life is for the living."

I was startled to see Taj standing there. When had he come in?

Dante's jaw clenched. He didn't even bother to turn around when he rebuffed Taj. "Those who do not learn from history are doomed to repeat it."

"Very impressive, Dante," said Candace, coming over to us. Even in her crazy heels she moved like a stealth bomber. You thought you were safe and then—*boom!*—there she was. "But you've made your delivery. I'm sure you have others . . . ?"

That was her unsubtle nudge for Dante to leave. I searched her face. If she wanted to chat about my unauthorized visit to her office, she didn't show it.

Dante stood. "I see you later, Bec." He didn't acknowledge Taj, whose mouth was quirked to one side.

"Okay." As he headed toward the door, Candace went upstairs into her office. Taj headed toward the kitchen and I was relieved to be alone. Suddenly Dante stopped, came back, and whispered in my ear, "Maybe I meet Mrs. Jennings sometime?"

Inwardly, I winced. "Sorry, but I don't know her schedule. It's kept secret for her protection. I never know when or where she's going to show up."

"You find out, I can come. Anytime."

Not him too!

First Taj with his subtle questions and now Dante with his sweet but disconcerting earnestness. People just didn't walk up to the First Lady like she was a celebrity. He wasn't stupid—he had to know that. Maybe Candace's CIA paranoia was getting to me, but their interest in Mrs. Jennings made me uneasy.

Sophie, Aldo, and Ortiz all came in.

"Bye, *bella*," said Dante.

"Bye, Dante." Sophie waved to Dante as he walked out. Then she sat next to me and bent close. "From the way he looks at you, I would say Dante likes you. And then yesterday, after you danced with Taj, there seemed to be something between you two. We need to have a long overdue chat." She smiled secretively. "I have some news of my own."

That brightened my mood. A night out with Sophie would be a great opportunity to see what she knew about Serena or if she'd noticed anything strange. I'd have to be very careful of my words. Last thing I needed to add to my chaotic life was a ticked-off Candace. "Want to go somewhere tonight?"

She sat down next to me. "I know a great market with a stall where you can get secondhand designer bags. You have to dump that backpack for something better. Maybe a Fendi satchel."

But I loved my backpack. It had served me well. Still, a new one might be a good idea. . . .

"Bec!" From upstairs, Candace's voice went through my head like a nail. She leaned over the balcony. "Sophie: you, Kevin, and

Serena are going over the final copy to make any last-minute changes. Now." She flicked a finger at me. "Your assistance is required for something else."

And just like that, our girls' night out–info session vanished like a puff of excess setting powder.

I made a sad face at Sophie. "Soon," I said with a sigh.

She nodded and, with palms up like "What can you do?" headed upstairs with me behind her.

It turned out that my assistance was required to help Candace pack the First Lady's blue silk suit and accessories to be brought back to the hotel. She called for a cab, not taking any chances of something happening to the clothing while walking it over. When we got to the hotel, she ordered me to stay in the taxi while she ran the suit up.

"Ristorante Divino," she told the driver when she got back in. Looking at me, she said, "I'm taking you out to dinner."

"Why?" I was a little confused—and leery—of her growing familiarity. And generosity.

"You've been working hard. You need a little break."

I wasn't buying it. My look may have suggested as much, because she added, "We can have some girl time. Chat, that sort of thing."

Girl time? With Candace? Was the Ice Queen finally melting?

"Uh, sure." She probably got around to talking with Varon.

The car rolled to a stop in front of a modern bistro, sleek and shiny. The maître d' greeted Candace warmly and ushered us to a quiet table near a back booth, away from the kitchen. Perfect place for an ambush, which I was sure this was, and I was the ambushee.

I fidgeted with my napkin, nervously expecting her to say my flight was already booked. The waiter bowed smartly and backed away. When Candace looked at me, there was an earnestness about her that was unnerving. It didn't help when I spied Ortiz at the bar— drinking coffee. I was sure that her presence wasn't a coincidence.

"The house chardonnay for me, and an *acqua frizzante* for my friend," she said to the waiter as he laid menus by our places. "Or would you prefer a Coke?"

Friend?

Whatever. I guessed a glass of wine was out of the question. It was probably for the best, although I thought I understood now what Mom meant when she said she could really use a drink.

"No, water's fine." We sat silently until the drinks arrived. Candace took a sip from her goblet, filled with a golden wine. Another waiter stopped by, putting down a dish of baby artichokes. The scent of garlic and crushed herbs made my mouth water. Under Candace's watchful eye, I took one and popped it into my mouth. She chose that moment to ask me a question.

"I know I've asked before, but this latest incident makes it so imperative that we have to be extra vigilant. Has anyone asked you for details about the First Lady?"

Who *hadn't* been asking? I chewed, swallowed, and cleared my throat.

"Taj wanted to take pictures of the outfit she's wearing tomorrow." That was true and didn't seem harmful in any way. I'd keep the part about him touching the suit to myself. It was only two fingers anyway.

"And what did you tell him?"

I tilted my head. "I said no. He can take some when she's in the square. You and the Secret Service squad can keep an eye on him and everyone else."

Candace smiled. "Good. And Dante?"

I didn't want to ruin Dante's life over something that might be nothing, but I wasn't going to stop being *mostly* honest. "Like everyone else, he wants to meet the First Lady."

That was true too—for lots of people. Let Candace and the Secret Service make of it what they would. It was their job to figure out if Dante was a threat.

Candace sighed, taking a big sip of her wine. "It's a nightmare trying to keep her movements and whereabouts quiet. She draws attention everywhere she goes, and she doesn't like to be crowded by bodyguards or have her movements restricted. We're hoping to get to the Vatican early tomorrow. The cardinals and the pope are more private and conservative about the news they share. I'm hoping we can be in and out of St. Peter's Square without much interference from the crowds." Candace chose an artichoke and chewed it slowly.

"Here's the deal," she said after swallowing. "There are extremists out there who threaten political figures or their families. Most of them are harmless. It's the few that are totally serious and might follow through that we have to find before anything happens. It's standard procedure for us to ask if anyone has been saying anything against the President or First Lady, either at the office, around Rome, or wherever you've been."

I shook my head vehemently. "No, not at all. I haven't heard anything bad or even critical about Mrs. Jennings or the President."

Candace leaned over, her gaze penetrating. "If you hear anything—and I mean *anything, from anyone*—that could be seen as a threat, no matter how silly it may seem, I want you to tell me. Or one of the Secret Service people if I'm not around. I'll make sure you have all the agents' numbers."

I sat up straighter. "Is something going on?" Candace seemed more intense than usual.

Our food arrived: a flaky fish surrounded by baby plum tomatoes, zucchini, olive oil, and herbs for her; lobster ravioli for me. She waited until the waiter left before she leaned forward to say softly, "Some anti-American groups have been more active on the Internet lately. And of course, there was the attack at the prime minister's, harmless as it may have seemed."

She paused to taste her food. I stuffed a ravioli into my mouth while I had the chance. She chewed carefully and swallowed, taking a small sip of wine before continuing.

"Can I depend on you?"

Now that was a phrase that wasn't used too often around me.

And even though it was coming from Candace—or maybe *especially* since it was coming from Candace—it took me aback. No one ever asked me to do anything important like they needed or *wanted* my help.

She's seen what you can do, and she respects that. Is that so hard to believe?

It was. But I did.

She didn't say it, but I knew that she expected me to rat out Dante or Taj if they asked for too much. I'd always questioned authority, gone against the system. I never liked people telling me what I had to do. But I really liked Mrs. Jennings and felt protective of Parker. I'd do what I could to keep them both safe.

I had to ask myself where Taj and Dante fit: friends or possible foes? Their actions would determine that, not me.

"Absolutely," I said. And as on that long-ago day when I had that heart-to-heart with Parker, I meant it. "I promise."

It was Ortiz.

Ortiz had searched my room.

And I was surprised at how unaffected I was by the discovery. Maybe it was because I had a better handle on what was going on now. But it did explain a few things—like why she opened up about the car possibly being tampered with. Maybe she felt guilty for constantly invading my privacy. She was only doing her job; I saw that now, and I'd make it a point to be nicer to her.

I'd have a good chance at St. Peter's. We were heading over to do Mrs. Jennings's last off-site shoot. I finished getting dressed and went out to meet Candace in the sitting room.

"You can't wear that," she said, examining my outfit with an über-critical eye.

I looked at the dress I picked out. It fell a little below my knee, so not too short, and the boat neckline was beyond modest. My legs were bare, but it was warm and no one wore pantyhose anymore except old ladies and British royalty.

"What's wrong with it?"

"It doesn't have sleeves and it's too casual. We're going to be in view of the Vatican with Theresa Jennings, not picnicking on the back of Romeo's Vespa. We're going to be seen by the entire world."

"It's Dante, not Romeo," I corrected.

"He's not important," she said. "The rules for dressing were outlined in the e-mail I sent out yesterday."

How could I forget? No bullet points, just paragraphs and paragraphs. I had no time to read through all of it; I was surprised she had time to write it.

"I went to the Vatican City Web site and checked the dress code—"

"You are representing *Edge* and are part of the First Lady's entourage." She fixed me with a stare. "Change."

Sighing, I went back to my room. *Sleeves . . . not as casual . . .*

I found a pair of simple black pants. Everyone wore them, and mine showed not so much as a centimeter of leg. Those, along with a silk tee and jacket, would have to work because I had nothing else that would be considered appropriate. All of me would be covered up. Candace would have to deal with bare toes—I wasn't meeting the pope, so my black studded sandals stayed. When I came back into the room, she nodded with approval.

"Much better. There's just one thing." She reached into a flat white box printed with gold lying on the coffee table and pulled out a wad of black. Shaking it out into a meshy, lace trimmed square, she popped it over my head.

"Hey!" I looked in the mirror. Goth was all very well, but it wasn't my thing.

"His Holiness sent these to everyone, a little gift. You don't have to wear it in the square or any cathedrals, but if you do visit one later, remember to keep your shoulders covered. They're very strict about it here."

"I will."

She sat gracefully on the couch. "It's going to be a long, difficult day."

I took the fluffy chair opposite. Candace didn't look her usual confident self but tired and a little older. Worry lines were visible across her forehead.

"Why?"

She eyed me for a few moments, as if she was weighing whether or not she should spill what was on her mind. "I tried to make Cardinal Tartoria see reason, but he wouldn't listen. We wanted to do today's shoot in one of the smaller buildings. The Vatican has a million nooks we could have used where we would have been out of the way, and it would have been much safer for Mrs. Jennings, but he wouldn't allow it. They won't give us access to any of the sites for pictures for a fashion magazine." Her tone changed to a deep rolling baritone, probably in poor imitation of the Cardinal's rough English: "The *Vaticano* is a holy site, for prayer and meditation, not for photographing women's dresses. Use the square—that is a public place."

I laughed, but Candace didn't join me.

"Anyone can just wander around the square—and after what happened at the prime minister's . . ." She looked out the window and inhaled deeply. "There'll be some Swiss Guards, and they'll help keep any crowds back, but still." She shook her head. "So many people . . ."

"Well, I'll do my part and cooperate," I said. "You can count on me."

She smiled. "I know."

Whoa, Bec! You're fraternizing with the enemy.

But Candace wasn't the enemy. Not anymore. And in a way, it was nice not to be at odds with her.

"That means no incidents, right?" she asked, bringing me back to the conversation. "No getting in the way, no disruptions, and no disappearing."

"Yes, ma'—Candace," I said.

She nodded approvingly and rose, opening the door for me. We went downstairs and out to the street where a line of cars waited—a string of taxis and the black First Lady-mobile.

"I'll see you there," she said, and I watched her as she squeezed into the special car with Mrs. Jennings and the other agents. I walked down the queue of taxis, looking for an empty seat.

"Bec! Over here!"

Sophie waved from the third car, a Fiat, like the one I rode in the day I arrived. She sat in the back with Kevin. Feeling like an intruder in an intimate moment, I slid into the seat next to the driver. When I shut the door the automatic belt almost strangled me as I clicked the one on my lap.

Our taxi flew down the Via di Panico and over a bridge that crossed the Tiber. Out the passenger window, I watched statues of men and saints flash by. When the driver hit the brake, I, like everyone else, lurched forward, the cross-body belt pressing into my chest as I strained against it. I heard Sophie gasp and on instinct, I stuck out a hand to brace myself against the dashboard. Looking up, I saw a group of tourists jump back onto the sidewalk. All of this happened in a matter of seconds.

"*Idioti!*" the driver shouted at them, then turning to me, said, "Sorry, *signorina*."

"It's okay," I assured him as I adjusted the belt, still tight across my chest. It had really held me in place, more than the lap belt.

The car turned onto another street, narrow and cobbled, the Borgo Santo Spirito, that ended abruptly at a white domed building that rose up like a glittering cloud.

Circling the building was the *borgo*, a mass of white marble, pointed cornices, and soaring columns. We pulled up to an ornate iron gate decorated with elaborate leafy scrolls and papal keys where two guards brightly dressed in Renaissance-era uniforms waved us through.

"Cute outfits," I said.

"They're the Swiss Guards," said Sophie. "They've dressed that way for hundreds of years."

Those were the guards Candace was talking about? The hats were silly enough with the giant feathers, but the yellow court-jester pantaloons and tights didn't exactly inspire respect. No way could they convince anyone that they were fierce or deadly.

Through the gates, our taxi joined a line of other cars depositing people at the edge of the vast plaza. I didn't realize how huge it was until I was out of the car—it was a mammoth place to keep an eye on. No wonder Candace was nervous. The dome looked like a giant crown when we approached it from the street, and I could just make out the row of white statues that balanced along the top. In the center, a huge obelisk partially blocked my view.

As I got out of the car I saw my hand, red and mottled from where I'd slammed it into the dash. On the heel of my palm was embedded distinctly the number *500*—the Fiat's logo.

"Come on, Bec!"

Sophie and Kevin were out of the car and heading into the square. Crowds of people wandered around, some carrying signs addressed to Mrs. Jennings like at the Pantheon, except a few of these weren't friendly. So much for the Vatican being secretive about who was coming to visit. We'd only just stepped inside the oval ring when a group of raggedy-looking kids came running up.

"The English-speaking tour starts in a few minutes!" they said. "We can give you the best tour. Cheaper too."

"Pickpockets," whispered Sophie.

I'd seen small groups of them wandering around when I'd gone out with Taj and Dante, but they had stayed away. Not so here—but then again, the plaza bustled with tourists taking pictures and buying overpriced souvenirs. I clutched my pack tighter to me and followed Kevin as he pushed past them, muttering something in Italian I was sure wasn't complimentary.

One of them, a boy, maybe twelve, shouted something back. I had no idea what he'd said, only that it couldn't be good. But somehow, it didn't sound so terrible in Italian.

"And in church too!" Sophie laughed.

Kevin grinned warmly at her. "Technically, we're not *in* the church."

"But it is holy ground," I said, and I wondered if this kind of thing went on during the public masses, or was there some honor code? Honor among thieves? Would they stay away from the First Lady's photo shoot?

We joined the other *Edge* staffers and Taj, who had already gathered in the square near the steps to St. Peter's Basilica. The photographers were starting to set up for the shoot.

A clutch of Swiss Guards stood in attendance not far from Mrs. Jennings. These guys were dressed more plainly but still oddly; all they needed to do was trade their floppy berets for tall hats and they'd look like pilgrims. They didn't seem formidable, although the tall sharp pikes they carried looked real enough. Still, what use could a spear be against some nut with a gun?

I walked up to Candace. "I can see why you were worried," I whispered. "They're not even armed!"

"Oh, they are," she said. "And so are we."

Good to know, but maybe I was catching her nervousness. I wished we had more agents with us. Chuck Norris would be even better.

"*Fatti gli affari tuoi, America!*" a group of protesters shouted. They waved signs and shook their fists.

"What are they saying?" I asked Candace.

"They're saying that America should mind its own business," she said. Her hand moved to her hip—where her gun was holstered under her jacket.

Suddenly the group pushed forward toward the barrier of Swiss Guards. Three of them moved fast, stepping up and blocking the rush with their pikestaffs. One of the protesters tried to go around them. Candace's hand now went under her jacket to her gun. My heart leapt into my mouth. I hated violence and didn't want to see anyone get hurt—but suddenly two more guards seemed to materialize from nowhere and grabbed the man by his arms. That sent the rest of the protesters back, although they continued to shout.

More guards appeared and grimly escorted the group out of the square. Watching the retreating protesters, I tried to calm the ner-vous flutter in my stomach. All these deadly weapons underlined the very real danger I was living with, and I didn't like it.

"Another close call." Candace shook her head. "Let's get this over with and get out of here."

She barked orders to the photographers to finish setting up. Ugi and Joe both prohibited me from touching their precious stuff. I'd done all that I could to help, so I moved out of the way and was on my own again for the moment. I looked around, wondering what I should do, when I saw Taj striding over to me.

"Come on," he said, "they're busy. I'll give you a tour, I've been here before."

I caught Candace's eye and motioned that I'd be walking around with Taj. She gave a brief nod and went back to hounding Aldo and Angelo.

Priests, nuns in habits, older ladies with lace-covered heads, shabby-looking teens, and wary-eyed guards moved to the shade of the columned cloister that ringed the plaza. We walked to the obelisk in the center.

"It looks Egyptian," I said.

"It is. The Emperor Caligula had it moved to Rome—you can imagine the things it's seen. But look, it's also a sundial and calen-dar. It's supposed to be quite accurate."

I followed the long, dark shadow as we walked a wide circuit around the obelisk, past more tourists and splashing fountains. It was getting warm. *Wouldn't it be nice to slip off my shoes and stick my feet in that cool water for just a minute. . . .*

"Bec!"

I turned.

Dante?

He ran across the square to reach us. Good eyes, to find us in this crowd, but I guessed my pink hair, especially in the bright sun-light, was a dependable homing beacon. I could never be a ninja—I was too visible.

"Hello," he puffed. It was a long run and a hot day.

"No deliveries today?" Taj's voice was sharp.

Dante's eyes darkened and the muscles in his jaw tensed. "My day off."

"What are you doing here?" I asked, "and how did you find us? Wait, don't tell me. Another cousin?"

He waved at one of the Swiss Guards, who signaled back with a bob of his pointy spear.

"Fabrizio," he said to me. To Taj, he said coldly, "*This is my Roma.* You are the tourist here. I will show Bec around."

Taj, his eyes stony and his hands clenched, took a step into Dante's personal space. "She's with me."

"She's with the *Edge* people," Dante countered.

"You mean Candace."

"I mean *not you.*"

"You want to do this here? Right now?" Taj threatened, his shoulders jutting forward, and stepping closer.

I rushed between them to prevent a confrontation. "It's so crowded. Too bad they wouldn't shut even a part of it down for Mrs. Jennings," I said, linking my arms with both of them before either could take a swing at the other, and more importantly, catch me in the middle. "Tell us something interesting about St. Peter's, Dante. Taj has been giving me a history lesson. You live here, so you have to know something cool about this place that's not in the guidebooks." I flicked my eyes at a passing Swiss Guard. "What can you tell me about these guys, since your cousin is one of them?"

"I know lots," said Dante, eyeing Taj, "but I'm sworn to keep secret. If I tell you, I have to . . . you know." He made a slashing motion across his throat.

"Oh, come on," I laughed uneasily. Dante had to be exaggerating, but there was a weird seriousness in his voice I didn't like.

"They are trained bodyguards, like your Secret Service—"

"Everyone knows that," quipped Taj.

"I didn't," I offered, hoping to stop them from squabbling as we circled back. Candace had said it was going to be a long, difficult day. I just hadn't thought she was talking about mine.

Suddenly Ortiz was there, and for once, I was glad to see her.

"I think we've all had enough history for today," she said, and before I could reply or thank her for saving me, she pulled Taj aside. They spoke in hushed voices. I wondered why didn't she lead Dante away. He wasn't staff, and he wasn't here to interview the First Lady. Why wasn't she patrolling or something, especially with the crowds making everyone jumpy?

My purse buzzed, and pulling out my phone, I read the text.

"Hey," I called to Taj and Ortiz, a few steps away. "Sophie says they're ready to start taking photos. I have to head back over to the basilica steps."

We walked quickly, dodging through the growing crowd. The Secret Service agents were plainly visible in their dark suits, earpieces, and sunglasses. In their midst was Mrs. Jennings. She must have been driving them crazy. From the moment she stepped out of her car, she paused to talk to anyone who stopped her. At the moment she was surrounded by a pair of nuns in full habit, suffocatingly hot wimples and all, and a gaggle of uniformed schoolchildren with their starstruck parents. She bent to hug and kiss them and sign notebooks. Gazing around, I noticed policemen in front of the barricades around our group. The one closest had his back to me. His silver hair glinted in the sun, and he paced back and forth with a long uneven stride. Looking closer, I saw one of his shoes had a thicker sole than its sibling. Before I could remember if I'd seen him before, Taj nudged me. When I turned he pointed slightly off to his left, where Mrs. Jennings stood.

When I caught her eye, she smiled and pantomimed for a bottle of water. The day had started out refreshingly cool, but all the surrounding stonework in the square made it feel like a convection oven, the heat radiating up off the paved travertine blocks. Where was Lidia? I searched the square. Case, Collins, and Mignone stood around the First Lady, their sides or backs to her so they could scan the area. Ortiz wandered through the immediate crowd. Varon stood with Ugi, Joe, and Sophie by the prep tent. And there was Lidia, leaning against the car, talking to Nelson. If anything happened, he was the getaway driver. Giving Mrs. Jennings the thumbs-up, I hurried over to the car to pass on the message.

"Mrs. Jennings wants a drink," I told her.

Lidia nodded, and as she fished a water out of the cooler, I looked at my palm again. The numbers were fading; I probably didn't bump into the dash that hard—it wasn't like I'd crashed into it.

Like Parker.

The mark on her chest—it looked like a shield, with a circle in it. . . . I pulled out my phone and typed in an image search. *Italian car logos.* When the images loaded, I scanned them, stopping at the logo for Lancia: a medieval shield with a circle inside it. I stopped, my breath caught in my throat.

The accident. *I knew what happened to Parker.*

And I had to tell Candace.

Now.

Turning, I searched for her—but saw only Ortiz looking around wildly, left and right.

"She's gone! She's gone!" she shouted, shoving people aside.

Suddenly there were shouts and screaming and people scrambling.

Panic shook me.

Where was Mrs. Jennings?

Ortiz put a hand to her earpiece as she ripped out her phone. With a swift glance, she took off, pointing for Case to go in a different direction.

My heart hammering in my chest, I turned around and around.

"Mrs. Jennings!" I called, and realized there was someone else I didn't see.

Someone who was by my side only a moment earlier.

Dante.

From the corner of my eye I saw Dante standing alone, nowhere near our tent, but next to the barricades.

No Fabrizio.

No Mrs. Jennings.

But that didn't prove anything . . .

"*Prima Signora! Prima Signora!*" It seemed even the schoolkids were upset.

Or not.

Theresa Jennings stood up, holding her hands up in apology, trying to calm everyone down. The children had enveloped her in a group hug, and she'd taken off her hat and the little cape. Lidia ran over to her, followed by Candace and Varon. Nelson, Mignone, and Collins surrounded the First Lady now, talking into their earpieces while scrutinizing the crowd and any movement in the square. Varon hurried to my side. His glare rooted me to the spot.

"What just happened?" he said, his voice uncannily calm.

"Mrs. Jennings was with the kids and she asked me to get her some water. I went over to the car and told Lidia. When I turned around, Mrs. Jennings was gone."

"And the first thing you thought to do was yell?"

"No!" I protested. "That was Ortiz." Damn. I'd ratted her out, but a withering glance from Candace froze the words in my throat. Both Ortiz and Case went running to look for Mrs. Jennings, I wanted to explain, but guessed it wasn't my place. They were the trained agents. Didn't they talk to each other?

Candace stood on tiptoe, scanning the plaza.

I went on anyway. "Ortiz looked like she didn't see her, then yelled, 'She's gone!' and everyone started to panic—"

"Fabulous!" snarled Candace. I guessed that Ortiz was going to get at least a loud lecture when she got back.

"I'm sorry, Candace, this was my fault," said Mrs. Jennings. "One of the children wanted to give me a drawing and a hug. And it's just so beastly hot out here. So I knelt down, took off the hat and cape. The agents must not have realized it. I didn't think about it. I'm very sorry if I caused anyone to panic."

The upset children were led away by the nuns and accompanying adults. Case, now back from his panicked run, handed Mrs. Jennings her hat. She put it on and looked around. The cape was gone.

"I knew this would be a disaster," Candace muttered, her face pinched. The square was getting crowded, and the agents were tense and edgy, their heads swiveling around, hands on the guns underneath their coats, searching for any suspicious movement. "We're finished. We won't be able to get any more good shots, not with all these people here." She turned to the First Lady. "I'm sorry, Mrs. Jennings, but I don't think it would be a good idea to continue in this crowd."

Mrs. Jennings placed her hand on Candace's arm. "I understand. Do we have enough photos from my audience with His Holiness and whatever we've taken so far?"

Candace rubbed her temple. "If we don't, we'll have to Photoshop the background in. Aldo and Angelo will be thrilled to take more in the studio. Somehow, we'll make do."

"Do you want me to try and find the cape?" I asked.

"Look around, but don't go too far. I've had enough missing people for today." She stopped and peered over Mrs. Jennings's head. Ortiz was striding through the plaza, dragging a scraggly looking boy by the collar in one hand and the cape in the other. Taj came jogging up behind her.

"Ortiz! Why did you leave the square?" Candace fumed.

"I lost sight of Mrs. Jennings. Then I spotted this little punk" —she shook the boy—"with her cape, across the square. I ran to check through the crowd he was in, looking for her, making sure she wasn't being dragged away," she panted. "Our earpieces went out, so I didn't realize she wasn't gone, just kneeling down. I couldn't take the chance." She took two deeps breaths. "I wouldn't have caught him if it wasn't for Taj. Guess my little friend here was trying to nab himself an expensive souvenir." She handed the cape to the First Lady. "You may want to have that cleaned before you wear it again."

Ortiz held the boy firmly by his collar. Mrs. Jennings gave her a pleading look and Ortiz loosened her grip a bit—but she didn't let go.

"What do we do with him?" Candace mumbled.

"Hai promess!" the boy squealed, struggling to get out of Ortiz's grip.

Candace eyed Ortiz. "What did you promise him?"

Ortiz glowered at the boy. "I told him we wouldn't cut him into little pieces and feed him to the pigeons if he came quietly. *Stai zitto!"*

"I'm sure he didn't mean any harm," Mrs. Jennings said and, despite Candace's sour face, extended her hand for him to shake. He smiled shyly and tipped his head as best he could with Ortiz still holding on to him.

"He's just a child. Please let him go." Mrs. Jennings's tone sounded as if that wasn't a suggestion, but an order.

"Fine." Candace crouched so that she was eye level with the boy. She pointed from her eyes to his and back with two of her fingers.

He didn't look scared, but I think he knew better than to laugh, especially with the Vatican guards, Secret Service, and a few police eyeballing him. I was willing to bet the locals knew the kid well. Ortiz released him, and he was gone in seconds.

"I'm in even better hands than I realized. Thank you all," Mrs. Jennings said graciously as the agents urged her back to the safety of the car.

Candace watched the limo speed off. Turning smartly on her heel, she called, "Kevin!"

He was standing next to Sophie but quickly ran to answer the summons.

"Ask Claudio if he got any good shots of Mrs. Jennings in the square. I want a contact sheet on my desk tonight."

Kevin bobbed his head and walked over to the where the extra photographer they'd hired to take candid shots of Mrs. Jennings stood, packing up his equipment.

Next to me, Candace didn't look too pleased.

"Everyone head back to the office! Bec, we have to talk."

Yes, we did.

She looked pensive, but once we were away from the others, she brightened a bit. "I have some good news that I got just before Mrs. Jennings disappeared. Parker woke up today."

I had to stop myself from hugging her, because it would be awkward on so many levels. "She did? Can I see her?"

"Yes, she did, and no, you can't. Not yet. Now don't give me a hard time, Bec," she said when she saw my face, knowing I was ready to argue. "I'm telling you this only because I know how concerned you've been and Parker and your mom are friends. Obviously your mother thought enough of her to put you under her care." Candace exhaled. "She keeps slipping in and out of consciousness, but the doctors feel it's progress. Once she stays awake you'll see her—again."

Uh-oh. Guess she knew about my prior visit. Maybe Ortiz wasn't as tight-lipped as I thought—and we'd made a deal on *that* piece of information! But it didn't matter. Right now, Parker was more important.

I touched her arm. "I think I know what caused the accident!"

Candace quickly looked around. "Not here."

I blew up my bangs. "Okay, but do you think Parker will be safe?" I'd found her, maybe someone else could too.

Candace started walking and put a hand on my shoulder. "We have people checking on her. As soon as she remembers the accident and can answer questions, we'll find out more. We're hoping she'll be able to shed some light on what happened—and on who wants to hurt the First Lady."

*I had to wait to share my theory about the acci-*dent with Candace because as soon as we got back, she called Ortiz into her office, barking a warning that she'd better not be disturbed, then slammed the door. My guess was that Candace had some serious explaining to do to the President and her bosses back on home soil—even though nothing really happened. A pickpocket hijacked a piece of Theresa Jennings's wardrobe. The First Lady was never in any real danger. I felt sorry for Ortiz. Candace was ripping the agent a new one, and everyone could hear it.

"Some excitement today, huh?" said Taj, coming over to me.

I'd just finished putting the light filters, which looked like little white umbrellas, back together for use on the final shoot. Aldo claimed his nerves were frayed and he had to get away because he couldn't function under such duress. He left a list of things to do. Aldo was just lazy and wanted to leave the grunt work of unpacking to others—specifically, me. I was thinking maybe Aldo's seat assignment was going to get switched from first class to coach for his trip home to Milan. These things happen.

At 5:00, Candace hadn't emerged from her office.

"It's a beautiful night, Bec. Want to go to our place and have some fun?" Taj said.

By "our place" he must have meant the Forte—our only place. And even though we'd only been there once, I liked him calling it ours. The fact that it was under scrutiny by several governments made it kind of fitting.

I looked up at Candace's still-shut door. I was dying to tell her my theory about Parker's car, but she was still closeted with Ortiz.

"Mrs. Jennings had her dinner and is tucked away safely in her hotel room, and we won't see her again until tomorrow for the final interview at one. We have plenty of time to take a little break. It's not like you don't deserve it, especially after Aldo skipped out, and Sophie and Kevin left for dinner. All of them left you to unpack almost everything."

"The glamorous life of an intern," I mumbled.

I wanted to talk to Candace so badly. And Ortiz needed to explain why she'd broken our deal. And as much as I wanted to spend time with Taj, the thought crossed my mind that it was odd how he knew the First Lady's schedule. I knew the interview was tomorrow, but Candace had only said around lunchtime and that I had to be at the office at the regular time to finalize any setup. Although he was interviewing her for all of twenty minutes, Taj wasn't official *Edge* staff, so how did he know where she was now—unless it was a guess, like where the interview would be?

And then there was Dante—always showing up with a cousin in every corner. Where would he turn up next?

No one seemed dangerous, at least not in an *I'm going to kill you for real* kind of way—but I was new to the Secret Service / spy business. And I wasn't so sure that I liked the responsibility of looking out for the First Lady's and Parker's safety. What if something I did caused trouble? *That* wasn't unheard-of. So many questions, too many people, one me.

I frowned. "I don't know. I really need to talk to Candace."

"You're very pretty when you frown, you know that?"

I blushed.

"Look, if you don't want to go across town, I can walk you back to your hotel—the long way. We can see some sights, get a drink. . . ."

That sounded nice. I smiled.

"And your smile's even prettier. I like that better."

"Bec!"

Dante? After hours? He couldn't be here with a package—and he'd said it was his day off.

"Must be a holiday, you haven't delivered anything all day," Taj quipped, scowling.

I glared at Taj before giving Dante my sweetest smile. "Hi, Dante. What's up?"

He came into the common room. "I wanted to see if you wanted to—"

Taj crossed his arms over his chest. "I'm sorry, she's already made plans for tonight."

Technically, I hadn't, and I didn't like anyone speaking for me. I was going to protest but Dante's lion-eyes glowed, like he was ready for a challenge—and if he decided to take it, it wouldn't end well, especially for Taj. I really needed these two to stay apart, but it was beyond my control.

"How about another time?" I suggested. "Like tomorrow, if Candace doesn't need me."

His brow furrowed, Dante glared at Taj, clearly unhappy with my answer, but he didn't argue. "*Sì*. Tomorrow. *Buonanotte*." He spun on his heel and left.

"I don't think he likes me," said Taj dryly.

"I think the feeling's mutual." I stood and dusted off my hands.

He checked his watch. "Let's go. It'll get your mind off things for a while and you can talk to Candace when you're both back in the hotel. I promise you won't get in late."

I was still a little annoyed about the way he'd treated Dante, but when I looked into his eyes to tell him, "Maybe another time," my resistance—and anger—melted away.

We left the office and strolled down a few streets, admiring shop windows and gently crumbling buildings, and then stopping at an outdoor stand to get icy granitas served in hollowed-out orange halves. Day was giving in to dusk.

When we came in sight of the hotel we slowed down, and putting his arm around me, Taj guided me out of the lights of the streetlamps. He stood against the wall, dimly visible. I leaned against him, my heart already beating faster in anticipation. His head dipped, and his lips captured mine.

I closed my eyes. The kiss was slow; he took his time exploring my mouth with his while he pressed me closer. I wrapped my arms around his neck . . . but it wasn't enough. My body wanted more.

A wolf whistle from some passing teens reminded me I was kissing hot and heavy on a public street. I started to pull back, but Taj murmured, "Not yet," and I couldn't disagree.

We shared a few more kisses until he drew back.

"We both have to go," he said. I could see the regret—and desire—in his stare. I know it was in mine. Putting a step of space between us, I nodded and brushed my hair away from my face. His fingers caught a strand and tucked it behind my ear.

"I'll see you tomorrow, Bec," he said softly and walked off.

He was staying somewhere close enough that he could walk. I'd never gotten the specific location from him. I bet Candace knew where he was staying, but I couldn't ask her. She had too many problems for me to bug her with questions like this. Then there would be the awkward, "Why do you want, or need, to know?"

I watched him head down the street, slowly being enveloped into the dark. Before he disappeared, I checked my watch—I had time. Keeping my eye on him, I yanked off my hoodie, turned it inside out, and slipped it back on so that the pale, pilled underside showed. I pulled my hair back into a ponytail and popped up the hood. Falling

into step behind a couple walking hand in hand, I watched him between their shoulders.

He only walked about a block in the direction of the *Edge* office
before he turned a corner. When my strolling couple passed by, I
turned down as well, staying in the shadows. I saw Taj slip into an
ordinary, stucco building and I continued walking past. I'd expected
a grander place from someone with his money and stature. Wouldn't
he want more luxury? Security? This looked like a student boarding-
house.

It was close to both the Hotel Beatrici and the office. Not too
surprising, considering that he was in Rome to work around the
Edge photo shoots, but shocking that it was so . . . plain. I looked
for a number, a name, any distinguishing feature, but there wasn't
even a clay pot on the doorstep. However, there was a bakery next
door to the hotel, Angelica's. It was separated from Taj's building by
a small twisty alley.

I stopped at the corner and bent as if to tie my shoe, checking
the place out. Candace said to keep an eye out for anything strange.
Taj knew my hotel, yet he never offered to tell me where he stayed.
Then again, it was the same with Dante. I stood, thinking that I
would look the place up when I got back to my room—and found
myself eye to eye with Ortiz.

I was still mad at her. She told Candace about my visit to Parker
when she promised not to. That was her job, but she'd *promised*.
And she was the one who searched my room. Candace said none of
the agents had been in there, but this was the Secret Service and
the CIA—and I was just a kid. They could do whatever they liked,
and they were under no obligation to tell me the truth if it didn't
suit them or if they thought it would interfere with their plans.

"Uh, about this morning—" I started, but she raised a hand.

"Candace told me you stuck up for me. Helped that the First Lady
did too—I appreciate that."

I smiled halfheartedly.

She looked at the building. "If you wanted to know where

Taj was staying, you could have asked—it would have been a lot easier."

I inhaled sharply and she laughed. "Let's get you back to the hotel before you turn into a pumpkin, Cinderella."

"I thought I was Juliet."

"Just trying to keep you out of trouble," she said, but her voice had lost its light touch. What did she mean? I wasn't in any trouble; I left that all behind with Dean Harding. I'd been golden here. Well, except for dropping in on Candace's secret meeting. And sneaking in to see Parker. And dropping rocks on Mrs. Jennings. And now getting caught tailing Taj by Ortiz. Okay, not so golden.

"I know it was you," I said as we walked.

"Me what?"

"You're the one who went in my room. You opened the envelope from Dean Harding. If you were going to open it, you could have at least done some of the math packet. Or you just could have asked," I said, throwing her words back at her.

She stopped abruptly. "How did you know?"

I'd managed to impress her again. First the car skills and now this. I liked that she seemed to appreciate it. Wonder what Mom would think of my "technology obsession," as she liked to call it. I'd wowed the Secret Service *and* CIA!

"Got your prints."

"How?"

"Black eye shadow, makeup brush, and Scotch tape. You can learn a lot watching police shows. It wasn't that hard really." Well, it was harder than it looked on TV, but the fun part about stuff like that was making everyone else think it was easy.

She blew out a slow breath. "It's part of the job. Protect the First Lady at all costs."

I glowered at her, curling my lips in a sneer. "Do you *really* think I'm such a threat?"

Her laughter was clipped. "One with your skills and rep? Yes!"

"I'm pretty sure I have some rights that are being trampled."

"I was following orders."

"Candace's?" I demanded, a sharp edge to my voice. "She said she didn't order it."

"There are people with more authority than Candace."

Oh God, who else had been digging into my past?

"I don't care," I said, jamming my hands on my hips. "You had no right."

She pinched the bridge of her nose. "True, but can you . . . do me a favor?"

She was asking for a favor? From me? Even when I was pissed at her? I tried to read her face, but couldn't. "Depends."

"The CIA and the Secret Service have to work together, and it's not always friendly. Candace doesn't like taking orders from anyone not on her team even if they are higher up, and she doesn't like to be kept out of the loop."

I could understand both sides, Candace's and Ortiz's. And it was interesting to know that as powerful as she was, Candace had others to answer to. "Go on," I said.

"She's still upset about what happened at the Vatican, even though I was following procedure. Once she goes through the chain of command I'll be cleared, but I'd rather not deal with . . . how should I say it? Her attitude. So can you keep this between us? For now—just until the First Lady's visit is over."

I feel your pain, Ortiz, I thought, but I still let her squirm a few long moments before I gave in. "Yeah, sure," I said, and was about to add, *even though you told Candace about my trip to see Parker,* when I realized that maybe Ortiz didn't tell Candace that I'd been to the hospital. Maybe in one of her lucid moments, Parker remembered me being there and told Candace herself. It was also possible that a staff member notified Candace that I'd been in Parker's room uninvited. I had promised Candace not to discuss anything about Parker, so I zipped it.

Ortiz grinned at me. "Thanks, Juliet."

In our suite, Candace was sitting in front of a laptop, but she quickly switched off the screen when I entered. Secret stuff, I got it. Dumping my backpack at my feet, I sat down on the chair opposite her, waiting to see what type of mood she was in. An empty wineglass was on the table next to her, but the accompanying bottle was mostly full. Was that good? Was she enjoying a single glass to unwind, or had she just gotten started?

Candace looked tired, dark circles under those famous hazel eyes. "Hello, Bec. Thank you for getting in at a reasonable time. I appreciate your being responsible and not making me chase you down."

"You have enough to do. Where's Varon?"

She laughed softly, and it made her look younger. "You're right about that. And Varon's out on a date with Joe. What about you? Was it Taj or Dante tonight?"

I tried not to be annoyed. I never got answers, yet she expected them. Sounded a lot like a certain blogger. "Taj. And just a long walk back to the hotel. Don't worry. I was careful."

"Have a good time?"

I relaxed a small bit with the easier camaraderie. "He's very interesting, been to a lot of places, but I still don't know much about him. You guys checked him out, right?"

She flashed a hard glance. "No one would come within an inch of the front door of this hotel or the office without clearance. Including you."

Uh-oh. That was a definite "yes and be quiet."

"I've dealt with hackers before." She held up her hands, seemingly aware that I was about to launch into defense mode, which I was. "I know that a good percentage of you are simply out to expose security weaknesses, but even you have to admit that can put people and information at risk, and there are a small number that use their skills to hurt and steal."

I had arguments against that too, starting with the fact that any information a hacker gained access to was already at risk, but I could see this wasn't the time for *that* discussion.

"You're basically honest," she continued. "We won't count changing your grades since it was only one class, one time, and I hear there were extenuating circumstances. If there's one thing being a celebrity has taught me, it's how to tell if a person is honest. In my experience, an honest person is rare."

"I know." I thought about all the phonies and liars at St. X's. I may have cheated by changing that one disputed grade, but I'd done the work. It was more like correcting a wrong. Still, it was funny coming from Candace. Not only was she was an authority figure, but her life was based on deception—using makeup, enhancing her looks, playing roles, and now, pretending to be an editor.

She searched my face. "You read people too, don't you?"

"People are like puzzles. I like to figure them out."

She nodded. "And you're compassionate. You have a good heart. You hack for fun, and, I believe, for what you think, maybe misguidedly, is justice."

I swallowed. Did she know about the Kevin debacle?

Candace poured herself a small amount of wine and swirled it around in her glass. "Now tell me, what do you know about Parker's accident?"

I frowned. "Someone tampered with the car's systems."

"We've figured that out. But which?"

"It was the seat belt," I said. "And the airbag."

"But Parker's seat belt was fastened—"

"The lap belt was. What about the one across her chest?"

Candace sat up straight.

"If it was an automatic belt, it didn't function properly. It should have held her back or she wouldn't have hit the dashboard so hard," I said.

"How do you know that's what happened?"

"When I went to see her—"

Candace narrowed her eyes at me, definitely not happy about that reminder.

"When I saw her," I began again, "she had this weird bruise on her chest." I looked around and, finding a pad and pen by the phone, quickly sketched it out and handed it to her. "I know what it is now—a logo. What kind of car was it?"

"A Lancia."

"A shield in a circle," I said. "So when Parker hit the dashboard hard, it left an almost exact imprint."

"If you're right, that would explain her chest injuries," Candace said in a tone that told me she wasn't completely convinced. "The airbag should have prevented that. It deployed in the crash."

I nodded. "Yes, and Ortiz said that the car was checked out before that day and everything was working fine. We know that all the safety features, the seat belt and the airbag, worked perfectly on the driver's side because although Ortiz was bruised and banged up, she walked away without being seriously hurt."

Candace blinked several times. Unsure if she was following where I was going with this, I continued, "Parker's seat belt had to malfunction for her to hit the dashboard. The injuries on her face and head came because the airbag was late being deployed. Along with the seat belt, I think the airbag sensor was also tampered with. It was like a one-two punch." I took a breath. "Anyone with the right know-how could do that with a laptop and a couple of cables. Whoever it was, they made the accident look legit by frying the system so that the seat belt hack couldn't be traced. After that, it was just a matter of a little offensive driving on someone's part—get in Ortiz's way on a narrow street."

She shook her head in wonder, then her eyes focused on me. "Keep this between us. Until we can verify this, trust *no one*. Do you understand?"

I nodded vigorously. "And there's another connection. Or maybe it's nothing."

She leaned forward, attentive. "Go on."

"When I was doing the expense reports I saw that Serena had bought these cables—the same kind that could have been used to hack Parker's car."

Candace relaxed a little bit. "Yes, Varon mentioned you were doing some recon. In my office."

I felt the blood rush to my face. "I didn't think it was *you,* I was checking to see if Serena bought the cables for one of the offices before I made any accusations."

"Serena? I don't think she's capable of anything that technical." She studied my face, realizing I was serious. "I'll look into it—we have to chase down every lead, even if it seems small. Or unlikely. She's been investigated, but it's possible we missed something."

I didn't respond. Every time I came up with an argument to connect Serena to the accident, a counter one cropped up: she was technically running the magazine now, but she didn't get to replace Parker. She bought the cables but didn't seem to have the knowledge to use them.

"I was going to ask Sophie if she knew or saw anything unusual about that day or Serena, but never got the chance."

One of Candace's sculpted brows rose. "Better that you didn't. We have enough extra noses in this situation." Tapping her chin with her index finger, she mused, "I don't know why Serena would need any extra technical equipment." Clearly the fact stuck in her head and puzzled her, as unlikely as Serena's involvement seemed at first. "If she was involved—and I'm not saying she was—I don't think she did everything herself."

I nodded. "That makes sense. But who would she be working with?"

"Has Dante ever shown any interest or aptitude for working with that kind of technology?"

I was taken aback, but the answer came quickly enough. "No!"

"But he is pretty agile on that Vespa. Enough to drive defensively. Maybe offensively," Candace countered.

He *was* slick on that scooter, but I was hesitant to either agree with her or defend him. It was getting harder to sort through the facts and not make guesses that could get people—maybe innocent ones—in lots of trouble. What if I was wrong about everything?

Taking a deep breath, I answered as honestly as I could. "That's true, but I've never seen him talk to Serena. I know what you're going to say: that I like him and I might not be thinking logically, and I admit that I don't know him that well. But I also don't want to accidentally help someone who might be involved. The only thing he said to me that might connect him to what happened is that he asked to meet Mrs. Jennings."

"Did he push hard? Pressure you?" Her voice was soft, but it felt sharp like steel.

"No, he didn't insist or offer me anything. I honestly think it's more of a 'meet a celebrity' thing."

Trying to meet the First Lady was something most people would want to do if they got the opportunity—I knew, because I was thrilled to get the chance. Could anyone really blame Dante? I waited, holding my breath, not certain I wanted to hear what she was going to say if it was going to be bad for him.

Candace replaced the cork, her long, strong fingers forcing it deep into the bottle neck. She appeared to be debating something. "I don't think I'm giving away any state or agency secrets by telling you that Dante came back with a clean record." She rested back in her chair, a slight upturn at the corners of her mouth that wasn't a smile but an expression of adamant determination. "We'll keep an eye on him."

That didn't sound too bad—not much different from what they were already doing with me. But there was still something else—I knew one person who had the know-how to use those cables.

"What about Taj?" I said.

"What *about* Taj?" She almost sounded defensive.

"Taj is . . . very tech-savvy." I didn't want to say how savvy. It might be nothing, and I didn't want to get him into trouble, any more than I wanted to get Dante into trouble—but I had to tell Candace everything.

"I'm aware of that—he also came back clean. And he has the curse of being a celebrity, which makes it easy to track his movements.

Always watched and never alone." I nodded, and she took a sip of wine, staring at me over the rim of her glass. "It's good that you're so observant, and it's smart that you're conscious of the company you keep, especially in this situation. That's a sign of good judgment, which I'm sure your parents and former headmasters would be thrilled to hear about, but, unfortunately, can't."

I gave her a wry look. "Too bad. A good word from you might help when my parents try to get me into a new school. They may even let me have a say where my next prison will be."

"I might be able to help with that, once this is all over."

"Thanks." I rose and picked up my backpack. "Good night, Candace."

"Bec? Don't worry. That's my job." She smiled grimly at me, and I felt a genuine concern—and realized that she was more worried than she wanted me to see.

For a job well done. Join us for the interview. Breakfast at the office. Please don't be late.
C.

The note I found when I woke up was written in Candace's elegant script. It had been placed on top of a hot pink dress, one of the coveted sample pieces sent to *Edge* by Dolce & Gabbana! There was also a little matching jacket and crystal-covered platforms that weren't so slanty that I felt like a leaning tower when I stood up. I was going to rock these.

I showered, put on a bit of makeup, then dried and curled my hair the way Joe had shown me. It looked almost as good as when he did it. Enjoying the stares I got as I wound my way up the street to the office, I felt like a native; I knew my way around, I was picking up the language. More than that, I was an asset. Candace had said as much.

Nothing in school, or what I'd done online, had been this intense. Changing a grade, putting my name first on the electronic sign-up list for concert tickets, and torrenting movies that were still in the theater were nothing compared to this. I had a new respect for Candace and the agents. It was kind of thrilling, being almost on the inside. My life didn't need any more complications and trouble, but being here in the middle of spies and plots and danger was exhilarating.

When I got within sight of the offices, a sudden anxiousness overtook me. When the shoot was wrapped up, would Parker be in any shape for Candace to hand me over to her? Not that I needed or wanted watching, but being a minor, I knew that was the way things had to be. Would I be going to New York as scheduled, or staying here? I was powerless to make a choice about what happened. All I knew was that the end of my time here also meant the end of my time with Dante and Taj.

God, I would miss Dante's golden smile. And clinging to him as we darted through the streets on the back of his Vespa. We could meet up in the states *if* he came over like he wanted to, and *if* it happened to be wherever my next school was, and *if* I wasn't kept under lock and key. Leaving would mean no more chats over shared gelato, strolling through quaint and quiet side streets, and sneaking up secret staircases.

And Taj . . . Without the Secret Service and Candace and the First Lady hovering in the background, we could just be us. He traveled the world: if he wanted to, we could meet up again.

And share tech secrets and tricks.

And kisses . . .

This had been the best week of my life—but who knew what would happen next?

Resigned to wait for my fate, I went into the office. Everything was ready for Theresa Jennings's last visit. All the porcelain coffee cups were sparkling clean and neatly lined up, and fresh pastries and fruit were laid out on pretty plates. There were full jugs of water and juice, and a professional barista in a uniform and apron manned the espresso machine. Maybe Kevin's OCD was actually coming in handy for once.

"Everything's in order! Don't even *think* about using the kitchen!" Kevin shouted when he stomped into the common area.

"Relax," Sophie said in a soothing voice. "Everything's fine."

He nodded and seemed to calm down. I saw her squeeze his hand before he left to check on something else. Everyone seemed to be on their best behavior today, and nobody was bickering. Ugi appeared to accept that Joe and Varon were a duo, and Joe wasn't as snippy to Ugi. Everyone seemed content.

For now.

"Bec, please get me the photos from Claudio," Kevin said, "in case we need to take additional shots. Aldo, are you ready?" Kevin rushed off to check on the photographer.

Wait. *Kevin*. Said *please*. To *me*.

I wondered if Taj had fixed his credit dilemma.

Shaking my head in amazement, I retrieved a stack of glossy prints from the photo editor's table and flipped through them. He'd marked a number of shots that he thought might work.

Mrs. Jennings with a handful of schoolkids in uniforms.

Mrs. Jennings with a pair of laughing nuns.

A little girl tugging on Mrs. Jennings's dress. Cute.

Same little girl, eyes opened wide as the First Lady smiled at her.

Mrs. Jennings taking off her cape, part of it flipped over and draped over her arm.

A small silver glint on the exposed lining caught my eye. Using a photo magnifier, I peered closer. A sharply inhaled breath caught in my throat. That bit of metal wasn't a snap or button—it was a mini GPS. A tracking bug.

Someone had tagged the First Lady.

I looked at the photo again, noting every little detail. Everyone looked so happy. The little kids, Mrs. Jennings, the nuns. Even the policeman in the background.

The policeman.

This time I could see his very distinctive profile. And then it hit me.

It looked like the Man from the warehouse.

His longish, silvery hair was the same as the policeman at the Pantheon and the security guard at the Forte.

He'd been everywhere. What were the odds?

After glancing around to make sure no one was watching me, I made a photocopy of the Man's picture, intent on showing it to Candace first chance I got. Taking a quick peek out the windows, I scanned all around: up and down the street, even straight across, trying to peer into the windows of the buildings across the way, looking for him. He was everywhere else, why wouldn't he be here now? And what was he up to?

Could he be the one who'd sabotaged Parker's car?

No. That would mean Candace was working with a kidnapper or worse. Anyone could be duped under the right circumstances, but there were things that didn't seem to fit—so many pieces to this puzzle. I tried to clear my mind and focus on each suspect, starting with the Man.

The first time I saw him, he was with Candace at the warehouse. The second time was at the Pantheon, and the time after that at the Forte, then again at the Vatican. At the Pantheon and St. Peter's Square, the Man played a policeman.

My heart skipped a beat.

Who was the other common denominator almost *every single time*?

Me.

And with the exception of the warehouse, Taj.

If there was any connection . . .

I *had* to tell Candace.

First, I found Kevin. "Here are the pictures from Claudio. Some look useable," I said, pushing them into his hands.

He rifled through them. "Hmmm. Maybe we can use one or two.

Serena will have to approve which ones. But there aren't enough."
He rubbed the bridge of his nose in frustration. "I'm going to have
Angelo take as many shots as he can here in the office during the
interview. We can crop some into head shots and Photoshop the
backgrounds." He handed the photos back to me. "Thanks, Bec. Put
these on Serena's desk when you get a chance." He gave my shoulder a squeeze, then marched off to talk with the photographer.

Wow. Who was this new and improved Kevin? Would it last?

I ran upstairs and dropped the photos on Serena's desk, then
knocked on Candace's door.

"Come in!"

She was on the phone but waved to me to sit in a chair. It was the
same one I'd sat in numerous other times to be yelled at, lectured
to, or ordered about, but this time I had valuable intel.

"Okay, fine. Yes, sir." Candace hung up and leaned back in her
chair. "I'll be glad when this assignment is over, Bec."

"Me too."

Her phone buzzed. "Make it quick," she said, as she looked at her
phone, then me. "Mrs. Jennings will be here soon." Sliding open
the desk drawer, she pulled out her gun and holstered it.

The sight of the weapon still unnerved me. Yes, she was CIA and
protecting the First Lady, so of course she'd have a gun, but it was still
chilling to see it—because I knew she'd use it if she felt she had to.

"I was going through the pictures from Claudio before I gave
them to Kevin and I saw—"

Her phone buzzed again and she quickly rose. "I have to meet up
with Mrs. Jennings's limo. Sorry, Bec. We'll have to talk later."

"But—"

She was out the door and gone before I could object. I couldn't
just leave this. It was too important.

I bumped into Case in the hallway.

"Agent Case, I know something about—"

"Later, Miss Jackson," he said, pushing by me to get downstairs
to meet Mrs. Jennings.

Collins simply held up his hands when he passed me as I opened my mouth. "Not now."

Really?

Frustrated, I sought out Ortiz, meeting her on the stairs. "I need to—"

"Mrs. Jennings will be here any moment." She started to brush me off, just like everyone else, but I wasn't going to be dismissed again. Besides, she owed me.

I grabbed her arm, stopping her. "It's important! I think I know what's going on—who's after Mrs. Jennings and who put Parker in the hospital."

That stopped her. She looked at me with agent eyes; they revealed nothing. "I have to stand watch by the front door, come with me. And keep your voice low, we don't want to get everyone all excited until we know what we're dealing with." She checked all the front windows and peered out the door, down the street. With a look of satisfaction, Ortiz strolled over to the front desk where, amazingly, Francesca sat for once. Ortiz spoke low, and slowly—the scary voice—and punctuated every word with a finger tap on the desk.

"Do. Not. Move. From. This. Spot. We clear?"

Francesca couldn't bob her head fast enough. Maybe Ortiz should've been Francesca's watchdog instead of mine.

The agent moved off to the side of one of the large windows, her eyes continuing to scan outside. "Spill."

"I was looking at Claudio's pictures. There was this man who was at all of the sites where Mrs. Jennings was having photo shoots, and I think that Mrs. Jennings's cape was bugged with a GPS. I have a photo—"

"What exactly did you see?"

Ugi and Joe passed by, arguing in Italian. I waited until they were gone to answer.

"A shiny, silver button. It looks like a tracking device."

She stared at me blankly for a moment, then did a fast glance around the room. Mostly everyone was upstairs; only Ortiz, Francesca, and I were in the front part of the building. She pulled me closer.

"*We* put it there, in case of something like what happened at St. Peter's Square. Whenever anyone in the First Family travels, we do that in case our barrier is breached and they're taken hostage. Unfortunately, there was a malfunction and I had to yell."

"Oh." Of course they would track her, especially in a large crowd, it made sense. That still didn't explain my silver-haired policeman. "But what about the guy? He—"

She made as if to put a finger to my lips. "There are more agents around than the obvious ones."

Right. Like Parker and Candace.

"*Don't* say anything. Mrs. Jennings hates being tagged, so we have to be subtle about it. And Candace will get angry if she even thinks that a layer of cover has been compromised."

Her fingers on my arm were almost painful. After the Vatican incident, the last thing Ortiz must have wanted was more alone time with Candace.

"Okay, Ortiz, loosen up." I pried her fingers off. She held her hands up and backed up a step.

"Sorry. This has been the worst assignment for bad luck."

I wouldn't argue that.

"Don't worry, Bec," Ortiz said, her voice calmer, "it's not a perfect system, but we have a lot of fail-safes."

I should have felt better, but I didn't. Their backup security measures hadn't worked in the square—that had been luck. But I took a little comfort that here in the office, and with the agents around, the First Lady would be safe.

"I should go help upstairs." Ortiz waved me away and returned to her vigil.

I helped Kevin and Sophie prep Mrs. Jennings's last wardrobe change, that simple sheath dress in effervescent green, paired with the oversized gold disc earrings and a gleaming pair of nude patent leather Louboutin pumps, the red sole shiny, new, and unworn.

I pushed the rolling rack with the dress and accessories into the models' changing room, which had been thoroughly cleaned just for Mrs. Jennings. Finished, I backed out, closed and locked the door.

Moments later, the other agents came in, surrounding Candace and the First Lady. The dressing room was inspected again before Mrs. Jennings and Candace went in. We stood by, waiting for them to come out, when I heard Nelson order Dante to wait by the door.

Earlier someone mentioned that today was payday; the checks were messengered over by the bank. Would there be one for me? I could use the cash.

I went down to the reception desk. There he was, holding a large envelope.

"Hello, Bec."

"You're early," I said as Francesca signed for it.

He peered past me at the agents milling about in the common area.

His eyebrows shot up. "She's still here?"

I drew in a slow deep breath, trying not to draw attention to us. Thank God she was leaving right after the interview. I was beyond ready for this all to be over with. Tomorrow I was declaring a free day and demanding to see Parker.

"Just wrapping everything up." I put my hand on his arm. "I'm sorry, but you can't be here now."

He leaned over to whisper in my ear, his lips brushing the lobe. It sent tingles down my spine. Only Dante—and Taj—could do that to me.

"Can I take a peek?"

Before I could refuse, his face suddenly hardened. He wasn't looking at me, but at someone behind me.

"I thought only authorized people were allowed in here today," said Taj.

He said it loudly enough for Case and Nelson to turn around— and come over to where we were all clustered together.

Through clenched teeth, Dante said, "See you later, Bec. After *everyone's* gone. Maybe we can go to a club tonight. By *invitation only*. My cousin Antonietta is the hostess."

"Maybe another time. I don't know how long this is going to take."

"*Ciao*, Bec." His voice was tight, but thankfully he didn't make a scene and left the office. Taj flashed his signature smirk. So much for easing international relations between those two.

I went upstairs just in time to see Mrs. Jennings come out of the dressing room looking more astounding than she had in the past three days.

"The best yet," said Lidia, a proud and beaming smile creasing her face.

Mrs. Jennings laughed softly, then made her way into the studio. I followed along with everyone else. Even though so much preparation had been done, it seemed like there was no end of things to do. Ugi and Joe fawned over Mrs. Jennings while Angelo adjusted his camera and grumbled at Aldo for the thousandth time for being lazy. I thought that Serena would be happy now that she was finally allowed to be in on things, but she only slunk around the studio frowning and demanding changes.

"Angelo!" she snapped. "We need more light on Mrs. Jennings. I don't want any shadows on her face!"

Angelo's neck turned red—I could see it from across the room where I tried to stay out of the way.

"You don't worry, Serena, Angelo Bardoluciano make her *perfetto!*" he boomed with a hand flourish. Then he began mumbling none too softly in Italian. I was guessing it was about knowing his job; Angelo didn't take instruction well.

Serena's next victim was Varon, standing next to the door, out of the way of the frantic traffic of Kevin, Sophie, and Aldo fetching things.

"You're in the way, we need space to work!"

While Mrs. Jennings raised a brow, Varon's face remained

impassive, but he crossed his arms over his chest. "I'm where I need to be."

Between the black look on her face and her screechy voice, we all knew Serena was wound tight today.

She peered at Mrs. Jennings, then walked with calm deliberation to Joe's station. She fumbled around with his stuff as he pleaded silently with Varon for help. Varon's gaze stayed on Serena. A second later, she was making a straight line—scissors poised in her fist—toward Mrs. Jennings.

I was frozen, but my mind raced. It *had* been Serena! She bought the cables taking out Parker's car, and now, demented, she was going after the First Lady.

Collins leapt forward, tackling Serena while Ugi screamed and threw himself into Joe's arms.

Thud!

Serena and Collins hit the floor. She was dazed as Collins yanked the scissors out of her hands, his knee on her chest, pinning her to the floor. Nelson and Case had jumped in front of the First Lady, their bodies protecting her and guns drawn. Ortiz and Mignone blocked doorways, also with guns aimed at the editor.

"A thread!" Serena wheezed. "There's a thread hanging from the underarm of her dress! It needs to be snipped! Everything has to be flawless!"

Almost everyone turned to look at Mrs. Jennings. She lifted up her arm, and there was the sinister string.

Poor Serena was still on her back, splayed out in an unflattering position with her arms and legs spread-eagled.

"I wasn't going to hurt her!" she cried. "I'm sorry! I only want to make sure it's perfect." She looked at Candace, frantic and wild-eyed. "Unlike some people, *I* care that it's perfect!"

Now she was all-out sobbing, and I felt sorry for her.

"Let her up, slowly," Candace ordered. Collins holstered his gun and pulled Serena up none too gently.

"Can . . . can I go to my office?" she stuttered. Tears streaked her face, ruining her teal green eyeliner.

Candace nodded. "Collins, get her out of here. And she's to stay in that office." Candace turned slowly around, her eyes resting on each person. "Everyone not needed, *out*. I will call you as you're needed. Joe, you stay and touch up Mrs. Jennings's hair. Ugi, you're next, so don't go far. Aldo and Angelo, is the equipment set up and ready to go?"

They both nodded.

"Wait in the hall. *Move it*, people!"

Sophie, Kevin, and I hurried out, Taj walking behind, unrushed.

"Taj, I'll call you in after our writer does her interview. Stay close," Candace said.

He nodded and joined our group outside. The door was left open enough so we could hear but not see the interview. Ortiz stood guard downstairs, Mignone at the studio door. Collins was probably keeping a sharp eye on Serena in detention in her office. Nelson, Case, and Candace remained with Mrs. Jennings.

"Can you believe Serena?" hissed Sophie. "What was she thinking?"

"That's the closest she's gotten to Mrs. Jennings since she arrived," Kevin mused wryly.

I shook my head. "And that's as close as she'll ever get." Was Serena involved in the plot?

"I'm going to check on her." Sophie looked at me and Taj, then elbowed Kevin in the ribs. "Don't you think you should *also*?" She wiggled her brows up and down.

"Uh, yeah. Of course, sure," said Kevin. Sophie rolled her eyes and grabbed his hand.

Taj and I were finally alone, but he didn't so much as look my way. I stood there, uncomfortable being so close and feeling so far. I swallowed and headed for the stairs, but he snagged my wrist, stopping me.

"Nerves," he said simply, crooking up one side of his mouth.
I nodded shakily, unsure of whether to stay or go.

He withdrew his hand. "I have to go over my notes." He stared at me a few long moments and turned away.

That was my cue to leave. I went downstairs to the common area, no longer caring about the interview. Obsessed with working out the clues I'd collected, I tapped them into the notes app on my phone:

1. Parker and the First Lady looked alike. It was easy for Parker to have been mistaken for Theresa Jennings.
2. Whoever caused the accident was tech-savvy enough to know how to access a car's electronic systems and alter them.
3. Serena bought computer cables that could be used to connect to a car. She put them on the company expense account, yet there are no new cables in the office.
4. Serena didn't have, or didn't *appear* to have, any kind of technical expertise, but how-to info is easily obtainable.
5. She'd been high-strung from the moment Candace and the agents arrived; she'd gone loco over a thread today.
6. Parker may have seen something or someone right before her accident, but she is in no position to tell us what or who.
7. The Man was present before *and* during Mrs. Jennings's visit, showing up almost everywhere, and wherever Taj was.
8. Taj is very tech-savvy. He could easily have pulled off the car hack, but he hadn't been here.
9. Dante is courteously persistent about meeting the First Lady.
10. Dante is a good driver and navigated Rome's treacherous streets with ease.
11. It had been Dante's idea to go up on the crumbling Pantheon roof and take pictures.

12. Dante had cousins throughout Rome, even in the Vatican guard.

13. Serena, Parker, and Dante all knew each other; and Taj, Candace, and Parker all knew each other, but there didn't seem to be any suspicious connections.

14. Kevin, Sophie, Ugi, Joe, Aldo, Angelo, and Francesca seemed to have no connection to any of this other than that they worked at *Edge*.

15. Taj is a virtual ghost—neither I nor any of my friends can come up with anything other than the most basic of info on him.

16. Was the cyclist at the Pantheon targeting Taj and somehow involved?

17. The cape Mrs. Jennings wore to St. Peter's Square was tagged by one of the agents, but they didn't seem to have any backup systems when it didn't work.

I scrolled through the list I'd made. Nothing seemed to connect. I couldn't point a finger at any one person, which meant the First Lady was still in danger and I was no closer to figuring out who caused the accident.

I felt like I had to do something. Walking as fast as I could without running and inciting the twitchy agents to tackle me, I went upstairs, ignoring the suspicious looks first from Ortiz, then Mignone.

I heard Taj's voice. His interview was well under way.

"Tell us the truth—did you really try to sneak into the Smithsonian and try on every available inaugural ball gown?"

Mrs. Jennings laughed, then demurely evaded the question. Taj asked one or two more, and then the interview ended with Candace thanking her. I was anxious for Mrs. Jennings to leave, even though it was kind of sad to see her go.

"Excuse me," said Taj as he followed Mrs. Jennings, Lidia, Candace, Case, and Nelson downstairs. "Would it be possible to get one picture of the First Lady across the street in the piazza? Just one—I can't use any of the *Edge* images. I need to have my own photos for the blog."

He looked respectable—and irresistible—in his pristine and crisply starched robin's-egg blue shirt, open at the collar, cashmere vest, and gray suit, which fit every angle and contour of his perfect body. Who could say no to him?

Candace.

Hands on hips, she turned to him. "You don't have any pictures from the last few days? Why not? You had plenty of opportunities."

"It's okay, Candace," Mrs. Jennings said. "Taj can take a few quick photos. It's the least I can do for him for helping retrieve my cape," she said, flashing a winning smile. "It'll only take a few minutes. And the cars are parked right there, aren't they, Case? I can duck right in." She started walking, which meant the matter was decided.

With a stony face Case muttered, "Yes, ma'am." He and the other agents weren't happy about this change of schedule, no matter how small.

"Thank you, Mrs. Jennings," Taj said, making a little bow.

Amidst the mumbling and frowns, Nelson and Case went ahead to check out the piazza, Ortiz led the escort, and Candace followed. Mrs. Jennings asked Taj to walk with her so they could talk, Collins and Mignone at their sides, while Varon and I followed last. Kevin and Sophie were upstairs babysitting Serena. I couldn't wait to see Mrs. Jennings get into the limo and drive away, safe.

When we stepped outside, it was late afternoon. The light was soft and the heat of the day was dissipating. Ortiz crossed to the middle of the street to divert any traffic while waving everyone over. Taj took a few candid photos of Mrs. Jennings with the rustic houses as a backdrop. Then he had Candace pose with her.

"Thank you so much, Candace. I know this visit wasn't easy," said Mrs. Jennings.

"It is always a pleasure to see you, Mrs. Jennings," said Candace. The First Lady turned to the rest of us. "And it was nice to meet and work with all of you. Try to enjoy the rest of your stay here—it is a beautiful city."

My smile felt forced, I was tired and fidgety.

Case opened the door of the car. Nelson was at the wheel. Mrs. Jennings paused and turned to Taj. "Did you get enough pictures?"

He motioned to her to stand in the middle of the street. "Just one more."

She posed in front of one house with boxes of dripping flowers. It would be a stunning photo. Taj lifted his camera to take the shot.

Bang!

An explosion of sound and smoke engulfed us. I heard screams and shouts and coughs. My eyes burned and teared as I gagged on the smell of sulfur. Even though my ears were ringing, I heard the pounding of frantic footsteps. I waved my arms frantically until at last the smoke began to thin.

And then it became really clear—Taj and Theresa Jennings were missing.

26

Panic erupted.

Ortiz, pulling out her gun, ran down the only alley right next to the offices.

Candace shouted directions to the remaining agents to spread out and scour the area and then ran off herself.

I didn't know what to do—and then I saw Varon, lying in the street, Lidia next to him, hysterical. I ran to him, slowing my steps as I came near. He was breathing . . . and conscious. He gasped and winced, a look of pure agony on his face. Bending closer, I saw why. His hand was wedged in the manhole next to him, the heavy iron cover crushing his hand.

I looked around wildly. "Candace!" I called. But she was gone. I crouched down.

"Oh my God, Varon!" He grimaced and together Lidia and I tried to move the cover but it was too heavy. Our clumsy efforts made him cry out.

"I'm sorry!"

"Mrs. Jennings," he panted. "They took her down there," he said, leaning his head toward the manhole.

"In the sewer?"

He nodded again. Suddenly Joe was at my side, Ugi and Aldo behind him.

"Varon!" Joe cried, cradling his head for a moment, then turning to the other men. "Help me get his hand out!" As the three of them worked to carefully lift the lid, Sophie and Kevin came running out.

"What happened? Was that a bomb?"

People from the neighboring apartments started pouring out into the streets. Joe, Ugi, and Aldo got the manhole cover off, then Joe helped Varon to stand. I didn't bother to answer Sophie but knelt by the manhole and wrapped my fingers around the edge.

"What are you doing?" Varon gasped and clutched his swollen, bloodied hand to his chest. Every finger was bent at an odd angle; all the bones had to be broken. I shuddered, not wanting to imagine the pain he had to be feeling.

I looked around for Candace or any of the other agents, but they were all gone. "I have to go after Mrs. Jennings. None of the agents knows she's down there."

Sophie and Kevin stood over me. I saw Varon nod reluctantly as I sat down on the street and dangled my legs in the hole.

"Are you crazy?" called Sophie as I clambered down a rusted ladder into the tunnel and dropped onto a floor paved with ancient-looking cobblestones. Miraculously, I didn't break an ankle. Thankfully there were no puddles or pools, but it was dark and damp and smelled of old sewage. It was all I could do not to vomit.

"Probably!" I shouted up.

"You can't let her go down there!" Lidia cried.

"Are *you* going to try and stop her?" Varon snarled. "We need someone to follow where it leads if Mrs. Jennings might be down there." He was pale and unsteady on his feet. Unhappily, that made me a better choice.

"No. But we're going with her." A second later, Sophie and then Kevin jumped down to join me.

"I thought you said I was crazy!" I retorted.

Sophie crossed her arms over her chest. "We can't let you go alone."

"Yeah," added Kevin, "what if there's another manhole cover to lift? You're going to need some muscle."

"Thanks," I said, glad to have them with me. I held my phone aloft to provide some light and something caught my eye.

Not far from where we stood there was a scuff of red—from the bottom of Mrs. Jennings's brand-new Louboutin heels. "Look!" I motioned with the light. "Mrs. Jennings left a trail. That mark is from her shoes."

We followed the arched tunnel using my phone to light the way, although every so often a beam of light came down from a grate in the pavement above. We moved at a maddeningly slow pace. It was hard to walk in the dark and on uneven ground in heels—platforms or not—and I didn't want to miss another clue if Mrs. Jennings left one.

Then we came to one place where part of the arched wall had collapsed. The fallen stones were scored with white streaks of lime. We had to pick our way over the tumbled rocks and ankle-deep muck that smelled like a Dumpster full of rotting food. Kevin moaned more than once about his ruined pants and shoes, and I tried not to think about the greasy water sliding between my toes. I thought I saw something move in the shadows, heard the scritch of tiny paws. Rats? I was okay as long as I didn't have to see them.

"We should call Candace or the police," said Sophie as she stumbled and just barely caught herself.

"She's right, Bec," Kevin gagged. "This is crazy! Whoever took her is desperate and dangerous!"

I looked at my phone, then held it up for them to see. "We can't.

No reception down here. And there's no time." I suddenly stopped short, and like a cartoon or bad movie, Sophie bumped me, having been bumped by Kevin, and I had to catch myself from pitching forward.

In front of us was a four-way divide: left, straight, right, and up a twisting flight of steps.

"Which way do we go?" said Kevin.

I focused the phone light. No red scuff, but I spied a small gleam. Rushing over to it, I picked up one of the golden disc-shaped earrings Mrs. Jennings had been wearing at the interview. It lay on the ground at the bottom of the steps.

"They took her this way!" I started to climb, but Kevin pulled me back.

"What if they have guns?"

I was not glad he thought of that little detail, but we couldn't stop here. "Then we have to be extra careful."

"So let me go first," he volunteered, but I scooted up before he could do anything, and the stair wasn't big enough for both of us at the same time. I heard him mutter something about ballsy interns. That almost made me smile.

I led the way as we crept up a long, crumbling spiral staircase. It was too dark to see the top, and the dull light from my phone barely illuminated the decaying stone. I prayed for another sign. I almost didn't see the next red scrape. Unless you looked for them, the scuffs were hard to spot. Either Mrs. Jennings was dragging her feet on purpose to leave a trail or she was putting up a good fight. She knew the CIA, Secret Service, and Italian police would be searching for her.

The kidnappers probably knew the trail well enough that they didn't need the light—and weren't looking for signs marking the way. If they had known what Mrs. Jennings was doing, they would have stopped her. That might be the case farther along. We'd know soon enough if the trail died.

One of the steps crumbled under my feet, sending down a noisy shower of rocks.

"Watch it!" Kevin yelled, coughing.

"Nice way to help us sneak up on them, Kevin," I retorted.

"Shut up, you two, before all of Rome hears you!" Sophie whispered fiercely.

"Help!" Taj's voice came faintly from above.

And I'd never been so glad to hear it.

"Where are you?" I called, "Is Mrs. Jennings with you?"

"Bec? Thank God! Mrs. Jennings is hurt! Come help. Who's with you?"

"Kevin and Sophie," I cried, stumbling up as fast as I could. "We're coming!"

His voice was getting louder, we were getting closer. By now all of us were breathing hard from climbing as fast as we could. I wanted to sprint up the stairs but after all the exertion, my legs were rubbery. I didn't even want to think about the return trip. Once we got to the top, I'd call Candace and fill her in.

"Hurry!"

I dug deep into my core and forced myself to run up the rest of the way, Kevin and Sophie at my heels.

"Almost there!" I called. My heart was pounding, my lungs screaming for a rest. We rounded a corner and there was another small glint—the other earring by a doorway. I was so glad we wouldn't have to pry open a manhole. A dark head poked hesitantly through the opening. I lifted the phone up and caught Taj's face—he looked anxious and shocked.

I scrambled up the remaining steps and bursting through, found myself in a small, tight alley with walls covered in peeling yellow paint and roofed by the blue sky far above—and Taj standing there.

I threw myself into his arms and hugged him to me tightly. I didn't care what sort of gunk was on me or how terrible I must have looked. "Are you all right?"

"Yes," he whispered. "Everything's fine now."

Behind me I heard Sophie come up. She gasped.

"What the—" said Kevin, but he didn't finish. I opened my eyes and pulled away.

Taj was not alone.

Mrs. Jennings leaned against the wall—held around the neck by Ortiz, who was pointing a gun straight at her head.

A quick glance around the alley told me exactly where we were: the narrow passage between Angelica's Bakery and Taj's way-off-the-beaten-path, hole-in-the-wall hotel. The crookedness of the alley prevented a direct line of sight from the street at either end. Ortiz stood blocking one way, a big goonish guy, the other.

"Mrs. Jennings, are you okay?" asked Sophie. The First Lady's dress was rumpled and had smudges of dirt smeared on the silky green. Her smile was shaky, though she tried to hide that fact.

"I'm okay."

Ortiz readjusted her grip on the gun she held to the First Lady's head. Sophie's indrawn breath next to me proved she was as riveted as I was on the pressure Ortiz's finger was putting on the trigger.

"Don't anyone do anything sudden or stupid," Ortiz warned.

"Please do what they say," Mrs. Jennings pleaded before directing a defiant gaze at Taj. "This won't end well for any of you. Let me go before anyone gets hurt."

The other guy laughed.

Kevin swore softly. I realized that one of us should've stayed behind in the tunnel until we knew what the situation was. Now there was no way any of us could go back for Candace or the police, even if we could find our way through the tunnels. What I wouldn't give for Dante to show up now with a pack of cousins. That Swiss Guard would work. Or Nunzio the ambulance driver. He looked like he could manage a takedown. Anyone! Please!

Taj's eyes didn't flicker with regret or indecision. "No. It's too late for that. Now everyone move away from the door. Slowly," he ordered.

"How did you know we were even here?" I demanded, stepping away from him.

"A little falling rock told him," said Ortiz. "And the yelling too. Not so quiet, are you?"

"I mean, that we'd follow you."

Ortiz gave me an incredulous look. "If there's one thing we've learned about you, Juliet, it's that you have a knack for sticking your nose where it doesn't belong and then figuring things out."

Disappointment and then rage rippled through me, and I guessed that Candace didn't have a clue that one of her agents had gone rogue.

I tried to piece together what happened in front of the office; someone threw a smoke bomb—I guessed it was this new guy—then Taj hustled Mrs. Jennings into the sewer. If he had to fight Varon off, he had the element of surprise. Ortiz lingered behind once Mrs. Jennings was snatched, giving false directions and making sure that no one could interfere with what they were planning, including me. She took off down the alley to meet up with Taj, this guy, and the captive Mrs. Jennings.

I assumed that meant that she had a hand in Parker's accident. Did she tamper with the car, or at least know it had been tampered with, and then crash it on purpose—knowing she would walk away and Parker wouldn't? As agents they would have both been trained on how to survive a car accident—unless, of course, the car had its safety features dismantled. If that was the case, having me show her how to control the car was just a big show. She wanted to see how much I'd be able to figure out, then shadow me to make sure I couldn't cause trouble. I scowled at her, but she only curled her lip and motioned with her gun.

"Follow Taj. Nice and easy, and real quiet. Remember I have the lovely First Lady in a choke hold and I can break her neck in a second—not that I want to," she added.

How polite. She didn't want to kill the First Lady—just threaten her, kidnap her, and possibly paralyze her.

We had little choice but to do as Ortiz said and follow Taj when he opened a little door in the hotel's wall and started climbing up a straight, narrow staircase.

Oh God, not more stairs! Up, up, up. These were steep and not easy to climb in my shoes with my tired legs. Taj stopped at a landing, then ushered us into a tiny hall, and then a large room with tall windows covered by elaborate grilles of scrolled iron. The high ceiling, peeling plaster, cracked molding, and tarnished silver mirrors on the wall gave me the creeps. I didn't want to die—especially here and now.

I hadn't really taken a good look at the other man in the alley, but I did so now. He was tall, and dressed in a fitted shirt and jeans and leather loafers. He had that same swarthy European look Taj had: olive-skinned, dark-eyed, and chestnut-haired. And like Taj, not quite placeable in any specific ethnic group. And I'd seen him before . . .

Oh my God. The biker at the Pantheon.

And the driver of the white car that almost took out Dante and me.

"*Em breve, Luca. Vamos,*" Taj said to him, and he nodded.

That wasn't Italian.

Mrs. Jennings was forced to sit in one of the chairs, and her hands were bound with zip ties.

"This way, please," said Taj, a courteous arm extended, indicating for us to move over to the grimy windows, as far away from the door and the First Lady as possible. Cautiously, we shuffled across the room, urged on by Luca, who nudged Kevin's shoulder with his gun.

"Hey, careful of the shirt! It's Marc Jacobs!" Kevin groused.

Typical. Here we were, facing international kidnappers who were holding the First Lady of the United States hostage and planning to do who knew what, and Kevin was worried about his clothes.

We were directed to sit on the floor with our backs to one of the wrought-iron window grates. Out came more zip ties.

Seriously?

"Why?" I demanded of Taj.

Luca shackled Kevin and then started on Sophie.

From across the room where he stood next to Mrs. Jennings, Taj's eyes met mine. I would have sworn a shadow of regret passed over them, but he'd fooled me too many times for me to care.

"I wish I could explain everything to you, but I can't. Just understand it's something that I had to do. If you were in my place, I think you'd do the same thing."

I snorted. "You think so? Then you don't know me very well."

Done with Sophie, Luca grabbed my wrists, forcing me to fall back against the railing. I glared at Taj, wishing him all kinds of terrible fates. As much of a long shot as it was, I hoped, somehow, that I could be a participant in the kick-ass payback he so deserved. Go viral with his photo and a caption saying he was a lowlife kidnapper who wore knockoffs. What would be worse for him? The felony or the fashion faux pas? Either way, it would be sweet.

"I think I do. You're rebellious, but loyal"—he gazed at the First Lady—"doing whatever you have to do to correct a wrong."

"I don't know what wrong has been perpetrated on you, Taj—" Mrs. Jennings started, but he silenced her with a squeeze on her shoulder.

"Everything will be made clear to you very soon, Mrs. Jennings."

I jerked forward, but Luca's fingers dug into my wrists, slamming me back against the railing.

"You *had* to kidnap someone? Not just someone—the American First Lady! What could possibly be that important?" I didn't think he would answer my question. He was all about secrets and lies. Even if he told me, I wouldn't believe him. Then a jolt of realization tingled through me.

What could possibly be that important?

He was wealthy, so it wasn't money.

Family? He had a brother. . . .

Taj could afford to pay a ransom—but if he orchestrated kidnapping the First Lady, the situation, whatever it was, had to be something that money alone could not solve. If he wanted the First Lady alive . . . did he want to make a swap? This brother—if that's what this was about—must have been very important, and probably very shady. But in what way?

Luca fastened the zip ties around my wrists. I didn't struggle; that would only make them tighter and give him an excuse to put me in a more awkward position. When he stood up, I tried moving my hands—yes! There was a little slack.

"What I don't understand," Kevin said, "is how neither the CIA nor the Secret Service found anything on you. They checked everyone out."

Taj shrugged and his features softened into an angelic innocence. "I'm just a fashion blogger."

"You used your blog to get close to Mrs. Jennings," I said, working it out. "Candace said she met you when you first started, so she could vouch for you. And you knew Parker too—but I guess you didn't set off any alarms with them. They knew you for several years." I glared up at him. "Who are you working for? How long have you been planning this?" I didn't believe that an eighteen-year-old would be the sole mastermind behind something this big.

He looked away. "Too long to let you ruin it now. And I'm not going to explain myself to you."

I sneered at him. "Well, congratulations! Your cover's been blown for good. Even if you get away, the whole world will know who you are. The U.S. and Italy will slap all your pictures on the most-wanted list!" I yelled. "Good luck trying to hide now!" My voice sounded shrill even in my own ears.

"I know," he mused regretfully. "But none of that matters. I have only one important thing I need to do."

I couldn't imagine planning something like this years in advance, then having to give up my life and identity forever.

"Is this about your brother?" I said. Maybe catching him off guard would get him to spill some details.

He didn't seem to acknowledge my question, but for a fraction of a second his lips twitched. Then he was all business again, motioning for Ortiz and Luca to move on. He wasn't giving that up, not here, not now. He might tell me other things if I worked on him.

"The biker at the Pantheon," I said, looking at Luca. "It was him! He wasn't going for Mrs. Jennings, he was going for you. But he almost took you out!"

Taj inclined his head at the gunman. "We passed a message."

"I didn't see you give him anything," said Sophie, "and I was looking right at you."

"Me too," added Kevin.

I narrowed my eyes in disbelief. "I didn't see anything."

"A few hand signals were enough. A wave, two fingers held up, a sweep of my arm indicated the time and place for the next move."

I stared at him, incredulous. "You told him all that by waving arms and fingers?"

Taj sighed, exasperated. "Come on, Bec, haven't you learned not to leave evidence? A note can be found if it's not destroyed. I don't leave anything behind that I don't mind others finding. Not on paper—and never electronically. E-mail and electronic searches can be traced, even if it's erased. *You* of all people should know that."

"Yes," I grumbled. The misadventure with Dean Harding seemed a lifetime ago, but it was going to haunt me forever.

"I had Ortiz put an antenna in your room and wear one on her to trace your movements and online activity. When she borrowed your phone, she planted a bug. I knew where you went, what you did, who you talked to." He chuckled. "Nice handle, Cap'nCrunch."

He got me there. He really was a master. I felt the blood rush to my face.

"But what about people—they can be evidence too," I insisted a little desperately.

Taj looked at Ortiz and Luca. "True. You can't eliminate all risk from a situation, but you can do your best to minimize it—involve as few co-conspirators as possible, pay them outrageously well, and have something on them to guarantee their continued loyalty."

I never would have thought not to trust Ortiz.

"Some things I had to do myself." He moved his fingers like he was rubbing something between them.

I gasped. "Mrs. Jennings's cape! When you touched it, *you* stuck the GPS on it!"

Taj's gaze settled on me. "Very good."

"You were going to take her there, at St. Peter's," I said, dumbfounded. On holy ground, in front of the Secret Service, tourists, the Swiss Guards, schoolchildren. It was so bold I could hardly believe it.

But something had gone wrong.

"I try to plan for all contingencies, but we couldn't account for her taking the cape off—and still less for it being stolen. Ortiz had the tracker. When it started beeping like crazy, she assumed that my friend here had taken Mrs. Jennings, and tried to send the other agents on a wild-goose chase. We followed the signal, and when we found the cape, Mrs. Jennings obviously wasn't with it. That light-fingered punk messed up everything."

I turned to Ortiz. "Why? Why do you help him?"

"Is it money?" Kevin asked with a sneer. And here I thought Kev was Mr. Materialism—but I guess even he had moral limits when it came to treason and kidnapping.

Ortiz didn't answer, only pressed her lips into a hard, thin line.

"Don't be too hard on her," Taj said. "Ten million dollars buys a lot of loyalty."

In the right place outside the U.S., Ortiz would be set for life like a rock star with that kind of money. Kevin cursed at her as he struggled against the ties, making them tighter.

"Stop jiggling or you'll cut off your circulation!" I snapped.

My mind ran through possible scenarios. It looked like Taj meant to trap us here and then disappear with Mrs. Jennings. If they were going to kill us, they would have done it already, not waste time tying us up. Taj might not have wanted to hurt anyone, but I wasn't anxious to see what he'd do if he became desperate. I thought about what happened to Parker. Did she just get in the way or figure out Ortiz was involved?

Wait.

Ortiz would have known all about Mrs. Jennings's schedule, so Parker wouldn't have been mistaken for the First Lady. Taj wanted Theresa Jennings, obviously—but he also must have wanted Parker out of the way. She was CIA. It would have been very risky having her in control. Get rid of Parker . . . and Serena was next in line. It made sense that she would fill in on such short notice; no one could have expected Candace to show up and take over.

"Is Serena part of this?" I asked, desperate to know that I'd figured it out. "She bought the cables to access the car's computer. She put them on her expense report."

"Stupid woman." Taj shook his head, a look of disgust on his face. "When you get out of here, make sure you tell Candace that Serena was more than willing to help us remove Parker Phillips as editor in chief of *Edge* so that she could replace her." He chuckled. "She had no idea that Parker was an operative, or what the ultimate plan was."

"This would have been a whole lot easier with Serena in charge of the magazine," said Ortiz. "She was manageable. But then Candace Worthington showed up." She turned to me. "And of course, let's not forget our Juliet. Nothing slows you down, not even being sideswiped on the way to the hospital."

Luca's lips twisted up wickedly. "It was just a little scare. I could have done worse."

Taj shrugged. "We still achieved our objective."

Taj, Ortiz, Serena . . . all scum. One good thought occurred to me, though. I didn't see Dante here. That could mean either he wasn't involved, which I fervently hoped, or he was somewhere else, maybe waiting with a getaway car. The whole "I can't stand to look at you" posturing between Taj and Dante could have been an act. At this point I didn't think I could trust anyone.

"You don't have to do this, *Agent* Ortiz," Mrs. Jennings said from her corner. I guessed she was trying to remind Ortiz she was sworn to protect and defend, but I didn't think Ortiz was about to have a change of heart, throw her life in with ours, and miss out on all that cash.

"It's not too late to make things right."

She didn't plead, but seemed to speak with real concern for Ortiz, as if she understood why the agent would take money to help Taj, for whatever he was trying to accomplish. Ortiz's eyes flickered, then she took her gaze to Taj.

He crouched down next to Mrs. Jennings. "Ortiz will do as she's ordered. She's too well paid not to. And there's no going back for any of us now." He frowned. "Tell me, Mrs. Jennings, why your government doesn't pay whatever it must to ensure that those closest to you and your husband remain loyal?"

"Some things should transcend money," said Mrs. Jennings. There was no desperation in her voice, only sad disappointment.

"We all have to make choices. Ortiz knew what she was doing," said Taj, rising and dusting off his pants.

Ortiz and who else? There was still one unexplained factor. The Man. Was Taj just not telling me about him? Was that his plan B? Not wanting to inadvertently give away any info, I kept my mouth shut. Last time I rushed into action I was hopping down the wrong rabbit hole, and this tea party wasn't so pleasant. The Man fit in here somewhere.

"Come." Taj helped Mrs. Jennings gently to her feet. Before he took her away, I had to let her know that the scuff marks from her shoes helped us track her, so that she could do it again.

"Did you have to be so rough, dragging her? Look what you did to her shoes! They're so scuffed, they're ruined!"

Taj looked almost offended. "If they're ruined, it's her own fault for fighting us. And look at yours. Not in the best condition either, and you weren't dragged."

I gave him a fierce glare. "They're not meant for running through sewers or climbing mile-long stone staircases."

"We do what we must." He turned his attention back to the First Lady. "This doesn't have to be painful, Mrs. Jennings. Don't make us drag you again. I might be forced to ask my associate"—he inclined his head at Luca—"to take the fight out of you. A little knock to the head and we'll carry you out of Italy. Either way, you're coming with us. And that warning goes for being quiet too. One scream . . ." The threat hung there, unmistakably clear.

He beckoned to Luca, who took his place next to Mrs. Jennings so he could shepherd her out of the room. She cooperated.

"Be careful," she called without looking back. "Thank you for all your help and concern. Don't worry, I'll be all right."

"Of course you will, Mrs. Jennings," Taj said. "We really don't want to harm anyone, as long as no one does anything stupid."

Kevin snorted and Sophie kicked him. Good for her. The last thing we needed was to make kidnappers with guns angry.

Taj came over to me and crouched down. I shrank away, but he bent closer, forcing me to listen to him as he whispered in my ear.

"I'm sorry, Bec—at least, for doing this to you." Gone was his arrogant, self-assured façade. He almost sounded truly regretful.

All part of the act, I told myself. Prison alone wasn't enough—and he was going there, for a long time, no matter what I had to do. Plans to expose him on the World Wide Web flashed through my mind. *Yes, I'm working on that now too. It's my mission. After I get out of here.*

I played it cool. "I find that hard to believe when I'm zip-tied to an iron railing and left to rot."

"Once we're safely out of the country, I'll tell someone where to find all of you. And it's okay to scream. The bakery's empty until early morning and all this stone deadens any sound."

"How thoughtful." While Kevin and I sent death glares, Sophie blanched from fear.

With a gentle finger stroke on my cheek, he said, "I really am sorry." He stood. Taking a last, lingering look at me, he said, "You're pretty, even when you're mad."

Mad, Taj? I was beyond being mad. "Hell hath no fury" didn't even *begin* to describe how mad I was.

"This is great. Just great," Kevin muttered when we all heard the distant slam of the door that led into the alley. He banged his head against the railing in frustration.

"It could be worse." I said.

"A *lot* worse." Sophie sniffed. "We could be dead."

She was right. We were still alive, and that meant we had a chance to escape and help Mrs. Jennings. Kevin wrestled in his ties, shaking the iron screen. I thought I heard the cracking of plaster.

"That's not helping," I snapped. "Do you want this thing to come crashing down on us? Every time you move, you make the zip ties tighter. These things are hard enough to get out of," I said.

Sophie's laugh was desperate; she was on the edge. "What are you, some kind of a ninja? What type of boarding school did you go to?"

"Probably juvie," Kevin said not so under his breath.

I shot him an evil look. "Well, my education is going to be worth more here than your extensive knowledge of fine Italian leather."

Sophie looked tearfully hopeful. "Can you really get us out?"

I felt a little smug. "I can."

"This I'd like to see," said Kevin. "Whatever you're going to do, make it quick. They could decide to come back. Not leave any witnesses . . ."

I gulped. Taj said he didn't want to hurt anyone, but I'd be an idiot if I believed him. Parker got hurt. Plus, he hadn't said anything about Ortiz or Luca. Mentally, I shook myself. *Focus!* I'd tensed up when my ties had been put on, knowing how to gain a few more millimeters of slack, all that I needed to work my way out.

"Hold still and don't ask any questions. I have to concentrate. And don't *move!*" I ran my fingertips along the railing. It was old and rusty with rough edges. Very cautiously, I rubbed the plastic band against the edges, up and down, as high and low as I could manage. Unfortunately, Luca bound us with thicker ties, the kind used for bundling electrical cords, not the nice skinny ones our gardener used to trellis the roses.

"Are you done yet?" Kevin whispered.

"Shut up and let me concentrate," I growled. "Work on your own ties. Rub them against the rough edges of the railing, but try not to pull on them or you'll make them tighter."

Snap!

I was free!

Scrambling to my feet, I dug in my pocket for my phone.

"What are you doing?" Kevin screamed. "Get us out first!"

"Trying to reach Candace."

I stopped. If I used my phone, Taj or Ortiz would know we were free because of the spy app she'd downloaded. And I couldn't take a chance that she hadn't done the same with Kevin's and Sophie's phones. I couldn't tell Candace anything until I could use a phone I was sure Taj hadn't touched.

Frantically I scouted around for scissors or a knife, but there was nothing in the room I could use to cut the ties. I was going to have to do it the same way I got out. I did Sophie first; it was so much easier and faster when I could see what I was doing.

"Cheap," I said as I freed Kevin. "You'd think with such an important job they'd know not to put us against something that could saw through the ties."

"They didn't count on you," said Sophie with a big grin.

I opened the door that led to the staircase and then the alley.

"You're not going after them, are you?" said Kevin incredulously, rubbing his reddened wrists. That's what he got for wiggling around and tightening the ties.

"Ortiz bugged my phone. She may have done it to yours too, if you loaned it to her once or left it lying around."

Their deflated faces told me all I needed to know. "There's no way to track them, so we have to follow." I ran down the stairs and was glad to hear Sophie and Kevin following me. I was tired, but I vowed to keep running. I could sleep all day tomorrow. Fear for Mrs. Jennings gave me the boost of adrenaline I needed.

"They weren't speaking Italian up there," I said as I clomped down the stairs.

"It was Portuguese," said Kevin.

I glanced over my shoulder at him. "How do you know?"

He arched a brow. "I work at *Edge*. World travel. International models. I pay attention."

Okay, so score one for Kevin.

"I thought Taj was from India," Sophie said.

"I think that's what he wants people to think. He could be from anywhere, but I think South America is a fair guess, maybe Brazil," I added, remembering his comment at the Forte about summering in Brazil as a little kid. Details dropped into place as we ran. If Taj was Brazilian, he'd done a good job of keeping it quiet. This whole operation wasn't amateur night; he'd hidden his tracks so well he'd thrown everyone off, even the pros. Who would be so bold as to kidnap the American First Lady? A common criminal couldn't pull it off, but someone with access to the world. And big money. That usually meant drugs. Or weapons. Or fraud of some type.

And then there was that brother; how did he fit in all this?

If you were in my position, I think you might do the same thing.

Family would be the only reason I would even think about doing something as crazy as this.

Why would Taj tell me anything at all? Could I believe anything he told me? But then why lie about a brother, of all things? Taj had told me things that I knew were true: the hacking skills, not leaving traces, little snippets like having a plan B. Why? Whether I wanted it or not, I was caught up in his scheme. There was no way I would sit back and do nothing.

Huffing heavily, we reached the alley. There was the barest hint of a red scrape on the ground by the door that led down into the tunnels. Chasing Taj and his crew wasn't the best way to help Mrs. Jennings. After all, they had guns. I should make sure Candace knew what was going on and what she was dealing with, as much as I could tell her.

We exited into the street. A crowd of people, both tourists and locals, shuffled past. No wonder they'd taken the sewer route. Luca and Ortiz could blend into the crowd, but Taj and Mrs. Jennings would be instantly recognizable. Looking around wildly, we crossed in front of the hotel. "Let's find Candace and—"

I slammed hard into someone who stepped into my path.

Dante!

"Nice dress, bella," said Dante uncertainly, checking me out, then Sophie and Kevin. What a sight we must have been; Sophie in a Creamsicle-colored top and skinny pants, Kevin in his powder blue silk shirt and tan slacks, and me in my pink dress—our clothes grubby with dirt and our shoes wet with sewer water.

"Do you have *any* idea how glad I am to see you?" I wanted to throw my arms around him but thought better of it. "Wait. What are you doing here?" The timing was disconcerting.

He held up an envelope and frowned. "Delivering a letter. Why are you here? This is—"

"—where Taj is staying," I finished for him. Of course Dante had to know—this was his delivery area. How often had he bumped into Taj? Did they have confrontations—or meetings—that I didn't see? I searched Dante's face. Could I trust him?

It was time for an executive decision.

"Dante—"

"We have to do something urgent," said Kevin brusquely, and then pulling me aside, added in a lower voice, "He's a *messenger*—you can't just tell him what happened with Mrs. Jennings. The Secret Service—"

"I know we can trust him," I said firmly. "We need his help." No one knew about Candace's real job; I never said anything and I'd only been told after I stumbled upon the meeting in that warehouse. I turned to Dante. "Taj has kidnapped Mrs. Jennings. Ortiz is helping him. He has at least one guy with him, but there may be more."

Dante frowned. "Where are they now?"

"We don't know where they were going, only that they're traveling underground. In the sewers."

Dante looked shocked.

"They only left minutes ago. I'm pretty sure they want to get her out of the city," I said. "Probably to an airport or a boat or something."

He spun around, studying the area. "These streets all around are too narrow for cars, everyone must walk. If he brought her out here, everyone would recognize the American First Lady," he said, thinking aloud and confirming what I thought.

Kevin nodded. "They definitely took her underground. We saw the shoe scrapes."

"They need a road where they can drive away. The closest street would be . . ." Dante's finger wagged as he concentrated. Suddenly he looked at me and grabbed my hand. "I think I know where they are—hurry!"

He pulled me with him. I looked over my shoulder at Sophie and Kevin. "Coming?"

"Wouldn't miss it," Kevin said dryly. He and Sophie stayed close behind as we pushed through the crowds, ignoring stares and curses when we bumped and jostled people out of our way.

My heart ached with Taj's betrayal. I tried not to think about the clues I'd missed, the plotting and planning that was happening right under my nose.

"Here," said Dante as we approached a cross street, a narrow one-way lane lined with cars. At the top, at a little distance from the other vehicles, we saw a sleek black van: nondescript, large enough to hold at least five people. The vehicle, unlike the other cars on the street, was occupied. An arm dangled from the driver's-side window.

We hunkered in a doorway, all mashed together.

"We can take him, there's four of us," Kevin whispered.

Finally, all of this adventure had gotten to him and he was thinking he was a superhero. Dante brought him crashing down to reality.

"You can run faster than he can shoot?" Dante asked doubtfully.

"No, it's not safe for Bec and Sophie. We must wait for the *polizia*."

The question was, if this was the getaway van for the kidnapping, how could it still be here? Taj left before us . . . Ah! But he was going *underground* with a bound prisoner. They'd have to climb ladders and go around fallen walls. Who knew how long that could take? I peeked around the corner again. No way could one of us walk over, check out the situation, and report back to the group. *That* wouldn't be suspicious!

But the question remained. If that was the van, what was taking Taj so long? Time was against them, they had to move fast. Soon the whole world would be scouring the country looking for Mrs. Theresa Jennings, American First Lady, political, cultural, and fashion icon, one of the most recognizable women in the world.

He would have to disguise her first, and that would eat up some precious minutes.

"I will call *polizia*," said Dante, pulling out his phone and stopping my logic train.

"Hold on," I said, stilling his hand. "We can't. If the police get here before Taj, he'll run scared, and we might lose him. I think that Taj might be trying to disguise Mrs. Jennings. Like you said, everyone knows her. The authorities have to be looking for her now. If that van is the getaway car, Taj could be here any second. We don't have much time. I have an idea. Quick!" I held out my hand. "Give me your phone!"

He passed it to me and I scrolled through the settings.

"I thought you said we weren't calling the police," Kevin said.

"I'm not. I'm calling a car."

"What?" Sophie laughed.

"You wanted me to show you something," I said, brandishing the phone. "Well, here's something. Watch this."

I showed her the settings screen. "First, you put the phone in promiscuous mode." Sophie raised both red brows. "Not that kind of promiscuous," I said, scowling. "When your phone is on its normal mode it only gets signals sent to you—texts, e-mails, you know."

She nodded.

"You put it in promiscuous mode, and it's open to everything—you pick up all the signals in the area—Internet connections, phones, and cars."

I flicked my finger across the screen. "And look. Here they are."

Sophie, and now Kevin and Dante, examined the list of numbers that came up.

"These are the numbers I've picked up. The ones with the 00876 prefix are phones. Prefix 0388 are land-based wi-fi connections, like for an apartment or business. And 00271 are cars—we've picked up five of those. One of them has to be that van."

"There's more than five cars on the block, genius," Kevin griped.

Holding my temper in check, I replied, "But it looks like only five are newer cars—ones that would have things like satellite radio, a built-in GPS—platforms that have to be connected to the Internet. We're only interested in the van, not the others,"

"So . . . you're going to . . . call the van?" Sophie said, working it out.

"Actually, I'm going to text—but it's going to be a bit of trial and error. I can't tell from the list which one is the van."

I copied the first car number, opened messaging, pasted it in, and tapped in a text. A few feet from us, there was a click.

"What was that?" Dante said.

I sent the text again, and the car, a Fiat, made the sound again. "That was me. I locked the door. Cross that number off the list."

"That is amazing," Sophie said with delight.

"I take back what I said." Kevin shook his head. "You are smart."

"I'll try the next one."

I flashed the lights on a Lancia and rolled down the window of another Fiat. Only two more possibilities.

I sent the text to the next number. The arm dangling out of the van jerked back.

Pay dirt!

We were too far away to hear if the van's door unlocked, but it was an excellent chance we'd found the right vehicle. To be sure, I made the lights flash on the last number on the list: a Porsche. We were good to go.

"I have the van's number," I said.

"Yes!" Kevin, Dante, and Sophie whispered, but then they turned to me. "Now what?"

"Watch."

I fired off a string of text messages, one after the other.

Passenger window down.
Headlights on.
Headlights off.
Headlights on.
Wipers on.
Lock doors.
Unlock doors.

I could see the head of the person in the van dart this way and that—he had no idea what was happening.

"And now, for the grand finale."

The van's horn blared out. Kevin shook his head and Dante laughed.

"Wait for it," I said as I hit send.

The horn sounded again. And again. And again and again and again.

"Oh my God, what did you do?" Sophie put her hand over her mouth.

"I told the horn to beep fifty times. Now, if I were him I would . . ."

Yes! He got out of the car and opened the hood. The beeping continued.

"Dante, I think you and I should help him out," said Kevin. "You up for it?" He flexed his appreciable biceps.

"Yes!" Dante replied, his face stony.

"Just make sure it's the right guy!" I warned.

Kevin nodded meaningfully, then he and Dante casually walked into the street and started making their way toward the van. His head under the hood, the driver didn't see them coming. When they reached the bumper, I grabbed Sophie's arm and tugged her along. The van was parked right in front of a manhole. So far everything added up: sole van on the street, manhole for access, only street wide enough for cars and vans.

We came around just in time to see that, yes, this was Taj's accomplice—and even better, to see Dante grab him from behind so that Kevin could deliver a stunning blow to his jaw, knocking him out cold. Kevin yelped and shook his fist.

Dante clapped him on the shoulder. "*Buono!*"

"Quick, get him inside!" I urged, looking around to see if anyone had witnessed our assault or was coming to check on the blaring horn. I didn't think so. Up to now, my plan was working, my guesses were good.

Sophie slammed the hood shut, and I texted the van to stop the horn.

Throwing open the van's back door, Kevin and Dante shoved Luca in, and Sophie and I tied him up with rope that was probably intended for the First Lady. There were also some zip ties, chloroform—no doubt in case she got feisty or noisy—and a blindfold, which I used to gag him. A deep breath and I was feeling better about the situation. The kidnapping supplies that no normal person carried were additional incriminating evidence.

"Dante, you have to drive, you know Rome better than any of us." I peeled the knit cap off Luca's head. "Put this on quick, and hide your hair." I threw the cap to him and he pulled it on, tucking up his pale mane. Dante was bigger than Luca, but hopefully Taj and Ortiz wouldn't notice that until it was too late.

I slid the door closed while Kevin settled next to Sophie. Luca lay immobile between us. Kevin looked thoughtful.

"You were able to control that car with your phone," he said. "And get out of zip ties. You're . . . a hacker."

And the train finally pulls into the station, Kev.

He gave me a frosty glare. "My credit card and bank account. Was that you?"

Okay, maybe he wasn't that slow. But I did have something on my side this time—the truth.

I shook my head. "Not me—but maybe you can ask Taj about it when he shows up."

He smiled evilly and cracked his knuckles. "Nice to know."

30

On Dante's phone, mine bugged. On Via di Panico, 1 way. Keep u posted. B

I hit send with shaking hands. The adrenaline was really pumping, and waiting for Taj was making me and the others, jumpy. This could work—or it could fail on an epic level.

A second later, a reply came back.

Why r u there? Know where TJ is?

I replied *Maybe* and hit send.

There was no time for a long explanation. I put Dante's phone in my pocket just as it buzzed again—possibly a reply from Candace. Quickly I pulled the battery from my phone—just in case Taj could track my movements. If I had any luck, he hadn't noticed that I'd already moved from the stone room. Besides, Candace couldn't send a rescue team before we got Mrs. Jennings.

We all heard the unmistakable grind of metal on asphalt. Someone was moving the manhole cover. Luca, now somewhat revived, writhed in his bonds, trying to rock the van to warn Taj, but Sophie plopped on his chest, knocking the wind—and the fight—out of him.

"Get ready," I whispered to Dante from the back. "Keep your head down a little, okay?"

He nodded and gripped the steering wheel. My heart pounded in my chest as I heard grunts and then footsteps and muffled voices.

The back door of the van opened, hinges creaking. At first, all I saw was Mrs. Jennings in a red wig—and she saw us. Her eyes went wide with surprise. Kevin leaned forward quickly and yanked her inside, leaving an astonished Taj alone at the bumper.

Taj tried to lunge into the back of the van. That's when I delivered the most bone-bruising side kick—the only thing I ever learned in tae kwon do—to his midsection. He oomphed as the air rushed out of his lungs and the force of the kick ejected him from the van. He stumbled back, slamming into Ortiz, who'd just climbed up into the street.

"Aahhhh!" she cried, and, pitching backward, fell into the manhole like a well-struck golf ball. Score!

Taj scrambled to his feet.

"You should've had a plan B," I yelled as I slammed the door shut. "Go!" I screamed at Dante.

I thought I heard Taj screaming and rose onto my knees to peek out the window when I was forced back down.

"What if he has a gun? Do you want to get shot?" cried Kevin as he yanked me away from the window.

Tires squealed as the van fishtailed, trying to get a grip on the uneven cobbles. With a lurch and a jerk, Dante pulled into the street and zoomed away.

Suddenly I remembered—

"Plan B! GPS!" I turned to Mrs. Jennings. "Taj put a GPS on you before. He might have done it again. I'm sorry, ma'am, but you're going to have to . . . um . . . take your clothes off. I mean, if they bugged you—"

"I'm so glad to see all of you unharmed, but this is dangerous. Call the Secret Service!" Mrs. Jennings urged, relief etched on her face, smudged with dirt.

"I've already let Candace know where we were, and I'll call her again," I promised as I worked off her zip ties, "but if there's a GPS on your clothes we have to get rid of it. Even if Taj can't chase us, we don't know if he has others who can. Hurry, please, Mrs. Jennings." I tugged off her wig.

Kevin's face went as red as a tomato as she started to unbutton her skirt. I guess it was one thing for professional models to strut around almost naked and another thing to see the First Lady in her lingerie.

"Close your eyes, Kevin," Sophie advised.

He nodded awkwardly but first helped us roll the tied-up creep against the side wall of the van. Kevin held him there with his back to the First Lady so she could undress with a little dignity—as much as she could get in the back of a cramped and speeding vehicle.

After hesitating for a fraction of a second, she kicked off her shoes, took off her jacket, and shimmied out of her dress, sitting there like a Victoria's Secret model in her matching sea green bra and underwear. Sophie passed the clothing to me and I handed them and the wig to Dante, who threw them out the window as he careened around corners. Bye-bye one-of-a-kind suit, now probably worth millions because of the action it'd seen.

I had no idea where Dante was going, but he'd proven himself to be a good spy-in-training, dodging cars, people, and Vespas as he drove. I risked a peek in the rearview mirror. No one seemed to be following us.

Yet.

Reaching over, I poked Kevin in the shoulder. "Don't turn around. Just give me your shirt and pants, please."

"What?!" He tried to twist toward me, but Sophie clutched his head tightly and forced him to remain facing forward.

"You're not going to make Mrs. Jennings walk around naked, are you?" Sophie demanded.

A huge defeated sigh escaped from him. "Fine." He started unbuttoning. "I hope people realize what a patriot I am when this is over!"

"Think of the fame and job offers," I said.

After an awkward face-plant on the side of the van from a quick right swerve, he handed over the shirt and pants—both filthy from our sewer run. I tried not to look at his toned body—for Sophie's sake—and helped Mrs. Jennings put on the too-big clothes.

Once the First Lady was buttoned up, I pulled out Dante's phone.

Report! NOW!

I texted Candace back.

We have her! Will turn on GPS so you can follow.

I changed the settings on Dante's phone. Seconds passed and I got a reply.

Tracking u. Police will follow soon. Go to hotel if u can.

"Hotel Beatrici!" I yelled to Dante.

He took a really sharp left turn, throwing all of us in the back across the van and slamming us painfully into the side. I think my knee ended up in Luca's rib cage. Pity.

"Hey, Mario Andretti! Take it easy!" Kevin shouted.

"I know him!" yelled Dante gleefully. "He's—"

"A cousin!" the three of us yelled back in unison.

Dante looked in the rearview mirror, confused. "No, his family and mine go to same church."

We heard the wail of sirens. The *polizia* were coming, as promised.

Dante drove faster.

"Slow down!" I yelled, clutching onto the back of the passenger seat. "Candace knows—she said the police were going to follow us!"

"Don't make them shoot us!" Kevin shouted. "When we get out of here, we're going to be surrounded!"

I couldn't stop myself from giggling. "And the world's going to see you in your Fruit of the Loom underwear."

Sometimes justice was too sweet.

I saw the flash of red lights through the van's windows. Police cars surrounded us now. The wailing sirens and the flashing strobes made me feel sick to my stomach. Suddenly, the van screeched to an abrupt halt. From my skewed view I could see we'd stopped in front of the Hotel Beatrici.

It was good to be home.

"Nobody move!" came a voice through a bullhorn. "We're going to open the back door. Put your hands up, slowly!" It sounded like Case.

I heard the tramp of boots all around the van. Not daring to move, I strained to see, and, from the corner of my eye, I saw that a gun was pointed at Dante's head. He held his hands out the window, barely moving enough to breathe. The back door of the van was flung open and a thicket of gun barrels were thrust in, red laser sights dotting everyone except Mrs. Jennings. We each very carefully and slowly raised our hands.

"Hold!" cried Candace, pushing forward. Peering in, she saw Mrs. Jennings. Like the others, I sat frozen in my place.

"Mrs. Jennings, are you all right? Do you need medical care?"

"No, Candace. I'm fine."

Candace offered her hand to Mrs. Jennings, helping her out. The police backed off and instantly Case, Nelson, Mignone, and Collins rushed forward.

Mignone put a hand to his ear and said, "We have Venus, Venus moving to Olympus. Over. Mrs. Jennings, come with me, please." He held out his hand to her, taking custody from Candace.

She nodded, her legs and smile shaky. After Dante's driving, I think we all felt the same.

"Thank you, and please take care of these courageous young people." They led her to a large black SUV with tinted windows. Once she was safely inside, it screeched off, a motorcade of police cars and motorcycles leading and following, lights flashing and sirens screaming. Only Case remained with Candace.

"Is anyone hurt, do we need a doctor?" asked Candace as Sophie and I climbed out of the van.

"No . . ." But then I remembered. "Ortiz—"

"What?!" Candace looked over her shoulder, searching. Of course, Ortiz wasn't there. "What about Ortiz?" she demanded.

"She was working with Taj, helping him!" Sophie gasped, indignant.

"Case, put out an APB for Agent Ortiz—"

"Actually, I don't think you're going to need to do that," I said.

They both turned to me. "Why not?"

"She had a little accident." I gave Candace and the agents a quick synopsis of everything that had happened, from discovering Varon to our takedown of Taj and Ortiz. "She fell down a sewer hole. She must be hurt. I don't know if she could get very far."

"She might, if Taj stopped to help her," said Candace.

Would he? After all I'd heard him say, I wasn't so sure about that. Candace asked the local police to search the area where she'd fallen and arrest her if they found her.

"Okay," she said, turning back to me, "do you have anything else I need to know?"

"We have one of Taj's accomplices in the back of the van, and, um . . . Kevin's probably a little chilly?" I jerked my head toward him.

Candace's mouth opened but nothing came out right away. "Blanket!" she finally shouted, and one was thrust into her waiting hand. She tossed it in to him and he emerged with it wrapped around his middle, leaving his chest bare. Sophie climbed out and put her arms around him. There were catcalls from some people across the street, and some girl wanted his phone number. Kevin turned furiously red—all over—and I had to laugh.

"Parker has to put you in a spread, Kevin," Candace snickered. I didn't think he could be more embarrassed, but he was.

Some officers came and took Luca away.

"C'mon, Bec," she said with a relieved look. She put her hand on my shoulder, then suddenly enveloped me in a crush-the-air-out-of-your-lungs hug. I went to hug her back and saw the police leading Dante away in handcuffs.

"Let him go!" I pushed Candace in their direction. "If it hadn't been for Dante, we never would have been able to find Mrs. Jennings and save her!"

Candace nodded to the officers and they reluctantly released him. Dante joined us and I gave him a hard hug.

"You're a hero, Dante!"

Now he blushed and smoothed back the sexy wayward shock of hair. Some girls called to him, taking pictures. *Sorry, ladies, not happening. Get your own hero.*

"And what about me?" demanded Kevin.

Sophie threw her arms around him and kissed his cheek. "You were amazing."

Kevin's ego did *not* need any more stroking, but if she could handle him, good for her. Then I thought, *Oh, what is my life going to* be like when things return to normal and I have to work for him every day?

I'd deal with that tomorrow.

Dante pulled me to him and tilted up my chin. I leaned forward into a long, delicious kiss. "I knew there were lots of reasons to like you, *bella*."

"Let's get inside," said Candace, exasperated, pushing Dante and me apart.

Dante, Kevin, and Sophie each went with new agents to be questioned.

The remaining police were left to disperse the crowd that had clustered around the hotel. People shouted and took photos with their cameras and cell phones. I hoped they didn't get one of me. I looked a mess. A tow truck pulled up, and men who looked more like government officials than mechanics started tending to the van. A good portion of the crowd backed away after that.

"How's Varon?" I asked as we made our way up the steps and onto the hotel's elegant porch. I felt a little out of place; my ruined shoes squished and my filthy dress hung in shreds. Plus, I'd worked up a sweat climbing all those stairs and running through the streets. It was a shame that Candace's gift was reduced to less than rags. I was tired and, as her wrinkled nose indicated, badly in need of a shower. My whole body slumped after all the excitement and tension. There couldn't be a drop of adrenaline left in me.

"His hand has numerous breaks, but other than that, he's recuperating."

"And Mrs. Jennings? Where are they taking her?"

"She's on her way to the American embassy. They'll take care of her there. As much as I like her, I'm beyond grateful that she's not my responsibility anymore."

I nodded, understanding all too well.

The doorman opened up for us, and we trudged into the lobby.

Candace put a gentle hand on my arm, stopping me. "Don't get too comfortable. You have to be debriefed first. We need to know everything you learned about Taj. I don't think his friend will be very cooperative. He's refused to ID himself."

"His name's Luca," I said.

"Well, that's a start." She took a deep breath. "Thanks. I can do your interview upstairs, after you've taken a shower—"

The lobby door flew open and a gang of suited men burst in— and with them, the Man. He moved quickly despite his uneven gait, and he held a badge aloft. Everyone froze.

"Inspector Frederic Poulet. Interpol. No one may leave."

"Great," Candace muttered, but flashed a wary, weary smile at the older man. "Inspector Poulet. So good to see you in the light for a change."

"Agent Worthington," he said tersely—and loped over to me. "We have to question this young woman. Miss, you'll be coming with us. We need to interview you about your dealings with Tajo Renan." His stony voice grated on my nerves.

"Tajo Renan?" Candace repeated the name like she'd never heard it before.

Inspector Poulet shook his head impatiently. "Known to you as Taj. Now, miss"—he turned to me again, holding out an arm—"come with us."

"I—" I started, not liking the idea of "accompanying" Inspector Poulet and his gang to some undisclosed location, but at the same time, dying to. I wanted to know everything there was to know about Taj/Tajo—and then use it to bury him. Interpol could catch up to him another time.

"Ms. Jackson is an American citizen and a minor in my custody. You can debrief her right here in the hotel," said Candace firmly, "under *my* watch." She wasn't taking no for an answer.

Thanks, Candace. I felt a small warm rush.

Inspector Poulet grudgingly agreed but wouldn't let me so much as pee first. We went right upstairs to the suite and the interrogation took place immediately, in the sitting room.

"I really don't know much about him," I said, hating the admission. Thinking about how he used and duped me and everyone else, including Candace, made my blood boil all over again.

Poulet frowned. "Tell me everything you can from the moment you met him. He could be out of the country by now, he's clever enough."

Only if you tell me everything you *know about him*, I thought. But the inspector was right; I was willing to bet next year's boarding school tuition that Taj was long gone.

"There's not much. He wasn't very open." I paused. "Tell me why you're chasing him, it'll help me be more specific."

The inspector and Candace exchanged a brief look.

Crossing my arms over my chest defiantly, I said, "I kept quiet about *everything* I heard about the First Lady. One problem I *don't* need is being stalked by official agencies—domestic or international. You know where I live. Trust me, I'll keep quiet about *this*."

I caught a flicker of amusement as Candace licked her upper lip. I think she was trying not to grin.

Poulet scrutinized my face, probably trying to judge if I was trustworthy. Finally, with a prim look, he said, "We've been following the Renan family for years. They're South American arms dealers."

"Brazilian?" I offered.

Poulet raised a bushy gray brow. "Yes."

Candace stared at me.

"When we were at the Forte, he mentioned a trip to a beach there, and then when we found Mrs. Jennings he was speaking Portuguese to Luca."

Poulet continued, "The father runs the operation, his oldest son made the deliveries. Santo Renan was captured several years ago by U.S. border patrol agents. Interpol has been waiting for them to make another misstep."

Candace pointed a long, steely finger at him. "We almost had an international catastrophe. If you'd bothered to share—"

"It looks like the crisis has been averted," the inspector interjected smoothly, "and I told you, I wouldn't and couldn't reveal anything that might have ruined my own plans, but now my mission is a failure. When we positively identified Tajo and followed him here, we believed he was planning to bargain for his brother's release. It looks like we were right, but now we're back to square one."

"Taj hacked Kevin's bank account, maybe you could use that," I suggested, even though I knew there'd be no link between the hack and Taj.

"She'll tell you everything she knows, Inspector. Hopefully it'll give you something to work with." Candace crossed her perfect legs, as if daring the inspector to disagree.

I didn't think anything I offered would be valuable. Taj had obviously eluded the police, Interpol, and the Secret Service when he was right under their noses, but then everyone I knew was focused on the First Lady. After we left him on his butt in the street, he had to have disappeared. It's what I would've done. But I would never try to kidnap anyone, no matter what. It was a special kind of desperate to think that kidnapping the President's wife would solve your problems. But I told Candace and Inspector Poulet everything I knew or even thought, realizing that Taj never left unsmudged fingerprints or DNA behind; he took his water bottles, didn't touch things that weren't his—and didn't let his personal belongings go far from his person. He didn't want to be traced or put into a data bank.

No evidence.

He'd always had a plan B.

I ran ahead of Candace into the hospital room, which was almost overflowing with flowers. Parker sat up in bed, looking weak, but very much awake. I wanted to cry, but instead, ran to her bedside and grabbed her hands, careful not to crush them with my enthusiasm.

"You're okay!"

"Easy! I want to get out of here, not stay longer!" she laughed softly. Embarrassed, I let go and backed up a step. After my interrogation with the inspector and a shower, Candace agreed that I'd earned a visit with Parker the next morning, as soon as the hospital would allow.

"Sit! I heard you turned my magazine—and Rome—upside down."

I wasn't sure if she was talking to Candace or me. It would apply in either case.

Pulling a chair up, I gave her the unedited version of what happened. She'd already been briefed and had given her statement. Candace stood, leaning against the wall across from Parker's bed, nodding and smiling in the right places, grimacing in others, and sighing tiredly and shaking her head at the end.

"I can't believe Ortiz sold out," I said, disgusted. "And she was the one who searched my room."

Candace looked taken aback. "What?!"

"Yep," I said and turned to Parker. "I dusted my room and matched up her prints. She even downloaded a spy app on all our phones so Taj could spy on us, to find out what he could about Mrs. Jennings and the places and times of the photo shoots."

Parker closed her eyes for a moment. "She fooled us all. And we're professionals, trained to look for the signs of a traitor. Anyway, she's in custody. You were right. She didn't get too far."

"How could she, with two broken legs?" said Candace.

"And she still wouldn't give anything up about Taj? Or Tajo, or whatever his name really is?" asked Parker.

Candace shook her head. "She and Luca Vitorio, his other accomplice, won't say a word. I'm surprised about Ortiz, though. She's keeping her mouth shut even after he left her down there."

"Ten million dollars buys a lot of loyalty," I offered glumly, not liking the idea that, whatever bargain they made, he'd just abandon her in a sewer. She could have died down there.

"We wouldn't have known about Serena's part in your crash without Bec picking up on the purchase of the electronic cables."

Parker exhaled, a sad look on her face. "Poor Serena. She only wanted to replace me at the magazine. She didn't realize what she was getting into."

I didn't feel sorry for Serena, and I didn't think Candace did either.

"From what Inspector Poulet told me, it's the way the Renan family operates," Candace added. "My guess is that Taj checked Ortiz out and promised to take care of her and her family if she got caught—the price of her silence. Same for Luca."

"So what happens now?" I asked, sitting on the end of the bed.

Candace and Parker exchanged a look.

"Hey, no secret spy signals!" I protested. "I went through a lot! I was zip-tied with Kevin, had guns waved at me, had to jog a marathon in wedges through nasty sewers, got slammed around in a crazy car chase, and *saved the First Lady.*"

"I think she deserves to know some," said Parker softly. "Without her, we could have lost Mrs. Jennings."

Yes! Let's trust Bec!

Candace deliberated a few moments. "Okay, but don't ask any more questions when I'm done. Agreed?"

I didn't want to concede, but I knew Candace wouldn't say a word until I did.

"Fine." I sounded surly. And I was. After everything, they still weren't going to let me inside the circle?

"Like Inspector Poulet said, Interpol has been watching the Renan family for a long time. He was actually the original officer assigned to the case. He's been tailing Taj because his superiors felt that the family was ready to make a move—"

"—because of Taj's brother," I said.

"That's right. Santo Renan, unlike his little brother, joined his father in the family business—arms dealing. He was caught and put into a supermax prison shortly before Taj emerged as a fashion blogger. This effort to free him has been a long time in planning."

"How did he manage to keep his identity so secret and for so long?"

Candace looked exasperated. "What did we say about questions?"

"Oh, come on!"

She sighed. "It seems that to protect them from law enforcement and rivals, the sons were raised separate from their real family—countries apart—but aware of their heritage and who their true parents were, and even saw them from time to time. They were always kept away from the public. There was never any concrete documentation of a visit, exchange of information, or even gifts."

I shivered, remembering what Taj had told me.

. . . haven't you learned not to leave evidence? A note can be found

if it's not destroyed. I don't leave anything behind that I don't mind others finding. Not on paper—and never electronically. E-mail and electronic searches can be traced, even if it's erased. . . .

It had been ingrained in him from birth.

"So everything was done through others," I said.

Candace nodded. "An ever-changing network of them, according to the inspector. Always a few that knew only so much—and then new people would be brought in. We're trying to trace the connection between the Renans and Taj's adoptive family in India, but it's a thin thread. The real question is whether Renan Senior was involved in this plot, or if Taj was acting on his own."

Rebellious, loyal, doing whatever he had to do to correct a perceived wrong . . . If Renan Senior went to this length to disassociate himself from Taj—for Taj's own protection—he wouldn't have hatched this or any plot that would have involved his son. My guess was that Taj was flying solo, and when Papa found out, he wasn't going to be pleased. But that was just a guess.

"Bec." Parker squeezed my hand, drawing my attention away from Candace. "If you ever hear from Taj again, you must report it. Immediately."

I nodded, but I didn't think he'd try. It wouldn't be worth the risk for him.

"So when do you get out?" I asked Parker, changing the subject.

"In about a week."

I glanced quickly at Candace.

Parker's eyes followed my gaze. "Candace will stay on until the investigation is finished, then she'll be reassigned. Kevin will take over *Edge* until I'm ready to go back to work." She tapped my hand with a finger. "Your spying days are over."

Candace had a car take me back to the hotel.

As I watched the scenery flick by, I thought about Dante and all that we shared. He was open and honest, he never withheld anything about his life or what he was thinking. He never used me. He jumped right in to help Kevin, Sophie, and me rescue the First Lady, even though it was dangerous. He'd been nothing but sweet and hot and exciting. Those memories made me happy and warm, especially that last searing kiss.

Then there was Taj.

He was absolutely wrong about us being the same. He clearly had no qualms about crossing certain boundaries that I wouldn't even dare to approach. But I couldn't deny that we had a few similarities. The hacking was part of it, but there was more. Being separated from his family, like I was from mine, made us both learn to depend on ourselves and trust few others. We were both mysteries even with our friends, to an extent. Dante, surrounded by his mother, sisters, and numerous cousins, would never understand the isolation.

Taj had taken things too far, though. Now he had multiple countries and agencies who would never give up on trying to find him. The seclusion would be a thousand times worse for him.

For now, at least Parker was healing quickly, the First Lady was safe, and I wasn't in trouble.

For once.

Dragging myself toward the elevator where Case no longer asked to search my backpack or demanded ID, I thought about sleeping for a week.

"Miss Jackson?" called the concierge at the desk.

I turned wearily. "Yes?"

"You have a delivery."

"Delivery?" The last thing I needed right now was more homework, but when he pulled it out from under his counter, it wasn't a manila envelope but a rectangular box.

"Would you like us to send it up?" he asked.

I shook my head. "No, I'll take it." I was immediately sorry as soon as I grabbed it. It was heavier than I expected. Staggering to the elevator, I went straight up to the suite. Once inside, I put it on the coffee table. Still overwhelmed by the last few days, my body demanded rest. I took a long, hot bubble bath, then pulled on my pj's even though it was only around three o'clock. I wasn't going anywhere, with anyone.

After a while, I turned on my laptop. I'd hidden it in the office as usual during Mrs. Jennings's interview and hadn't thought of going back for it in the chaos after she went missing. It turned out to be a good thing. I couldn't imagine having to drag my backpack through the sewers, up all the stairs, and then on the wild car ride. Once the interrogation by Inspector Poulet was over, I had asked Candace about it, and she'd had one of the agents retrieve my gear.

When I signed into my e-mail account, the monitor went black, and a message in green letters came up, filling up the entire screen.

Bec,

I'm sorry for the way things had to turn out, but I did it
to save my brother. I can't tell you more than that. This
message is as much as I can or am willing to risk. It's
very important to me that you know I wasn't going to
let anyone get hurt.

Especially you.

One day we will meet again and I hope to convince
you not to hate me. I'll do whatever it takes. . . .

Taj

The message blinked on the screen, refreshing itself over and
over. I read it again and again, growing angrier with each pass. Taj
was looking to swap Mrs. Jennings for his brother—and he wasn't
going to let anyone get hurt? Was he kidding? Then why the guns?
And what about Parker? And the threats? We were all put in danger. And now I would *have* to hand my laptop over to Candace—
after I wiped my personal things and not-always-so-kosher stuff
from it. I didn't want to mess with Taj's message in any way. The
Secret Service or Interpol tech people would be able to trace the
e-mail, see where he sent it from, see—
    Blip!
    The message disappeared. And a string of commands popped
up.

Erase all file folders . . .
Erase all program folders . . .

    "No, no, come back!" I practically shrieked, furiously tapping
commands on the keyboard while yelling them too.

"*Stop!*

"*Cease!*

"*Halt!*"

I watched helplessly as file after file was erased. Programs, music, and movies I'd bought/stolen/borrowed, photos, homework files. Then the command doubled back, erasing itself like a snake eating its tail. One by one the strings of text disappeared until it was a single line, then a handful of letters, and finally, a big, black nothing.

I fumed, and, grabbing the laptop cover, was about to slam it shut when the screen went bright green. There was a crackle and hiss and the smell of burning plastic. I pulled my hand away.

My baby!

My hand flew to my mouth as I heard the slow draining sound of machinery shutting down. A final crackle and the screen went black again. I scrambled for my backpack and pulled out my tool kit. Flipping the laptop over, I pried open the back case, but I knew it was hopeless even before I saw the motherboard. The circuitry was nothing but a silver blob with plastic bits sticking into it like sprinkles on melted ice cream.

My eyes filled. Oh, I had backup files on a flash drive for almost everything, and this one time I was lucky I had done all of my homework on paper, *but still!* Apart from the machine, I probably hadn't lost much, but that wasn't the point. This was mine, and Taj destroyed it on purpose. Those bots that he planted did one last lethal job—kill any evidence in my possession.

Taj was right; I was a pathetic hacker.

And he was sorry. Yeah, okay, sure.

The delivery box resting against a chair caught my eye. I studied the label; there was no return address. Taking out my phone—always good to have a plan B for accessing the Internet—I entered the tracking information. The box had been sent from the United States only two days before. I thought back. *The day Mrs. Jennings was supposed to be swiped from the Vatican.* There was no name under sender because it had been paid for in cash.

Carefully I peeled off the label and opened the box.

Holy moly . . .

It was a factory-sealed, direct from the manufacturer, M14x Alienware laptop. Top-of-the-line, with a backlit keyboard in—what else?—neon pink.

I searched the packing slip. It had been ordered directly from Alienware and came with a lifetime warranty and upgrade package. If I had a problem, I could always send it back and have them send me a brand-new one. Should I trust it?

Because I knew who it was from—name or no name.

The Edge *office remained closed so the new Se-*cret Service detail could do their thing: clean up, gather evidence, and conference with their colleagues back in the U.S. This gave me a chance to examine and reconfigure my new laptop. Having determined that it was, indeed, clean, I installed the new version of Ninja Assassin and retrieved the latest messages in the virtual meeting room.

Looks like T-bone is 1337, said DR#4.

1337—"leet"—the hacker term for the best there is. Taj better hope that he really was elite; he had a lot more than pulling pranks at stake. Unfortunately, I couldn't share everything I'd learned about Taj/Tajo, but I'd planted a seed. Fashionistas weren't the only ones interested in him now. This would be a constant itch for the off-grid community. They'd be searching for his signature and wouldn't stop until they found him.

When the magazine was cleared to resume operation the day after, Kevin took over the editor's office. Candace had given Sophie the day off, but she went in to help Kevin move his stuff. Varon stayed behind to make sure everything ran smoothly while he recouped. He had Joe to keep him company and take care of him. Ugi was planning to move to a high-end salon for a change and a fresh start. Aldo and Angelo were still arguing and still being pestered by Francesca for a photo op.

Candace took me out as a reward. We stopped in boutiques where she insisted I needed this Miu Miu dress and that Prada wallet—all next season's, of course, and written off on the *Edge* expense account—on the condition I didn't mind keeping quiet about the whole matter. Since I hadn't gotten paid, I felt I deserved it.

"What I want to know is how you managed to keep everyone and everything quiet," I said, reclining back, letting the stylist at Contesta Salon reenvision my hair. "Somehow, even with all those people gaping and taking pictures, there was nothing in the news about the First Lady or you guys, or Dante, Kevin, Sophie, or me . . . anywhere."

Candace cocked a sharp blonde brow at me, her face unreadable. "Sometimes what seems like an interesting story turns out to be nothing; some kids playing pranks with smoke bombs, or the police showing up at the wrong house in response to a family squabble."

Unbelievable, I thought, but I didn't mind being out of the limelight. The last thing I wanted was to be famous. I'd done the ant-under-the-glass routine, and it was really overrated. But I intended to work my heroine status to my advantage a little longer: I wanted to choose my next school—or maybe no school. I liked this "independent learning" thing. A private tutor might be the way to go. Both Candace and Parker had promised to back me up. How could my parents object?

"What's going to happen to Serena?" I asked. Everyone else was accounted for—save for Taj, of course.

Candace closed her eyes in spa bliss. "Serena is having an extended vacation in an Italian jail, but I hear she has a nice view and is getting the help she needs."

I nodded, hoping that for Serena's sake, they allowed eyeliner in prison.

"You ready?" Pia, the stylist, asked.

I nodded.

I kept the pink, but just a little. When we stepped out into the perfect sunny afternoon, my hair was chin-length, and instead of the neon pink, it was a pearly platinum blush and swished softly around my face. Maybe I'd start a new trend. I was so over neon.

For now.

"Hungry?" Candace asked as we strolled down Via del Pigneto.

Shopping bags banged against my legs. It was hungry work, being pampered and carrying all this loot. "Famished," I said, working a "poor, pathetic me" look.

She grinned. "I know a good place close by." Smoothing back her own salon-fresh hair, she looked at me. "Mrs. Jennings has extended an invitation to you, Kevin, Sophie, and Dante to visit her and the President at the White House."

"Will you be there?" I asked.

I hoped this wasn't the last I'd see of Candace Worthington. She'd grown on me—in her odd, bitchy way.

She leveled a secretive smile at me. "You know I'm going to show up. Sometime. Somewhere."

Acknowledgments

First, to my agent, Natalie Lakosil of the Bradford Literary Agency, because she brought the *Blonde Ops* team together: editors Peter Joseph and Kat Brzozowski, and of course coauthor Natalie Zaman. To family, friends, the writing community, bloggers, and book lovers who have encouraged and anticipated this book. I wish I could name you all, but you know who you are. To my family for putting up with leftovers or pizza and a messy house, and my cats for missed playtime, and my garden for letting the weeds take over—thanks for your patience and support. And no, sons, I'm still the only one getting the Lamborghini (eventually). And finally, a huge thanks to Google, who made research on everything from the Secret Service to what a certain street in Rome looks like possible while sitting at my laptop in my jammies.

—Charlotte Bennardo

Working on *Blonde Ops* has been such a great experience, and I have so much to be grateful for, especially the people who made it possible. Huge thank-yous to:

Super-agent Natalie Lakosil, for making it happen and connecting Char and I to our amazing editors, Kat Brzozowski, Peter Joseph—and Tristan, somewhat anonymous but always insightful.

Leanna Renee Hieber, Molly Cochran, Shannon Delany, and Kristi Cook, for reading early drafts of *Blonde Ops* and for their kind words.

The book blogging community, and especially Tanya Contois and Bridget Connors, who supported us from Sirenz and beyond.

Audrey Jankucic and Suzanne Garris, for sharing your Italian adventures with me.

Emma Coleman, sartorial guru.

My friends and family, who put up with my moods, ever-changing schedule, and general mayhem—especially Raz and Asim, for technical expertise and patience with my endless questions and repeated requests for explanations of how things work.

The folks at Hack a Day, *2600* magazine, and the organizers of H.O.P.E.

And of course, my coauthor, Charlotte Bennardo—because there is no "I" in team. ♥

—Natalie Zaman